The Living Stone

More Handheld Classics

Betty Bendell, *My Life And I. Confessions of an Unliberated Housewife, 1966–1980*
Algernon Blackwood, *The Unknown. Weird Writings, 1900–1937*
Ernest Bramah, *What Might Have Been. The Story of a Social War* (1907)
D K Broster, *From the Abyss. Weird Fiction, 1907–1940*
John Buchan, *The Runagates Club* (1928)
John Buchan, *The Gap in the Curtain* (1932)
Melissa Edmundson (ed.), *Women's Weird. Strange Stories by Women, 1890–1940*
Melissa Edmundson (ed.), *Women's Weird 2. More Strange Stories by Women, 1891–1937*
Zelda Fitzgerald, *Save Me The Waltz* (1932)
Marjorie Grant, *Latchkey Ladies* (1921)
A P Herbert, *The Voluble Topsy, 1928–1947*
Inez Holden, *Blitz Writing. Night Shift & It Was Different At The Time* (1941 & 1943)
Inez Holden, *There's No Story There. Wartime Writing, 1944–1945*
Margaret Kennedy, *Where Stands A Wingèd Sentry* (1941)
Rose Macaulay, *Non-Combatants and Others. Writings Against War, 1916–1945*
Rose Macaulay, *Personal Pleasures. Essays on Enjoying Life* (1935)
Rose Macaulay, *Potterism. A Tragi-Farcical Tract* (1920)
Rose Macaulay, *What Not. A Prophetic Comedy* (1918)
James Machin (ed.) *British Weird. Selected Short Fiction, 1893–1937*
Vonda N McIntyre, *The Exile Waiting* (1975)
Elinor Mordaunt, *The Villa and The Vortex. Supernatural Stories, 1916–1924*
John Llewelyn Rhys, *England Is My Village, and The World Owes Me A Living* (1939 & 1941)
John Llewelyn Rhys, *The Flying Shadow* (1936)
Malcolm Saville, *Jane's Country Year* (1946)
Helen de Guerry Simpson, *The Outcast and The Rite. Stories of Landscape and Fear, 1925–1938*
Jane Oliver and Ann Stafford, *Business as Usual* (1933)
J Slauerhoff, *Adrift in the Middle Kingdom*, translated by David McKay (1934)
Ann Stafford, *Army Without Banners* (1942)
Amara Thornton and Katy Soar (eds), *Strange Relics. Stories of Archaeology and the Supernatural, 1895–1954*
Elizabeth von Arnim, *The Caravaners* (1909)
Sylvia Townsend Warner, *Kingdoms of Elfin* (1977)
Sylvia Townsend Warner, *Of Cats and Elfins. Short Tales and Fantasies* (1927–1976)
Sylvia Townsend Warner, *T H White. A Biography* (1967)

The Living Stone
Stories of Uncanny Sculpture, 1858–1943

Edited by Henry Bartholomew

Handheld Classic 35

This edition published in 2023 by Handheld Press
72 Warminster Road, Bath BA2 6RU, United Kingdom.
www.handheldpress.co.uk

ISBN 978-1-912766-76-5

1 2 3 4 5 6 7 8 9 0

Series design by Nadja Guggi and typeset in Adobe Caslon Pro and Open Sans.

Printed and bound in Great Britain by Short Run Press, Exeter.

Contents

Note on the texts

The texts of all stories were proofread against first editions. Some consistency was introduced to the spellings of some words where there was variation in the original. Obvious typographical errors have been silently corrected.

Acknowledgements

My thanks, first and foremost, to Kate and the Handheld Press team for agreeing to publish another anthology with me. Special thanks to S T Joshi for helping me on matters Lovecraftian, including sourcing scans of the elusive *National Amateur*. I am grateful, also, to R B Russell for sharing his expertise on Arthur Machen and Oliver Onions, and for helping me clear up some editorial points concerning 'The Ceremony'. Begun in the UK and finished in China, I have worked on this book in a variety of places and at strange hours. Throughout, I have been blessed by my wife Eleanor's endless encouragement and the benign indifference of our cat, Wilhelmina.

Henry Bartholomew is a lecturer in the Department of Literary and Translation Studies at Xi'an Jiaotong-Liverpool University. He is the editor of Algernon Blackwood's *The Unknown: Weird Writings, 1900–1937* (2023) and *Dangerous Dimensions: Mind-bending Tales of the Mathematical Weird* (2021).

Introduction

HENRY BARTHOLOMEW

This is a book of stories about the uncanniness of stone or, rather, sculpted stone – stone that has been shaped to resemble something or someone, or carved to serve some purpose. As the stories collected here demonstrate, once stone has taken a shape, it is remarkable how easily it can become a vessel for all manner of hopes, fears, terrors, and desires. 'Thou shalt not make unto thee any graven image', the God of the Old Testament commands jealously, and it is easy to see why. There is something divine (or perhaps demonic) about sculpture. As the Prussian philosopher Johann Gottfried von Herder put it in 1778, 'the sculptor stands in the dark of night and gropes toward the forms of gods' (quoted in Forster 2022). Statues have a strange, perhaps even dangerous, vitality, one capable of inspiring a range of responses, from devotion to destruction, obsession to repulsion.

This vitality has occasionally taken on supernatural proportions. Indeed, stories of statues coming to life have a long history. In the West, the foundational myth of this type is the ancient Greek story of Pygmalion. As told by the Roman poet Ovid in his *Metamorphoses*, the sculptor Pygmalion, offended by the wickedness he sees in the prostitutes of the city of Amathus, sets about sculpting an ideal woman and soon falls obsessively in love with his creation. After praying to Venus for a bride in the likeness of his sculpture, he returns home and kisses his statue only to find warm lips and supple flesh; Venus has made his fantasy a reality. The story has inspired countless imitations, adaptations, and reinterpretations, including Shakespeare's *The Winter's Tale*, where a 'statue' comes to life at the close, reuniting a king with his long-lost wife.

This is only half of the picture, however. For while this book is about stories of stone 'come to life', it is also, and conversely, a book of stories about the transformation – whether real or figurative – of people and things *into* stone. The literary scholar Patricia Pulham has shown how this theme of 'reverse pygmalionism' is used metaphorically in a range of nineteenth-century realist novels by notable authors like Thomas Hardy, Nathaniel Hawthorne, Henry James, and George Eliot (Pulham 2022, 12, 34). For this editor, however, it is in supernatural fiction, not realism, that this idea finds its most powerful expression. After all, when people are scared, they 'turn to stone'; fear *petrifies* us. From the myth of Medusa whose gorgon stare was the terror of the ancient world to the White Witch in C S Lewis's *The Lion, the Witch and the Wardrobe* (1950) – who decorates her palatial grounds by transforming her enemies into stone – becoming lithic is often depicted as a fate worse than death. Embodying the inorganic, stone represents in many ways a kind of anti-life – unchanging, inscrutable, inhuman. It is no wonder that the most terrifying *Doctor Who* villains of recent years are the statue-like Weeping Angels – alien entities who can only move when they are not being observed and who, in one episode, seemingly turn the Doctor herself into stone.

These two themes – stone come to life and life frozen into stone – give shape and substance to the stories presented here, all of which deal with the darker consequences attending to the creation and admiration of sculpture. The majority of them coincide with the 'golden age' of the ghost story (roughly, the 1880s to the 1920s) and the concomitant rise of weird fiction in the first half of the twentieth century. Of all the arts, sculpture, it must be said, lends itself especially well to weird fiction's emphasis on materiality, on strange matter, or rather, the strangeness *of* matter. Unlike the relatively flat surface of a painting, sculpture occupies space three-dimensionally. Our sensory experience of it, especially of large statuary, is never total. It cannot be experienced from a single viewpoint but retains haptic depths and surfaces that reveal themselves as the viewer changes their position. Circling Bernini's Baroque masterpiece *Apollo and Daphne* at the Borghese Gallery in Rome, for example, one could almost believe that the 'front' and 'back' are two different statues entirely, such is the revelatory power of the shift in perspective.

In this regard, sculpture is often more physically present than other kinds of art – more bulky, durable, and long-lived. It possesses strange temporalities, too. Many of the world's most famous sculptures are relics of a distant past – the hands that shaped them, the culture that encircled them, long since passed from the world. 'Look on my Works, ye Mighty, and despair!', reads the inscription on the pedestal of a shattered statue in Percy Shelley's poem 'Ozymandias' (1818), but the pharaoh's 'Works' have long since disappeared, lost to time and the desert sands: 'Nothing beside remains. Round the decay / Of that colossal Wreck, boundless and bare / The lone and level sands stretch far away' (Shelley [2014], 311).

As Shelley's poem powerfully dramatizes, sculpture can outlive its historical moment. Two of the oldest carved figurines ever discovered – the 'Venus of Hohle Fels' and the 'Lion Man of Hohlenstein-Stadel', both shaped out of mammoth ivory some 40,000 years ago – date from an almost unimaginably distant past when *homo sapiens* still shared the planet with the last Neanderthals. Even here, however, one can see plainly the imprint of a mind, a vision, a purpose that connects the past to the present, making it tangible, real; a past you can touch. Sculpture is explicitly physical. Of course, in order to preserve these objects, visitors to museums and galleries almost never get to touch sculpture, despite tactility being one of the distinguishing sensory draws of the medium – a proscription developed largely in the nineteenth century in response to increasing visitor numbers (Pulham 2022, 24).

The Victorians, for their part, were bombarded with all manner of carved and sculpted objects, from bric-a-brac to ancient monoliths, academic statuary to cheap souvenirs, architectural reliefs to figurative statuettes. Homes, cemeteries, parks, museums – stone-work could be found almost everywhere and at every scale. Nor was its creation the sole purview of solitary artists working in bohemian studios in the hope of winning acclaim at one of the prestigious Academy or Salon exhibitions in London and Paris – even if several of the stories here depict just such a figure. Most shapers of stone were masons or stonecutters – artisans, designers, and tradespeople working in an industry dedicated to quarrying and shaping the material.

And yet, despite the ubiquity of the stuff, sculpture itself remained enigmatic. As the critic Angela Dunstan puts it, sculpture was 'hauntingly present but rarely interrogated, monumental yet mundane, and, above all, disconcertingly difficult to read'

(Dunstan 2016, 3). Nor was it confined to stone. New techniques and technologies meant that desirable pieces could be reproduced in bronze at a more affordable price for the thriving middle-class market (*op cit*, 8). Wood was another ubiquitous material, but more outré mediums were also in use, including glass, clay, ceramics, precious metals, wax (Madame Tussaud's waxworks was founded in London in 1835), and even animal skin (Ross 2020, 117).

Stone, however, served a particularly wide range of purposes in the period – commemorative, aesthetic, structural, and ornamental. In fine art circles, stone sculpture was typically neoclassical and looked to Antiquity for its models and methods. The initially controversial naturalism trailblazed by the French sculptor Auguste Rodin (1840–1917) reoriented the field, and by the end of century movements like Symbolism and the New Sculpture were revitalising the artform – as seen in works like George Frampton's *Lamia*, a polychromatic bust first displayed at a Royal Academy exhibition in 1900. Its innovative combination of ivory, bronze, and opal infuses the figure with an allusive witchery.

Outside the rarefied halls of the Royal Academy of Art, neoclassicism had already lost some of its lustre thanks to the ongoing Gothic revival in arts and architecture. Beginning in the late eighteenth century but really gaining steam in the nineteenth, the Gothic Revival marked a re-energised interest in Britain's medieval past. The Gothic – the chief architectural style for large ecclesiastical buildings in the Middle Ages – was positioned as Britain's indigenous artistic heritage – a 'northern' style better suited to the country's political and religious history than classical architecture (which was seen by its detractors as a foreign, Mediterranean import). The revival generated fresh interest not only in new kinds of medieval-inspired objects, ornamentation, and architectural projects (the Houses of Parliament, for instance), but in the original medieval works themselves – the sepulchral effigies of long-dead knights found in churches up and down the land, for example (and used with chilling effect in E Nesbit's 1887 story 'Man-Size in Marble').

The Gothic Revival also spurred the 'restoration' of parish churches – a practice that reached its zenith in the 1860s. Under the influence of the Cambridge Camden Society (later the Ecclesiological Society), described by one historian as 'the most influential undergraduate society of all time' (Watkin 1980, 70), almost every parish church in the country requiring refurbishment was overhauled according to the rules and strictures promulgated by the society in their pamphlets and printed proceedings – an approach now considered to have been, in many cases, overzealous, if not downright destructive. Ecclesiastical restoration was occurring elsewhere in Europe, too. The chimeras peering over the parapets of Notre Dame cathedral in Paris (see the front cover of this book for an illustration) are not medieval but date to refurbishments begun in 1844 by the architects Eugène Viollet-le-Duc and Jean-Baptiste Lassus, who were keen to revive the cathedral's Gothic majesty.

Alongside building (and rebuilding) upwards, the Victorians were also busy digging downwards. As the century progressed, archaeology replaced antiquarianism as the most salient means of understanding ancient artefacts, and innovations in the field were numerous. To give just one, somewhat macabre, example, in the 1860s the Italian archaeologist Giuseppe Fiorelli developed a technique for making plaster casts of the cavities left by the decayed bodies caught in the volcanic eruption at Pompeii in 79 CE. Images of these casts, many taken by the photographer Giorgio Sommer, together with speculative details of the victims' terrifying final moments, circulated throughout Europe and America (see, for example, Hopley 1870). Though not stone *per se*, the casts have a poignant statue-like quality, their semi-molten forms – some details in sharp relief, others disturbingly blurred – are notably uncanny.

For an account of British archaeology in this period, the reader is encouraged to look at another Handheld Press title: *Strange Relics: Stories of Archaeology and the Supernatural, 1895–1954*, edited by Amara Thornton and Katy Soar. As their introduction makes clear, the nineteenth and early twentieth century was an exceptionally active period for archaeology. New research, societies, and digs – including a series of major excavations at Stonehenge by William Hawley in the 1920s – were putting Britain's pagan past in the cultural spotlight. The influence of this past can be seen in several of the stories reprinted here, including those by Arthur Machen, N Dennett, Eleanor Scott, and E R Punshon.

During the colonial period, Britain's archaeological interests also extended overseas. As the British Empire expanded and new 'discoveries' were made, an enormous amount of money and effort flowed into the collecting, itemising, and displaying of world sculpture, much of which was acquired by or gifted to the British Museum, whose Department of Antiquities was established in 1807. The Parthenon Marbles, removed from Athens to London by the British Ambassador to the Ottoman Empire, Lord Elgin, between 1802 and 1812, were bought by the Crown in 1816 and placed in the museum shortly thereafter. Hoa Hakananai'a – a moai basalt megalith stolen from Rapa Nui (Easter Island) by an English commodore in 1868 – was gifted to the museum the following year by Queen Victoria. The Amaravati sculptures – decorated limestone slabs from one of the most important Buddhist shrines in ancient India – were received by the museum in 1880 following the dissolution of the India Museum in London (the official museum of the East India Company between 1801 and 1879). The Benin Bronzes – a collection of decorated plaques and sculptures made in the West African Kingdom of Benin between the sixteenth and seventeenth century – came to the museum in 1897 following a brutal military invasion of Benin city by British colonial forces earlier that year.

The list of these sculptures is long, and the history of their acquisition shameful, but the accumulation and display of them attest to a public and institutional appetite for the sculptural productions of the colonies and beyond, an appetite reflected in other public displays such as The Great Exhibition of 1851 (moved to the purpose-built Crystal Palace in 1854), where, in rooms like 'The Grecian Courts' visitors could find reproductions of famous sculptures rendered in plaster of Paris (Pulham 2022, 5). For some, however, these imitations weren't enough. While the souvenir 'trade' may have been limited at the beginning of the nineteenth century to Grand Tour aristocrats winding their leisurely way through Europe, by the end of the century new railway and steamship infrastructure had given birth to an energetic tourism industry. The opening of the Suez Canal in 1869 made Egypt an especially popular destination. Gripped by a fascination with all things Egyptian, unscrupulous Victorians started taking souvenirs – from scarabs to mummified remains – back home with them (Edwards 1891, 51–52). Howard Carter and Lord Carnarvon's sensational unearthing of the tomb of Tutankhamun in 1922 further cemented Egypt's reputation as a destination of choice for the intrepid tourist.

The ghost story and the weird tale responded enthusiastically to this influx of 'exotic' objects and artefacts, often using them as a mechanism for curses, apparitions, and revenants of all kinds. Typically, these narratives exploit fears around 'reverse colonisation' which is to say, fears that the subjugated colonial Other might return in spectral, monstrous, or displaced form to terrorize British subjects (often in their own homes) or destabilize British society (Arata 1990). I have consciously avoided overloading the book with stories of this type, many of which are, by dint of their historical moment, xenophobic if not explicitly racist. E F Benson's 'Bagnell Terrace' has been included as a less egregious representative of this type. Nevertheless, published just three years after the media frenzy surrounding Tutankhamun's discovery (and the supposed curse it unleashed), it echoes the orientalist prejudices of its time.

As weird fiction started to cohere into a discrete genre in the first half of the twentieth century in American pulp magazines like *Weird Tales*, statuary began to take on cosmic, extra-terrestrial aspects. Strange monoliths, 'Cyclopean' bas-reliefs, and Elder God idols are regular features in H P Lovecraft's tales, while Mary E Counselman's wonderfully bizarre 'The Black Stone Statue' (1937) features a sculptor who steals an alien creature for its power to turn everything it touches into unbreakable black stone. Clark Ashton Smith was a sculptor as well as a writer and painter, and produced several hundred figurines from rocks sourced near his home in Auburn, California. With names like 'The Sorcerer Eibon', 'The Mysteriarch', and 'The Moon-dweller', these small, hand-carved pieces were often inspired by (or the inspiration for) his own writings and those of his circle, including work by Lovecraft, who owned several pieces. Smith's sculptures are an underacknowledged medium for high strangeness, suggesting, as they do, that 'the weird' should be understood not merely as a literary phenomenon but as a more encompassing artistic movement. The statues certainly loomed large in the imaginations of other weird fiction writers, including the director of Arkham House publishing, August Derleth, who alludes to them directly and by name at several points in his intertextual short story 'Something in Wood' (1948).

While to contemporary eyes many of Smith's figurines may appear comical rather than nightmarish, there remains something highly suggestive about them. Smith understood the mysterious ambiguity at the heart of statuary. In his prose poem 'The Statue of Silence' (1922), an unnamed narrator wandering an Olympian hall spies a statue veiled in drapery. Uncertain as to its form and meaning, the narrator asks Psyche for an answer, to which she replies: 'The name of it is Silence, but neither god nor man nor demon knoweth the form thereof, nor its entity [...] and the gods and demons of the universe are mute in its presence, half-hoping, half-fearing the time when these lips shall speak' (Smith 1922, 139). Even the gods, it would seem, are not immune to that strange blend of fear and desire that halos statuary.

Psyche's response is also a testament to the paradox of stasis and activity that characterises the uncanniness of sculpture, and 'uncanny' is an important term here. The subtitle of this book is 'Stories of Uncanny Sculpture', but what is the uncanny, precisely? While most people know what it is to *feel* uncanny, definition has proven elusive. Sigmund Freud defined it as that strange sensation of the familiar suddenly becoming unfamiliar, or vice versa, and he lists an impressive number of possible triggers for the experience including déjà vu, dead bodies, misrecognising oneself in a mirror, and, in a bizarre anecdote, the inability to escape a red-light district in a small Italian town.

For Freud, uncanny feelings are the result of the return of a repressed anxiety or belief. In his famous reading of E T A Hoffman's short story 'The Sandman' (1816) – which follows the plight of a man who falls blindly in love with an automaton – Freud's diagnosis is that the protagonist is suffering from a repressed castration anxiety, relayed symbolically through the man's fear of eyes and eyesight. It is perhaps worth mentioning that Freud was himself a great collector of statues, idols, and figurines, and kept an assortment of them in his office – including twenty phallic amulets. A recent exhibition at the Freud Museum in London suggests that these objects acted as spurs to his own thinking and may have even informed the development of various psychoanalytic theories and methods (*Freud's Antiquity*). Another instance of sculpture's compulsive power.

Still, if you don't find Freud's argument particularly convincing, you may prefer the theory put forward by Freud's precursor on matters of the uncanny, Ernst Jentsch. Jentsch claimed that we feel uncanny when we experience something that we can't grasp intellectually or psychologically. As soon as we 'master' the experience – for instance, when we realise that the shambling ghoul in the bedroom corner is just a coat being blown by the wind from an open window – the uncanny feeling dissipates. However, for a fleeting moment, Jentsch claims, we are exposed to the true nature of things: nothing is *really* what it seems – familiarity is a psychic structure or procedure that protects us from the primordial otherness of reality. The most reliable trigger of the uncanny, Jentsch says, is 'doubt as to whether an apparently living being really is animate and, conversely, doubt as to whether a lifeless object may not in fact be animate' (Jentsch 2008, 221). For the tale of terror, this doubt becomes a literary device, a lever by which to turn something ordinary into something profoundly disquieting.

Of course, readers must decide for themselves whether these psychoanalytic explanations hold water. Some critics have argued that psychoanalysis should be thought of not as a science or a therapy but as a kind of Gothic fiction or ghost story in its own right. It is certainly intriguing that the uncanny should coalesce into an object of study at the beginning of the twentieth century – the peak years of the ghost story's 'golden age' (see Luckhurst 1999). Nevertheless, if there is a thread that runs through all of the stories gathered here, it is precisely this troubling of the boundaries between the animate and the inanimate, the human and the lithic. Each author, in their own way, makes use of the strange life/death we find in, or project onto, sculpted stone. As Jeffrey Jerome Cohen reflects in his book *Stone: An Ecology of the Inhuman*, 'stone brings story into being' (Cohen 2015, 4). This book collates some of these stories, acting as a monument, a monolith in words, to the remarkable potency of the material and the strange influence it has exerted on the darker facets of the human imagination.

The stories

The first story is 'Master Sacristan Eberhart' by Sabine Baring-Gould, an Anglican priest as well as a prolific author. With interests ranging from hymnody (he composed the lyrics to 'Onward, Christian Soldiers') to werewolf lore, this story first appeared in the December 1858 issue of *The Hurst Johnian* – the school magazine for Hurstpierpoint College in West Sussex, where Baring-Gould worked as a Master between 1855 and 1864. Subtitled 'Not Quite a Ghost Story', this creepy tale pivots on a strange friendship between a sacristan and a beloved church gargoyle. While the story was likely conceived as a bit of ghoulish Christmas fare for students and colleagues like many of Baring-Gould's tales it deserves a larger audience.

W W Fenn's 'The Marble Hands' is the first of two stories with this title republished here. First published in the two-volume collection *Woven in Darkness: A Medley of Stories, Essays, and Dreamwork* (1885), it tells of a young sculptor who receives an unexpected gift from an old friend. In a cruel twist of fate, the 'gift' is linked to a shocking family legend and the sculptor must reckon with the phantasms of his ancestry. The story's author, William Wilthew Fenn, was a painter until his sight began to fail him. He was diagnosed with amaurosis and by his mid-thirties was completely blind. His several collections of stories and essays – produced with the help of his wife, Elizabeth Bowles – were all published after the loss of his sight. Artists and artworks are, unsurprisingly, a recurring theme.

Robert W Chambers' story 'The Mask' is taken from his seminal collection of weird decadence, *The King in Yellow* (1895). A sculptor has developed a liquid for transmuting any object into pure marble; calamity ensues when a painful truth is unexpectedly revealed. Born in Brooklyn, New York, Chambers trained initially as an artist and illustrator and studied for several years in France. Inspired by these years abroad, 'The Mask' is a blend of Beaux-Arts, chemistry, and a love triangle gone awry – all set in the heady atmosphere of a Parisian art studio at the *fin de siècle*.

Not much is known about Nellie K Blissett. Her father worked for the African Commissariat, and census data shows that she lived on the Isle of Wight (Bassett 2023). Between 1896 and 1905, she wrote eight novels, including *The Sea Hath Its Pearls* (1901), *The Bindweed* (1904), and *The Silver Key* (1906). The story included here is 'The Stone Rider! A Short Story of the Weird' – a pacey Gothic tale of secrets, villainy, and comeuppance first published in *The Harmsworth Monthly Pictorial Magazine* in 1898. Aside from a 1998 reprint in the short-lived horror zine *Enigmatic Tales*, the story has sunk into obscurity. Its reprinting here should solidify its reputation as one of the quintessential narratives of its type.

'A Marble Woman' by the American author William Chambers Morrow presents a disturbingly literal account of reverse pygmalionism. A man's desire to keep his wife forever young and beautiful, to keep her skin perpetually smooth and pale, leads him to carry out an unorthodox chemical experiment. As her skin begins to harden, the fantasy soon turns into a nightmare. Morrow's early stories appeared in papers like *The Argonaut* and the *San Francisco Examiner* (putting him in contact with another author of the weird, Ambrose Bierce), and a volume of his collected tales, *The Ape, the Idiot and Other People*, appeared in 1897. 'A Marble Woman' was one of his last stories and first appeared in the June 1899 edition of *The Penny Pictorial Magazine*.

The next entry is from the Pulitzer Prize winning author Edith Wharton, best known for her satirical exposés of upper-class American socialites in novels like *The House of Mirth* (1905) and *The Age of Innocence* (1920), and for her bleak New England narrative, *Ethan Frome* (1911). While Wharton's short stories have received less attention, they are of remarkable quality and much beloved by ghost story afficionados. 'The Duchess at Prayer' first appeared in the August 1900 edition of *Scribner's Magazine*. Touring the country mansion of a seventeenth-century Italian ducal family, the narrator is shown a remarkable Bernini sculpture in a private chapel, but something is wrong with her face, terribly wrong. A story told to the caretaker by his grandmother may hold the key to the statue's extraordinary expression.

An artist by training, the Yorkshire-born author Oliver Onions published three stories concerning sculpture, each one involving a different medium – 'The Smile of Karen', 'Resurrection in Bronze', and the story featured here, 'Benlian'. Published in *The Fortnightly Review* in January 1911 and collected in *Widdershins* shortly after, it tells of a sculptor who requires a witness (and worshipper) for an experiment involving a misshapen statue in his studio. As the story progresses, the reader, like the narrator, must grapple with Benlian's magnetic personality. Wrapping an innovative take on the theory of metempsychosis around a masterfully executed character study, this is Onions at his very best.

At under a thousand words long 'The Marble Hands' by Bernard Capes is the shortest story in the collection, but no less potent. An author, journalist, and editor, Capes published some forty books in a range of styles and genres, and his work appeared regularly in many of the leading papers and periodicals of the day. Despite this, his stories remain perennially underappreciated. 'The Marble Hands' originally appeared in the journal *The New Witness* along with several other tales. These were then collected together into a single volume titled *The Fabulists*, published by Mills & Boon in 1915. The book employs a classic framing device in which various narrators take it in turns to tell a tale. 'The Marble Hands' is narrated by the enigmatically named Raven, and tells of a peculiar grave in a village cemetery, and the fate of the woman it commemorates.

Howard Philips Lovecraft needs little introduction. The doyen of weird fiction, his stories are a veritable pop-cultural phenomenon and despite the toxicity of the man himself (he was an ardent racist and white supremacist) his influence on the genre's philosophical and aesthetic commitments is unparalleled. 'Hypnos' comes from his early to middle period. A young sculptor in London is fiercely drawn to a beautiful 'godlike' man he meets in a crowded train station. The man becomes his friend and teacher and the two commence a series of drug-fuelled cosmic dream quests into unplumbed spheres with dramatic consequences. Is the sculptor's friend real or just a projection from the wish-fulfilling unconscious of a chronically lonely and unstable young man? Readers must decide for themselves. A characteristic example of Lovecraft's breathless, catachrestic diction, it was first published in *The National Amateur* in May 1923.

Arthur Machen's interest in ancient statues and artefacts can be traced back to his boyhood in Gwent, South Wales, and the unearthing of pagan finds by some local archaeologists. Statuary would go on to feature in several of his major works, including *The Great God Pan* (1894) and, more directly, *The White People* (1904). The story published here, 'The Ceremony', is a clear precursor to the *The White People* in terms of theme and content, but is more of an atmospheric vignette than a full story. A masterpiece of suggestion, it was written in the 1890s but didn't see publication until 1924 in a collection titled *Ornaments in Jade*. As this title suggests, Machen saw these particular writings in an ekphrastic register in which prose might be wrought into a kind of ornamental sculpture.

Edward Frederic Benson OBE, is perhaps best known for his series of six playful social satires known collectively as the Mapp and Lucia novels. For horror fans, however, these are eclipsed by his several volumes of 'spook stories', which stand as some of the best in the genre. His father was the Archbishop of Canterbury from 1883; his mother, Mary, was the sister of Henry Sedgwick, a Cambridge philosopher and the first president of the Society for Psychical Research. Edward graduated from Kings College, Cambridge with a degree in archaeology and was involved in several excavations in a professional capacity before taking up writing full time. His sister, Margaret (Maggie) Benson was an amateur Egyptologist and conducted the first woman-led excavations in Egypt in the 1890s. Edward visited her site in Luxor, helping where he could. Maggie's finds were significant, and a book detailing the excavations, co-authored with Janet Gourley, appeared in 1899. The story published here, 'Bagnell Terrace', is one of several that draw on his experiences in Egypt. A mysterious neighbour and a strange statuette of a cat brought back from the Valley of the Kings lead to a terrifying climax. The story was first published in *Hutchinson's Magazine* in July 1925.

'At Simmel Acres Farm' by Eleanor Scott, the pen name of Helen Leys, is one of the more subtle and sinister tales in the collection. Appearing in Leys' single volume of supernatural fiction, *Randalls Round* (1929), it tells of two Oxford students vacationing in the Cotswolds. It soon becomes clear, however, that the name of the farm they're staying at may refer to something far less bucolic, a *simulacrum* or, in Middle English, a simulacre: 'an image (of a god, etc) to which honour or worship is rendered'. While Scott's debt to other ghost story writers (including most notably M R James) is inarguable, her rich atmospherics are uniquely effective. With folk horror back in the limelight, Scott's pioneering work in the genre is beginning to receive the acclaim it deserves.

'The Maker of Gargoyles' by Clark Ashton Smith is the fourth of a dozen or so stories set in Averoigne – a fictional medieval province in France. As mentioned above, Smith was himself a maker of 'gargoyles' – small outlandish statues hand-shaped out of local stone, so the theme is not an unexpected one. Largely self-educated, Smith was wildly creative if something of a recluse. His first published book was a well-reviewed volume of poetry titled *The Star-Treader and Other Poems* (1912), produced when he was just nineteen. A correspondence struck up with H P Lovecraft in 1922 introduced Smith to the weird fiction scene, and would see him go on to produce over a hundred short stories for various pulp magazines. 'The Maker of Gargoyles' tells of a shunned mason who pours too much of himself into the two gargoyles he has been commissioned to carve for the city's cathedral. An unflinching tale about lust and hate made manifest and the ultimately self-destructive consequences of these emotions, it first appeared in the August 1932 edition of *Weird Tales*.

'The Man of Stone' by Hazel Heald tells of a jealous husband (descended from evil wizarding stock) who uses arcane knowledge gleaned from the Book of Eibon to wreak vengeance on his wife and her suspected lover. While Heald is credited as the sole author, the story had in fact been heavily edited and revised by H P Lovecraft, who occasionally offered his services to aspiring weird fiction authors. While the exact nature of their relationship is unknown, they collaborated on at least five published stories, 'The Horror in the Museum' (1933), 'Winged Death' (1934), and 'Out of the Æons' (1935) among them (see Derie 2021). Lovecraft claimed to have all but ghostwritten these stories, but it is Heald's voice, not Lovecraft's, that shines through in 'The Man of Stone' – their first collaboration and Heald's first ever story – not least because it features a young woman with guts, intellect, and agency, a virtual impossibility in stories of Lovecraft's own devising. The story made its debut appearance in the October 1932 edition of *Wonder Stories*.

'The Menhir', by N Dennett, begins with the arrival of a church curate in a small rural village in which he is to take up his new position. His indignation is roused when he observes the local villagers paying superstitious deference to an ancient carved pillar in the church cemetery. But there is something … malignant about the stone menhir, and soon his own faith and sanity are put to the test. A masterfully wrought slab of English weirdness, the story traps the reader in an ever-tightening spiral of claustrophobic dread. Nothing is known about N Dennett – a strong indicator that the name was a pseudonym. Richard Dalby proposed that Dennett might be another of Helen Leys' pen-names, an attribution echoed by Aaron Worth, who includes this story in his recent edition of *Randalls Round*. Still, as there is no conclusive proof for this attribution, the theory remains speculative for now. The story was first published in *Panics: A Collection of Uneasy Tales* (1934) – a book in the 'Creeps' series published by Philip Allan between 1932 and 1936. Notably, the jacket illustration for the book, designed by Philip Simmonds, shows a man fleeing from a menacing carved figure behind him; clearly 'The Menhir' was a standout story. The Creeps series was edited by Charles Lloyd Birkin, who prefaced this story with the following tag: 'The power of the Old Gods and of Evil still lingers in quiet corners of England'.

Birkin's line would not be an inaccurate description of the next story either, Ernest Robertson Punshon's 'The Living Stone', first published in *Cornhill Magazine* in September 1939. A professor of comparative religion on a trip to Cornwall starts asking questions about local missing persons cases. Teaming up with a chief inspector from Scotland Yard, the pair discover a curious granite monolith known only as the Hunting Stone. The professor has his suspicions, but some horrors have to be seen to be believed. The initial set-up of this story would have been a familiar one to fans of Punshon's work. Though he produced several short stories over his career, this London author was known primarily for his detective novels, of which he wrote almost sixty. The chief inspector, for example, would not be out of place in one of Punshon's thirty-five 'Bobby Owen' novels, in which a policeman rises up the ranks from constable to commander. Some foes, however, defy natural explanation.

The final story in the anthology is James Oliver Causey's 'The Statue', published in the January 1943 edition of *Weird Tales*. Jerome Winters, a callous moneylender, seizes a sculptor's unfinished statue as collateral for a failed repayment. An ultimatum issued by the desperate sculptor is dismissed by Winters, but things change when he starts waking in the night to sounds of a chisel at work. Stranger still, the statue's limbs seem to be in a different position each morning. Born in California, Causey wrote at least three stories for *Weird Tales* in the 1940s, of which 'The Statue' was the first. In the 1950s, he pivoted to science fiction and crime fiction, producing several stories for various science fiction pulps and a number of hardboiled crime novels with titles like *The Baby Doll Murders* (1957) and *Frenzy* (1960). 'The Statue' is an expertly self-contained revenge story. For all its straightforwardness, it is perhaps the quintessential example of our theme, and it is hoped the reader will leave this story, and thus the book, feeling decidedly uneasy.

Note

Two stories that deserve a place in the volume but are not to be in found in its pages are Edith Nesbit's 'Man-Size in Marble' and Mary Elizabeth Counselman's 'The Black Stone Statue' as they have already been published in other Handheld Press titles (*British Weird: Selected Short Fiction, 1893–1937* and *Women's Weird 2: More Strange Stories by Women, 1891–1937*, respectively). Various other tales made the longlist but ultimately had to be left out. These include Lady Emilia Dilke's 'The Shrine of Death' (1886), Thomas Hardy's 'Barbara, of the House of Grebe' (1891), 'The Black Statue' (1899) by Huan Mee (the pseudonym of Charles and Walter Mansfield) – a story flagrantly plagiarised a quarter of a century later by Laurence D'Orsay in a 1925 issue of *Weird Tales* – Margery Lawrence's oneiric 'The Shrine at the Cross-roads' (1932), and A N L Munby's 'The Alabaster Hand' (1949). In the case of Vernon Lee's stories, of which at least five feature sculpture or statuary, it was felt that as they have now been reprinted several times in recent years, including in a prestigious Oxford World Classics edition, space should be given to lesser-known tales. Nevertheless, if, after finishing this volume, the reader is hungry for more, the above stories come with the editor's recommendation.

References

Arata, Stephen D, 'The Occidental Tourist: "Dracula" and the Anxiety of Reverse Colonization', *Victorian Studies*, 33:4, 1990, 621–645. For the pulp magazines of the early twentieth century, one can replace Britain here with white America.

Bassett, Troy J, 'Author: Nellie K. Blissett', *At the Circulating Library: A Database of Victorian Fiction, 1837—1901*, 25 June 2023. https://www.victorianresearch.org/atcl/show_author.php?aid=3053

Cohen, Jeffrey Jerome. *Stone: An Ecology of the Inhuman*, University of Minnesota Press, 2015.

Derie, Bobby, 'Her Letters to Lovecraft: Hazel Heald', *Deep Cuts in a Lovecraftian Vein*. 31st March, 2021. https://deepcuts.blog/2021/03/31/her-letters-to-lovecraft-hazel-heald

Dunstan, Angela, 'Reading Victorian Sculpture', *19: Interdisciplinary Studies in the Long Nineteenth Century*, 22, 2016.

Edwards, Amelia B, *A Thousand Miles up the Nile*, George Routledge & Sons, 1891.

Forster, Michael, 'Johann Gottfried von Herder', *The Stanford Encyclopedia of Philosophy* (Summer 2022), Edward N Zalta (ed). https://plato.stanford.edu/entries/herder

Freud's Antiquity: Object, Idea, Desire. 25th February to 16th July 2023. Freud Museum, London.

Hopley, Howard, 'Pompeii', *The Leisure Hour: A Family Journal of Instruction and Recreation, January 1852–December 1876*, 981, 1870, 660–663.

Jentsch, Ernst, 'On the Psychology of the Uncanny', translated by Roy Sellars, in *Uncanny Modernity: Cultural Theories, Modern Anxieties*, (eds) Jo Collins and John Jervis, Palgrave Macmillan, 2008, 216–228.

Luckhurst, Roger, '"Something Tremendous, Something Elemental": On the Ghostly Origins of Psychoanalysis', in *Ghosts: Deconstruction, Psychoanalysis, History*, (eds) Peter Bruse and Andrew Stott, Macmillan, 1999, 50–71.

Pulham, Patricia, *The Sculptural Body in Victorian Literature: Encrypted Sexualities*, Edinburgh University Press, 2022.

Ross, Alan S, 'The Animal Body as Medium: Taxidermy and European Expansion, 1775–1865', *Past & Present* 249:1, November 2020, 85–119.

Shelley, Percy Bysshe, *The Poems of Shelley, Volume Two: 1817–1819*, (eds) Kelvin Everest and Geoffrey Matthews, Routledge, 2014.

Smith, Clark Ashton, 'Ebony and Crystal: Poems in Verse and Prose', *The Auburn Journal*, 1922.

Watkin, David, *The Rise of Architectural History*, Architectural Press, 1980.

First publication details

Sabine Baring-Gould, 'Master Sacristan Eberhart: Not Quite a Ghost Story', *The Hurst Johnian*, 7, December 1858, 283–250.

W W Fenn, 'The Marble Hands', *Woven in Darkness: A Medley of Stories, Essays, and Dreamwork*, Kelly & Co, 1885.

Robert W Chambers, 'The Mask', *The King in Yellow*, F Tennyson Neely, 1895.

Nellie K Blissett, 'The Stone Rider! A Short Story of the Weird', *The Harmsworth Monthly Pictorial Magazine*, 1:1, 1898–9, 30–37.

W C Morrow, 'A Marble Woman', *The Penny Pictorial Magazine*, June 17th 1899, 64–67.

Edith Wharton, 'The Duchess at Prayer', *Scribner's Magazine*, August 1900, 151–64.

Oliver Onions 'Benlian', *The Fortnightly Review*, 89:529, January 1911, 164–78.

Bernard Capes, 'The Marble Hands', *The Fabulists*, Mills & Boon, 1915.

H P Lovecraft, 'Hypnos', *The National Amateur*, May 1923, 1–3.

Arthur Machen, 'The Ceremony', *Ornaments in Jade*, Alfred A Knopf, 1924.

E F Benson, 'Bagnell Terrace', *Hutchinson's Magazine*, July 1925, 14–20.

Eleanor Scott, 'At Simmel Acres Farm', *Randalls Round*, Ernest Benn Limited, 1929.

Clark Ashton Smith, 'The Maker of Gargoyles', *Weird Tales*, August 1932, 198–207.

Hazel Heald, 'The Man of Stone', *Wonder Stories*, October 1932, 441–45.

N Dennett, 'The Menhir', *Panics: A Collection of Uneasy Tales*, Philip Allan, 1934.

E R Punshon, 'The Living Stone', *Cornhill Magazine*, September 1939, 321–33.

James Causey, 'The Statue', *Weird Tales*, January 1943, 20–26.

1 Master Sacristan Eberhart (1858)

SABINE BARING-GOULD

The much respected Master Eberhart, Sacristan of the ancient church of S Osbaldus, lived, as others of his profession have done before, and do still on the continent, in the tower, above the big bells. His office was to keep his keen eye upon the villages around; and, should he detect the rising smoke and flame from a house on fire, to sound the alarum on a separate bell in the turret above his chamber.

This chamber, by the way, requires description. It formed one stage in the square tower; four windows commanded the points of the compass, glazed with the coarse old fashioned glass, called in some places 'bull's eye', with the exception of one light in each, that was filled with quarries, and that was just the one to peep through. In the corner of this room rose a crazy wooden stair, leading to the leads; below it, descended another to the belfry. There was a table of common deal, a large slope-backed armchair, and another chair for visitors, if they should come, but they didn't. Against the wall, as is the custom with pious people abroad, there hung a crucifix. Now the Sacristan was a pious man, though he was odd too — at least 'the people down below' called him so — *I* think he was very sensible, but as we may differ on the point, I leave you to judge for yourself. The good old man lived very much to himself up there in the windy old steeple, and very seldom descended into the wicked world, except to hear mass of a morning, and to fetch his bread and milk; and these were brought for him as far as to the tower door. No one ever thought of going up the three hundred and sixty-five steps leading to the Sacristan's room, except the bell-ringers just occasionally; and they tried the old man's temper dreadfully — they were so earthy; and the Priest called now and then, but Master Eberhart, although he respected and honoured him, (I said before he was very pious) — yet from being only associated with the birds and the old gurgoils — (those are the old carved spouts) he talked to him, not as if he were flesh and blood, but as if he were a stone man; not a gurgoil exactly, but a church monument. I don't think the Priest quite liked that.

Master Eberhart had a way of making friends too; but then they were not the ordinary friends 'people down below' make. You shall hear who they were. On the top of the tower below the broach of the spire, were four carved figures, life-size; one was a horse, another a dragon, a third an eagle, the fourth a monk, and the frost had taken his nose off. These statues had their mouths wide open, and were intended to spout the water off from the spire; but they never did, the rain always ran off another way down an ugly lead pipe. Yellow lichens marbled these grotesques all over, even over their faces. The monk turned west, and at sunset a red light covered him. He looked very terrible then, as if dipped in blood. It was not to be expected that Master Eberhart should care much for the three animals, at least not more than the people below would for their horses — they haven't got dragons or eagles — or for their guinea-pigs and fancy pigeons. But it was quite another matter with regard to the monk: the Sacristan loved him dearly, and had long conversations with him — only the talking was all on one side, but that was the pleasanter. On a sunny day, it was so agreeable to sit on the leads, leaning against the battlements, right over against the monk, and discuss the world below: a genial light irradiated the stone face, and it looked quite smiling; if it had not lost the nose, it would have been even handsome. On a moon-bright night also, when the lights were going out, one after another, in the windows far below, like sparks on a bit of tinder, the Sacristan loved to kneel in the shadow of the stone man, whose cowl and mutilated face would be cutting the moon's disk, and chant clearly some beautiful Psalm, finishing with his hymn 'Te lucis ante terminum'. The old man thought sometimes that the shooting lips of the figure moved, but of course we who live on the earth know well enough that it was only his fancy. For a long time Master Eberhart did not know his friend's name, as he had never told him, but he found it out at last; for one day the priest of S Sebaldus came up to visit him, bringing under his arm a big book bound in hogskin, and having a quantity of leaves in it. The Sacristan had never seen more; he thought there must be about a thousand, five hundred, and something over. The Priest talked to the old man a great deal, chiefly about some Egyptian saint whose life he was going to read to him. The Sacristan loved stories, so he listened with all his ears; the life was that of S Simon Stylites, who lived — I don't know how long — on the top of a pillar, ate nothing but leeks, and was never once blown off, however high the wind was. As he heard the account, a clear gleam of light shot into the old man's brain, and looking up through the little door at the top of the stairs, at the monk who was just visible, nodded friendly to him, with a 'Good morrow, Father Simon!' After that day, the Sacristan always called the gurgoil man 'Father Simon'.

Master Eberhart had his notions concerning things in general; they were bright and expansive, as the view from his belfry; but as in that he looked over the rising gables of the church below — each topped with a cross, so in every view he took of earthly matters, the cross was in them. It was quite wonderful how clear and panoramic his ideas were; quaint fancies surrounded them, and they were like the gurgoils, from among which he saw the earth. We do not get these broad theories below, for somehow, a neighbour's garden wall, or a granary gable, or sometimes merely a twig, debars us from taking a general sweep of the horizon.

The old man was one day sitting on the leads, looking up to his stone monk. 'I think,' said he, 'that the people down below are very self-sufficient, they fancy that all Creation is made to do them service; for that purpose called into being, and may be trimmed and pruned just as suits their wayward fancies; as if the handiwork of God were not made first to do Him praise and glory, and only secondly to rejoice the heart of man. I wish the folk down on earth would know their Benedicite a little better, and remember that all God's works praise him! Do you not agree with me, Father Simon? I know you do; why — a scud of rain cannot break over this fair spire, and the water trickle down these runnels, but the men down there think it is sent just to clear their gutters and sewers; as if there were not first the yellow lichen stain to rejoice and the pretty moss to make glad, before ever it reaches them.' A ripple of golden sunlight ran over the weathered face of the gurgoil — 'Heaven knows,' sighed the old man, 'I do not, the exact way in which all the works of God praise Him; perhaps it may be in being always cheerful; perhaps in fulfilling what their mission is; perhaps in having no thought of themselves; but being beautiful; they work so steadily till they have done all they can, and till they are perfectly beautiful— and how cheerful they always are! There are those men down below. They seek their own interests, their self-advancement, and, if they be the least religious, their own feelings, forgetting all about the duty of praise; and that lifeless — I mean what *they* would call lifeless — things which cannot praise any other way, praise by doing their duty.' A bird perched on the monk's cowl, and sent forth a stream of song. 'There! there!' exclaimed the Sacristan — and he was undoubtedly going on to moralise, when, for the first time, he noticed a long crack at the back of the old carved spout. 'Bless me,' gasped the good man in alarm, 'Father Simon is breaking from the spire; what shall I do? The next high wind or frost, and he will be off— horrible! into the naughty world below. I will save him from that; what shall I do?' Master Eberhart rushed down the stairs; and catching the rope, sent forth peal after peal on the alarm bell. The folk on earth said, 'There surely must be a whole village on fire somewhere,' — but it was only the gurgoil which was cracked. Up the stairs ran the sexton to know what was the matter; and the terrified Sacristan implored him to send a mason and his men at once, that his friend the monk might be saved. The sexton growled and went down the tower, he was quite disappointed that *that* was all; he had made up his mind that Altdorf was in flames. What men we are!

Well! — next day there came the mason and one man; and they pulled down the stone man, and laid him on the leads. 'You had better bring him into my room,' said Master Eberhart. 'What shall we do next?' asked the mason, when he had done so. 'Put him in my visitor's chair; wait — one moment — let me move my cash box.' The Sacristan pulled a tin coffer containing all his savings, from the seat, and laid it on the table; then the gurgoil was lifted into the place. 'When shall he be put up again?' asked the old man. 'Put up?' exclaimed the mason, 'He ain't worth the expense. What's the good of an ugly bit of stone like that, up aloft? Why he might have tumbled and welcome, but that people feared for their heads.'

'Not put back up again!' groaned the Sacristan. 'Never mind my box, leave it alone,' said he sharply, to the mason's man, who was lifting it. 'I don't care what it costs, I'll pay for him; and if I haven't enough, why the monk shall wait till my death, and all my savings shall go to put him back again; he shall be my monument.' The mason laughed, and would have brought his hammer down on the head of the monk, but that the Sacristan withheld his hand.

'You haven't got enough to pay for replacing that thing,' said the mason's man.

'I do not know that,' answered the old man, 'What would it cost?'

'Why there's a new block to be let into the spire, and the figure to be rivetted with iron clamps —'

'Iron clamps!' moaned the Sacristan.

'Don't know what it would come to exactly,' replied the mason. 'Good evening, master.'

Eberhart sat down to supper, in his slope-backed chair, on one side of the table; on the other, in the visitor's chair the stone Friar squatted on his haunches, hands on knees, head thrust forward, the mouth protruding and wide open, the cowl half drawn over the dull eyes, the nose, I said before, was gone. The wind moaned at the window, but that it always did; the little fire burned brightly, and Master Eberhart looked lovingly and with a serene brow on his guest. 'I never have a meal quite to myself,' said he. 'There's a mouse or two generally comes out at supper time, and a robin is at the window of a morning; it is very strange that my mice do not come tonight! I cannot eat all by myself, I should feel as if doing wrong, not to share with some creature. Father Simon, will you have some?' he laid a piece of bread before him, but the courtesy passed without any acknowledgment.

'I always say my prayers after supper,' said the Sacristan, 'and then to bed; would that you could join!' Then he cleared the victuals from his table, moved to it his book of devotions, swept away the crumbs, and knelt down. Long and earnestly did the old man pray, his silver hair trailing over his thin fingers. He said his prayers aloud and sang a psalm or two on his knees, then remained silent for a moment or two — A shadow fell along his book — something cold touched his head — he felt two heavy hands on his hair — like a priest's, blessing him; then they were withdrawn and Master Eberhart rose joyously from his knees. 'That is just as it ought to have been,' murmured he, in his happy heart. Afterwards he undressed and went to bed. It might have been three hours after this that the old man awoke, hearing a heavy tread about the floor, he opened his eyes. The moon lighted up the interior of the room, shining in at one of the four windows: in the corner stood Father Simon, going down the stairs into the belfry. Shortly after, Master Eberhart heard him groping among the bells, every touch of his fingers sounding on them, for those fingers were stone; then up he came again. The old man chuckled, and said to himself — 'Friend Simon is curious to know how the bells are hung and worked; he has heard them so very long without having seen them.' The figure was again in the room, crossed it and coming up to the bedside laid itself down on it. The old Sacristan did feel a little startled, the weight seemed so great, bending down the outer side of the bed; and, as he put his hand to the figure, it was so cold, so bitterly cold; but he drove away these foolish fears, and said 'Father, if you are chilly take the coverlid.' The statue remained immovable, so the old man sitting up, folded the counterpane over his bedfellow, then turning his face to the wall, tried to sleep. Now and then, however, he cast a furtive back-glance at the monk. The moon was on his face — that was cold, white and rigid with deep shadows in the eye sockets, the monstrous mouth gaping wide.

Master Eberhart dozed off, and when morning dawned, the figure was crouching in the visitor's chair, looking before it out of the opposite window. The day passed, as days usually passed in the tower top; at half past seven the old man went down to hear Mass, after which he received his bread, milk, and leeks at the door. Breakfast followed; but the bird was not at the window ledge, as was its wont; nor did the mice appear all day. In the evening, the fire was lighted, and Master Eberhart warmed himself at the blaze; he would have moved the monk to the fire, only he was not strong enough. At nine a bell rung in a distant church tower; they had no clock in S Sebaldus' steeple, but that of S Lorenz had one. The Sacristan wiped his table, brought out his book and said his evening prayers. Again the shadow fell across the page, and two cold hands were laid in benediction on his head. Strengthened heart, and soul, the old man rose from his knees, and undressed by the fire; for some time he remained sitting before it, meditating, till at last he grew sleepy (people generally do get sleepy sitting over the grate) and crept to bed. Ten o'clock struck faintly and sweetly in the distant tower, and then the chimes began to play 'Willkommen, du seliger abend,' plaintively. 'I am thankful we have no chimes in S Sebaldus,' muttered the Sacristan half dozing. 'They are like emperors playing spellikens. Bells were made to be pealed, not to be hammered about with little knockers.' Somehow, now that he was in bed, he could not sleep. First he turned his face to the wall, then the other way; then with great misgivings tried his back. In that position he may have slept for a half hour or an hour; I do not know, nor did he; but he was again awake, and his eyes opening fell on the fireplace. Then he brisked up thoroughly, for he saw, seated before the hearth, the monk, his hands on his knees, the crimson glare of the embers seeming to saturate his maimed face, cowl, and robe with blood, red, blood red. He had the blue grey of the room for a background, and through the window, the indigo sky, in which sparkled one bright frosty star. The foregoing night, Eberhart had felt but little fear; but now, a cold shudder quivered his old flesh; it was so awful, the face of his friend was changed, the brow seemed to be contracted over eyes no longer dull, but burning as iron from a forge; the vast mouth was closed and the lips firmly set. The features were no longer grotesque, but resolute, inflexible, determined; that was what paralyzed the Sacristan. The monk had some errand to perform; he saw it in that unwavering face, on which the reflection of the embers was steady, however it might flicker on cowl and robe. The clock of S Lorenz struck twelve, and then the chimes played a simple hymn, now sounding clearly as the wind bore the notes, then feebler as it died away. A falling star glided past the opposite window without haste. The bright star was beyond the window frame, another appeared. A slight clatter from below reached the Sacristan's ears; an owl must have got in among the bells; but for that stone figure he would have risen to drive the bird out. Slowly the monk rose from his seat and walked deliberately to the head of the stair ladder, stationing himself a little on one side, slightly back. On the other side there was but a narrow strip of flooring to the wall, sufficiently wide for a chest to stand, on which was placed the Sacristan's cash box. Again, a noise below. 'Well,' said the old man half audibly, 'Father Simon will not hurt me I know; and I must see what is going on among the bells; those owls and jackdaws' — he put one leg out of bed, 'No —! I hear a step on the stair.' The monk turned his head cautiously round and beckoned with his stone finger. Master Eberhart understood his meaning and settled himself in bed again. There *was* a stealthy tread on the stair. Surprised and terrified the old man sat up in bed. Thirteen — fourteen — fifteen — whoever it might be, he must be near the top: there! — a head rose through an opening in the floor, and Eberhart recognised the mason's man by the firelight. The shadow of the slope-backed arm-chair crossed the corner where the old man sat so as to conceal him. The fellow crept nearly to the top; a large knife was in one of his hands; his eyes roved about the room, seeking something in the obscurity: in an instant they kindled up; he saw, and put out his hand to grasp the money coffer. A heavy tread behind him made him turn sharply round, and a fearful shriek broke from him, as his eyes encountered the stone monk leaning towards him, the cold eyes fixed on his, the granite hands extended, the knees bent as if for a leap. The mason stood benumbed with horror — the knife fell from his fingers and clattered down the steps, till it struck a bell. The gurgoil stooped further forward, sloping towards him; the cold hand touched his throat — in a moment those fingers collapsed; the figure became rigid; there was a gurgle, a fall, a furious bounding and crashing down the ladder; one wild jangle on a tenor bell, droning off fainter, fainter, faint, lost.

Not a sound to be heard, but the breath of the wind on the window panes, and its hum through traceried battlements over head, a sweet Æolian wail. Then scarcely audible came the horn of the watch from the great square; a bat dashed against the glass; all was still again. One o'clock struck far off in S Lorenz tower: something moved on the bed, it was only a mouse, it scrambled down the coverlid and trotted across the floor. The last embers grew cold. A moth fluttered against the window top, and would not be still; the death watch ticked in an old beam; the cinders fell together in the grate! Morning came at last: 'Thank God' sighed the Sacristan. The chair was in front of the extinguished fire; the cash box safe; no gurgoil-monk to be seen. 'It cannot have been a dream,' faltered Master Eberhart. Then he rose from his pallet, slowly dressed, said his prayers, and hesitated at the top of the stairs, for he feared to descend. First he peeped down, but there was only sufficient light to distinguish huge rounded shapes of bells and massive rafters. 'I will wait until it is a little lighter,' muttered he.

The sun rose, bars of yellow shone through the luffer boards on the bells. 'I must go and ring for Mass,' said the old man, 'that is a duty, I *must* go now.' So down he went. In the belfry, under one of the largest bells, lay a heap — the stone monk on top, crouching, one hand on his knee, the other clenched at the mason's throat, the large mouth gaping as of old; and the man — he lay, his feet doubled under his back, his hands clutching the stone arm, the head slung unnaturally on one side, for his neck was broken. The gurgoil, too, was snapped in half.

The old man said gravely to himself, 'I dare say that all creatures in nature, or in art, whatever they may be, cheerful flowers, happy birds, or only bits of stone, may become to us angels of good, if we only love them with true heart and reverence; but then we must love them because they are true, and good, and not because we may see in them reflections of our own selves, our feelings, and passions.'

2 The Marble Hands (1885)

W W FENN

A bye-street off the Hampstead Road, not a promising locality for poetry and romance, but rather suggestive, perhaps, of grime and squalor, and more grimy and squalid thirty years ago than now. Yet here Carlo Juliano Rossi had his studio, and Carlo Juliano Rossi was, at the age of four-and-twenty, one of the most imaginative and poetically-minded young sculptors that you might meet with in a long day's march. But in the face of high aspirations he had to contend with poverty, and whilst filled with an intense desire to devote himself to the production of work which should live for the benefit of mankind through all time, he had to earn his daily bread in a stonemason's yard, and this from the age of fourteen.

Charley Rossi, as he was familiarly called by his English friends, was very English also, in spite of his name and descent, having been born and brought up in London. There was some tradition about his being of noble family, albeit his father, like himself, worked with mallet and chisel in the neighbouring Euston, then the New Road. My acquaintance with him began when he was not above seventeen. Then I went abroad, and lost sight of him for a time. Meanwhile I heard from a friend of the death of his father. He had been deeply affected by the event, said my correspondent — so deeply, indeed, that for a while fears were expressed lest his reason should give way. He fell into a state of gloom and melancholy from which nothing could rouse him, and which was due, the rumour ran, to his having become possessed of some terrible secret, confided to him by the poor stonemason on his death-bed.

Well, after a long residence in Rome, I returned to find him steadily triumphing over all obstacles, and established, as I have said, in a studio in the unpromising region aforesaid. Still labouring with mallet and chisel at monumental urns and prosaic effigies of impossible animals, he, nevertheless, had contrived to produce several notable groups, busts, and medallions on his own account. To do this he had hired from a sculptor who had gone on his travels the lofty, capacious, but barn-like room in which I found him. Its owner, an unsuccessful man, had left in it a great number of his somewhat gigantic failures in plaster, and these statues, with busts and casts of all descriptions, considerably encumbered the apartment, and formed a ghostly array beneath the high, broad window, particularly at night, and when the moonlight streamed in from above, as it was doing when I first looked up my old young friend.

'The place suits me for the present,' he said, when our hearty greetings were over, and we came to discuss his prospects and mine. 'You see I sleep here. There, in yonder corner, is my crib behind the screen — a bedroom quite sufficient for my wants. Besides, I like to sleep in the midst of my work, it makes me dream of it; and often when I wake with a new thought I spring up, as Goëthe used, and capture it. This moonlight, now is it not very suggestive? I always let in as much of it as I can through the farther window. Does it not stir the heart of an artist and a poet? See how wondrously the shadows fall from that group of poor Smithson's. It even gives an air of poetry to the 'Sibyl', as he calls that tall, strangely-imagined figure; and the 'Dancing Fawn' yonder — in this light it almost looks well modelled.'

Carlo was pointing about the room with an eager enthusiasm whilst speaking, as we sat smoking our pipes in the winter evening by the glimmer of a dim light near the stove.

'Ah! talking of modelling,' said I, 'that reminds me. I have brought you a trifling present which I think you will like. I picked it up at a sale that was going on in an old palazzo when I was in Rome. It is a little damaged, for it is very old, though, of course, not an antique. The notion is very quaint, and pleased me, besides being exquisitely beautiful in execution.'

Carlo's dark eyes sparkled with delight, as he caught the idea that I had brought him some work of art, and his curiosity grew so amusing that I refused to tell him any more as to the nature of my offering.

'No, no,' I went on; 'have patience; it has not arrived yet. It was too heavy to bring as personal baggage, and is coming round by sea.'

'Then I can guess,' he cried. It is a piece of sculpture. Oh! my dear fellow, how good of you! Yes, you have brought me some exquisite gem, no doubt. When — when will it come?'

'It should be here in a couple of days now,' I said; 'and directly —'

'Yes,' he interrupted, gleefully, with the quiet apprehension of his race, 'you will bring it up here. But remember, I am away all day; you will not get in unless you let me know — or, stay — yes — I have a duplicate key of this room; you shall have that, and then you can superintend the arrival, and I shall come home some night and find it standing, say here — place it here, do you see? I must see it first by moonlight.'

'I also heard,' I said to him, 'a strange story in connection with — well, with what I am going to give you, but I shall not tell you even that now.'

I hardly know what possessed me to adopt this tantalizing method of announcing my gift. Say it was a freak due to a foolish impulse of the moment; or perhaps, because, Charley Rossi appearing to be a little gloomy and grave on my first arrival, I wished to communicate some of my high spirits to him. In this I thoroughly succeeded, and we parted for the night with much of the old, cordial, jovial *camaraderie* which had always existed in our set.

✕

Three days later Rossi's wishes were carried out. The exquisite gem of art was placed in the precise spot he had indicated, and I awaited the result of his fanciful notion of getting the first sight of it by moonlight with some curiosity. I was not prepared, however, for the effect it seemed to have produced, and was startled beyond measure by the wild, scared, and haggard expression of the young fellow when he burst into my room the following morning while I was at breakfast. I never beheld such a sudden alteration in a man in my life. He looked years older; his usual pallor was intensified a thousand fold; his face was as white as the marble in which he wrought; whilst his black hair and eyes by contrast appeared quite unnatural, and gave him a most ghastly aspect. As he sank exhausted into a chair, his broad forehead was heavily bedewed with the moisture of some mental agony, and for many minutes he could not answer, save with a gasp, my earnest inquiries as to the cause of this alarming appearance and manner. Only after some time was it that he grew sufficiently calm to give me anything like a coherent account of himself. Even when he did so, it was so interrupted by wild ejaculations of bewilderment and terror, and by my own expressions of astonishment at what he told me, that in order to make his statement intelligible I must endeavour to reduce it to a far more matter-of-fact narrative than that which actually fell from his lips. In substance, then, what he said was this:

'With high anticipations,' he began, 'I returned unavoidably later to my studio last night than usual; and although this was a trial to my impatient curiosity, I did not regret it, because the moon, I thought, would be shedding her light with more power the later the hour. The side window of the room, not always unshuttered, allows her at her full, as she is just now, to penetrate more clearly, and earlier of course, than the window to the north. This, therefore, I had opened before leaving home in the morning, because in such clear frosty weather and bright nights as we are now experiencing I always look to getting my fancy stimulated, as I have told you. I prepare for it — look forward to it; besides, it is almost the only natural light which comes into the studio in the winter — at least, that is of much use to me. My heart beat loudly as the key turned in the lock. Full of joyful wonder, I peeped round the screen which shields the door and my bed, and, delighted as I knew I should be with what your friendship had devised for me, I nevertheless did not expect such a dream of beauty as that which met my gaze. My dear fellow,' continued Rossi, 'my whole soul went out to you in gratitude for the rare and exquisite treat which you had prepared.

I could not have expected, great as my anticipations were, that you would have brought me such an important and valuable treasure of art as the statue appeared to be at that first glance. Little could I think it was to vanish like a dream, although I have likened it to one. It is all a mystery and a marvel, yet it seems to have had a meaning — must have had — as you will say when you hear all.'

What the poor young fellow could be alluding to at this point I was quite unable to divine. Was it possible that the reports which had reached me concerning his mental condition were only too well founded?

'Statue!' I cried, looking at him in amazement.

'Yes, a statue,' he repeated, as an additional dazed and puzzled expression came over his face. 'I saw it plainly, as palpably as I ever saw anything in my life: the figure in marble of a kneeling woman, life-size, at prayer, her hands crossed on the top of the *prie-dieu* chair, with face, drapery, and all details chiselled with rare and masterly power. I examined it, passed round it again and again. The flood of moonlight in which it stood was so ample as to show it me clearly without any other aid. True, I did not touch it; I wish to heaven I had! for then I could have brought another sense, another witness in proof that I was not deceived — that it was not some ocular illusion or mental hallucination. Further — in the calm and beautiful features I could trace a likeness to that unhappy ancestress of ours, whose story and whose dreadful fate, although I have never talked about it to anyone, has been a tradition to me since I was a child, and which, from the first moment I heard it, impressed me with a wondering terror which I have never forgotten, and which was revived with startling vividness as I stood in the presence of this lovely statue. I seemed to recognise the likeness instantly, as I knew it in the picture — a miniature — which my father left me — gave me on his death-bed, and which had passed down to him through many generations of our family. I have it still, and will show it to you.'

It is very difficult on paper to give an adequate idea of what I may call — to use a theatrical expression — the business of this strange scene between my romantic, and, as I thought, demented young friend and myself. Moreover, so far I could not make head or tail of what he was driving at, and I said so repeatedly. But in spite of his intense excitement and mental distress, and the unintelligible nature of his speech, it produced a strange impression on me. His words seemed in a mysterious manner to be leading up to some fact or circumstance with which I also was acquainted.

'Go on, my dear Carlo,' I said at length, endeavouring to soothe and comfort him. 'Try and quiet yourself, and be more explicit.'

He made a strong effort to do so, and steadying himself, continued after a while with greater deliberation and calm.

'Well,' he said, 'there, where we had settled you should place your gift, I found it last night, as I have said — a beautiful kneeling statue of a woman, and, although much disturbed and overcome by the remembrance which the face provoked, it did not lessen my admiration of it as a work of art, or make me forgetful of my gratitude to you. For a long time I was absorbed by emotions of wonder, delight, pleasure, and pain. Finally, having moved aside the screen the better to watch the play of light around the statue, I threw myself upon my narrow bed without undressing, just as the neighbouring clocks were tolling midnight. Their clangour boomed with unnatural loudness in my ears, and added another element of confusion to the whirl already in my brain. I lay there for I know not how long, regarding your gift with a dreamy sense of amazement and awe. As the shadows changed and fell in weird mysterious shapes across the floor, or mingled with the other objects in the room, and as the moon gradually passed away, leaving only the dim reflection of her light upon the walls, my fancy, as it is my pleasure to indulge it, and as it has often done before, led me into a dreamy belief that the place was peopled. The statues standing around became for me endowed with life, slowly moving to and fro, and posing themselves in divers ways suggestive of new and valuable combinations and compositions. Unless you can bear with me and understand this vagary of mine, and accept it as a common habit, you will think it silly, childish, useless; but, as I said before, I have owed to it much of the poor success I have hitherto attained in my art. Be this as it may, however, I was in the full indulgence of the practice, and may have been, as often occurs, on the point of falling asleep in its midst, when I fancied suddenly that the figure of the woman had disappeared, and that the marble chair on which she had been kneeling was empty. A gloom had fallen over that part of the room, only leaving a dim outline of the vacant seat visible.

'Assuredly the figure was no longer there! But this circumstance produced for the moment little or no surprise, for have I not said that in the mood I then was, I could imagine, nay, I believed, that the statues lived. Certainly then, at first, I was neither terrified nor amazed, and might still have fallen asleep in the conviction that the effect was only one of the phenomena with which dreamland and the border-land which separates it from consciousness is filled. I might, in short, have looked upon it but as one of the dreams it is my pleasure to encourage, had it not been that I suddenly beheld the figure — the marble statue — kneeling now close to me beside the bed, in precisely the same attitude as it had when on the chair, but now without the hands, and by some strange and terrible paradox, blood was issuing from the wrists, there, where the hands had been cut off! Now, truly a great panic seized me. Half paralyzed, I continued to glare in frantic amazement at this awful spectacle. My horror was increased as I saw the cold, white stone gradually warm into tones of life — the marble turned to flesh and blood — the blood no longer being a matter of astonishment to me, for had not the hands been cut off, as I have said? It was a living, breathing figure of a woman that I was looking at! Her hair was brown and soft, her eyelids quivered, whilst the folds of the drapery, like the flesh, became real, and assumed the pliant look and colour of human garments. Before I could reassure myself that my senses were not playing me false I fainted, or slept, I know not which, but I became unconscious, yet still aware of what had happened, for in this horrible circumstance of the handless arms, I recognized the crowning tragedy of our family tradition, and the link which binds the portrait with the statue.'

Fully convinced by this time that the poor fellow, in addition to some return of his mental malady, was suffering from the effects of a horrible nightmare or dream, I nevertheless felt that his words now had a strong significance in them. They were developing a very remarkable coincidence with what I had to tell him of the legend associated with my poor present, but of which, as yet, he could know nothing. Before I could speak, however, he was proceeding with his story, with more wild excitement and gesticulation than ever.

'I know what you would say,' he urged, holding up his hand in deprecation of any interruption; 'you would say I had simply been dreaming — that is what most people would say. I might have said so myself, perhaps, but for what follows. Hear me out, and then you will see as plainly as I do that it was no dream. The proof that it was not is there — in my studio. When at length I awoke from my trance, or whatever state it was into which I fell, and recovered my senses sufficiently once more to remember the horrible sight I had witnessed, I started up with a feeling of depression indescribable. The pale feeble dawn of the winter's morning was just creeping in, and then for a moment I admit I thought I had been dreaming, but as my eyes turned towards the spot where you placed the statue, and I saw that it had disappeared — that nothing remained but the empty chair, with merely the hands in marble as before, crossed on the top — cut off as it were by the wrists — when, I say, I saw this, I knew it could be no dream. You may see the hands and chair for yourself, if you will go back with me to the studio; but what the meaning of it all can be, heaven alone knows.'

'The meaning, my dear boy,' I broke in, as the young sculptor sank back on his seat exhausted, and trembling from head to foot, 'the meaning is just what I expected. However much you may doubt, and however strange the coincidence may be, your fancy and imagination have played you a sad trick this time, whether in dreamland or not; for I brought you no statue — nothing more than the quaint device you have just described:

a pair of most beautiful woman's hands resting on the top of a *prie-dieu* chair, the whole exquisitely wrought out of one block of the purest marble. When you can calmly examine it, and look at the strange composition in its integrity, and without any of your wild imaginings, you will see that it is merely an odd original idea on the part of the artist, whoever he was, which tickled my fancy. I bought it for a song, and brought it to you because I thought you would like it. That it may have had a meaning is possible, and that it is associated with a tradition similar to that at which you have hinted is also true, perhaps; but that you ever saw in your studio the statue — the figure belonging to the hands — is impossible, simply because I did not bring it — it never was there!'

Rossi remained silent, and for a minute appeared surprised, and somewhat relieved by this statement; but presently the old look of terror and bewilderment returned to his face as he said:

'You explain one fact, perhaps, but you do not explain what strange fate it was which induced you to bring this horrible device to me — to *me* of all men in the world! Nothing that you have selected throughout the whole of Rome's antiquities could have had such a terrifying effect upon me as these armless hands have. Even now as I think of them I shudder, and can see the figure of the suffering woman, first as she appeared kneeling in the chair, and then in life at my bedside. A phantom of the brain, or vivid dream I suppose I must admit it was, after what you tell me; but anything more real and palpable you cannot conceive. Strong imagination may play us all tricks at times, but nothing in the whole world, I repeat, could have so stirred mine as this gift of yours.'

'My dear Carlo,' I began, 'it grieves me beyond measure to think I should have been the cause of such distress; but pray believe I am your friend, and, as such, tell me how and why you are so moved. Can it be that because, by a marvellous coincidence, this family tradition of yours is identical with that which was told me of the origin of this work of art, and which at the most, I treated as a mere idle story — can it, after all, be that there is any truth in it, and that it is actually the same as that to which you have alluded? If it be, why then, indeed, no such unlucky fate ever befell a friendly act.'

Although I could not, except upon the hypothesis that Rossi's mind was deranged again, conceive that he would take the matter so much to heart, I deemed it wise to humour him by this conciliatory tone.

He seemed to pass through some mental struggle before he answered me, but at last he said: 'Well, tell me exactly what legend there was connected with this fanciful creation, as you imagine it to be, and if your supposition is correct, and the story be that of my family, you will see, I think, that the device is no mere idle whim of the sculptor, but the outcome of a more terrible tragedy.'

'Surely,' I answered, as I took out my pocketbook. 'Here is what was told me by the auctioneer's clerk when I bought the piece of sculpture; I noted it down at the time. Then I read as follows:

'In Rome, ages ago, a heartless, unscrupulous libertine of noble birth, but who at the same time had a great genius as a sculptor, professed to have fallen in love with a model who sat to him for her hands, which were very beautiful. He was betrothed, however, to a girl of his own rank, and never contemplated marrying the model. Finding after a while that she was growing troublesome, and was likely to interfere with his matrimonial prospects, he determined to put her out of the way. Through his instrumentality she was denounced to the Inquisition as a heretic, and that infernal tribunal condemned her to have her hands, of which she was very proud, cut off. The hellish cruelty of this act was increased by the fact that she was near her confinement, which it brought on prematurely, together with her death. Years afterwards, a strange piece of sculpture, a woman's hands crossed on a *prie-dieu* chair, was found in the noble villain's studio, but under what precise conditions it had been executed is not known, nor is it known whether his child lived.'

'Yes, it did live!' suddenly shrieked poor Carlo in my ear, as I finished reading. 'Yes, it did live, and that hapless baby boy was my great ancestor — the ancestor from whom my family sprang — and from whom has descended through many generations such talent as its members have from time to time shown in the sculptor's art. Great God! what an inheritance!' added the poor young fellow, as he cast a despairing glance upwards. 'And to think that it should thus have been brought home to me by the possession of the actual monument — the hideous record of that miscreant's act, wrought probably by his own despicable hands.'

✕

Here is the romance of that bye street off the Hampstead Road, and to which, with an ill-luck unparalleled, I was the innocent means of putting the finishing scene. Were it not that I am assured by the highest opinions among the faculty that the confirmed melancholia into which Carlo Juliano Rossi sank after that sad time would in all probability have come about under any circumstances sooner or later, I might almost have fallen into the same condition myself from the dreadful reflection that it was due to my unfortunate gift.

As it is, at the worst, I must endeavour to think I only accelerated the catastrophe. The hateful cause of it all has been shivered into a thousand fragments this many a day.

3 The Mask (1895)

ROBERT W CHAMBERS

CAMILLA: You, sir, should unmask.
STRANGER: Indeed?
CASSILDA: Indeed it's time. We all have laid aside disguise
   but you.
STRANGER: I wear no mask.
CAMILLA: (Terrified, aside to Cassilda.) No mask? No mask!

— *The King in Yellow*, Act 1, Scene 2d.

I

Although I knew nothing of chemistry, I listened fascinated. He picked up an Easter lily which Geneviève had brought that morning from Notre Dame and dropped it into the basin. Instantly the liquid lost its crystalline clearness. For a second the lily was enveloped in a milk-white foam, which disappeared, leaving the fluid opalescent. Changing tints of orange and crimson played over the surface, and then what seemed to be a ray of pure sunlight struck through from the bottom where the lily was resting. At the same instant he plunged his hand into the basin and drew out the flower. 'There is no danger,' he explained, 'if you choose the right moment. That golden ray is the signal.'

He held the lily toward me and I took it in my hand. It had turned to stone, to the purest marble.

'You see,' he said, 'it is without a flaw. What sculptor could reproduce it?'

The marble was white as snow, but in its depths the veins of the lily were tinged with palest azure, and a faint flush lingered deep in its heart.

'Don't ask me the reason of that,' he smiled, noticing my wonder. 'I have no idea why the veins and heart are tinted, but they always are. Yesterday I tried one of Geneviève's goldfish — there it is.'

The fish looked as if sculptured in marble. But if you held it to the light the stone was beautifully veined with a faint blue, and from somewhere within came a rosy light like the tint which slumbers in an opal. I looked into the basin. Once more it seemed filled with clearest crystal.

'If I should touch it now?' I demanded.

'I don't know,' he replied, 'but you had better not try.'

'There is one thing I'm curious about,' I said, 'and that is where the ray of sunlight came from.'

'It looked like a sunbeam true enough,' he said. 'I don't know, it always comes when I immerse any living thing. Perhaps,' he continued smiling, 'perhaps it is the vital spark of the creature escaping to the source from whence it came.'

I saw he was mocking and threatened him with a mahl-stick, but he only laughed and changed the subject.

'Stay to lunch. Geneviève will be here directly.'

'I saw her going to early mass,' I said, 'and she looked as fresh and sweet as that lily — before you destroyed it.'

'Do you think I destroyed it?' said Boris gravely.

'Destroyed, preserved, how can we tell?'

We sat in the corner of a studio near his unfinished group of 'The Fates'. He leaned back on the sofa, twirling a sculptor's chisel and squinting at his work.

'By the way,' he said, 'I have finished pointing up that old academic "Ariadne" and I suppose it will have to go to the Salon. It's all I have ready this year, but after the success the "Madonna" brought me I feel ashamed to send a thing like that.'

The 'Madonna', an exquisite marble for which Geneviève had sat, had been the sensation of last year's Salon. I looked at the Ariadne. It was a magnificent piece of technical work, but I agreed with Boris that the world would expect something better of him than that. Still it was impossible now to think of finishing in time for the Salon that splendid terrible group half shrouded in the marble behind me. 'The Fates' would have to wait.

We were proud of Boris Yvain. We claimed him and he claimed us on the strength of his having been born in America, although his father was French and his mother was a Russian. Everyone in the Beaux Arts called him Boris. And yet there were only two of us whom he addressed in the same familiar way; Jack Scott and myself.

Perhaps my being in love with Geneviève had something to do with his affection for me. Not that it had ever been acknowledged between us. But after all was settled, and she had told me with tears in her eyes that it was Boris whom she loved, I went over to his house and congratulated him. The perfect cordiality of that interview did not deceive either of us, I always believed, although to one at least it was a great comfort. I do not think he and Geneviève ever spoke of the matter together, but Boris knew.

Geneviève was lovely. The Madonna-like purity of her face might have been inspired by the Sanctus in Gounod's Mass. But I was always glad when she changed that mood for what we called her 'April Manœuvres'. She was often as variable as an April day. In the morning grave, dignified and sweet, at noon laughing, capricious, at evening whatever one least expected. I preferred her so rather than in that Madonna-like tranquillity which stirred the depths of my heart. I was dreaming of Geneviève when he spoke again.

'What do you think of my discovery, Alec?'

'I think it wonderful.'

'I shall make no use of it, you know, beyond satisfying my own curiosity so far as may be and the secret will die with me.'

'It would be rather a blow to sculpture, would it not? We painters lose more than we ever gain by photography.'

Boris nodded, playing with the edge of the chisel.

'This new vicious discovery would corrupt the world of art. No, I shall never confide the secret to anyone,' he said slowly.

It would be hard to find anyone less informed about such phenomena than myself; but of course I had heard of mineral springs so saturated with silica that the leaves and twigs which fell into them were turned to stone after a time. I dimly comprehended the process, how the silica replaced the vegetable matter, atom by atom, and the result was a duplicate of the object in stone. This I confess had never interested me greatly, and as for the ancient fossils thus produced, they disgusted me. Boris, it appeared, feeling curiosity instead of repugnance, had investigated the subject, and had accidentally stumbled on a solution which, attacking the immersed object with a ferocity unheard of, in a second did the work of years. This was all I could make out of the strange story he had just been telling me. He spoke again after a long silence.

'I am almost frightened when I think what I have found. Scientists would go mad over the discovery. It was so simple too; it discovered itself. When I think of that formula, and that new element precipitated in metallic scales —'

'What new element?'

'Oh, I haven't thought of naming it, and I don't believe I ever shall. There are enough precious metals now in the world to cut throats over.'

I pricked up my ears. 'Have you struck gold, Boris?'

'No, better — but see here, Alec!' he laughed, starting up. 'You and I have all we need in this world. Ah! how sinister and covetous you look already!' I laughed too, and told him I was devoured by the desire for gold, and we had better talk of something else; so when Geneviève came in shortly after, we had turned our backs on alchemy.

Geneviève was dressed in silvery gray from head to foot. The light glinted along the soft curves of her fair hair as she turned her cheek to Boris; then she saw me and returned my greeting. She had never before failed to blow me a kiss from the tips of her white fingers, and I promptly complained of the omission. She smiled and held out her hand which dropped almost before it had touched mine; then she said, looking at Boris,

'You must ask Alec to stay for luncheon.' This also was something new. She had always asked me herself until today.

'I did,' said Boris shortly.

'And you said yes, I hope,' she turned to me with a charming conventional smile. I might have been an acquaintance of the day before yesterday. I made her a low bow. 'J'avais bien l'honneur, madame,' but refusing to take up our usual bantering tone she murmured a hospitable commonplace and disappeared. Boris and I looked at one another.

'I had better go home, don't you think?' I asked.

'Hanged if I know!' he replied frankly.

While we were discussing the advisability of my departure Geneviève reappeared in the doorway without her bonnet. She was wonderfully beautiful, but her color was too deep and her lovely eyes were too bright. She came straight up to me and took my arm.

'Luncheon is ready. Was I cross, Alec? I thought I had a headache but I haven't. Come here, Boris,' and she slipped her other arm through his. 'Alec knows that after you there is no one in the world whom I like as well as I like him, so if he sometimes feels snubbed it won't hurt him.'

'À la bonheur!' I cried, 'who says there are no thunderstorms in April?'

'Are you ready?' chanted Boris. 'Aye ready,' and arm in arm we raced into the dining-room scandalizing the servants. After all we were not so much to blame; Geneviève was eighteen, Boris was twenty-three and I not quite twenty-one.

II

Some work that I was doing about this time on the decorations for Geneviève's boudoir kept me constantly at the quaint little hôtel in the Rue Sainte-Cécile. Boris and I in those days labored hard but as we pleased, which was fitfully, and we all three, with Jack Scott, idled a great deal together.

One quiet afternoon I had been wandering alone over the house examining curios, prying into odd corners, bringing out sweetmeats and cigars from strange hiding-places, and at last I stopped in the bathing-room. Boris all over clay stood there washing his hands.

The room was built of rose-colored marble excepting the floor which was tesselated in rose and gray. In the centre was a square pool sunken below the surface of the floor; steps led down into it, sculptured pillars supported a frescoed ceiling. A delicious marble Cupid appeared to have just alighted on his pedestal at the upper end of the room. The whole interior was Boris' work and mine. Boris, in his working clothes of white canvas, scraped the traces of clay and red modelling wax from his handsome hands, and coquetted over his shoulder with the Cupid.

'I see you,' he insisted, 'don't try to look the other way and pretend not to see me. You know who made you, little humbug!'

It was always my rôle to interpret Cupid's sentiments in these conversations, and when my turn came I responded in such a manner, that Boris seized my arm and dragged me toward the pool, declaring he would duck me. Next instant he dropped my arm and turned pale. 'Good God!' he said, 'I forgot the pool is full of the solution!'

I shivered a little, and drily advised him to remember better where he had stored the precious liquid.

'In Heaven's name why do you keep a small lake of that gruesome stuff here of all places!' I asked.

'I want to experiment on something large,' he replied.

'On me, for instance!'

'Ah! that came too close for jesting; but I do want to watch the action of that solution on a more highly organized living body; there is that big white rabbit,' he said, following me into the studio.

Jack Scott, wearing a paint-stained jacket, came wandering in, appropriated all the Oriental sweetmeats he could lay his hands on, looted the cigarette case, and finally he and Boris disappeared together to visit the Luxembourg gallery, where a new silver bronze by Rodin and a landscape of Monet's were claiming the exclusive attention of artistic France. I went back to the studio, and resumed my work. It was a Renaissance screen, which Boris wanted me to paint for Geneviève's boudoir. But the small boy who was unwillingly dawdling through a series of poses for it, today refused all bribes to be good. He never rested an instant in the same position, and inside of five minutes, I had as many different outlines of the little beggar.

'Are you posing, or are you executing a song and dance, my friend?' I inquired.

'Whichever monsieur pleases,' he replied with an angelic smile.

Of course I dismissed him for the day, and of course I paid him for the full time, that being the way we spoil our models.

After the young imp had gone, I made a few perfunctory daubs at my work, but was so thoroughly out of humor, that it took me the rest of the afternoon to undo the damage I had done, so at last I scraped my palette, stuck my brushes in a bowl of black soap, and strolled into the smoking-room. I really believe that, excepting Geneviève's apartments, no room in the house was so free from the perfume of tobacco as this one. It was a queer chaos of odds and ends hung with threadbare tapestry. A sweet-toned old spinet in good repair stood by the window. There were stands of weapons, some old and dull, others bright and modern, festoons of Indian and Turkish armor over the mantel, two or three good pictures, and a pipe-rack. It was here that we used to come for new sensations in smoking. I doubt if any type of pipe ever existed which was not represented in that rack. When we had selected one, we immediately carried it somewhere else and smoked it; for the place was, on the whole, more gloomy and less inviting than any in the house. But this afternoon, the twilight was very soothing, the rugs and skins on the floor looked brown and soft and drowsy; the big couch was piled with cushions, I found my pipe and curled up there for an unaccustomed smoke in the smoking-room. I had chosen one with a long flexible stem, and lighting it fell to dreaming. After a while it went out, but I did not stir. I dreamed on and presently fell asleep.

I awoke to the saddest music I had ever heard. The room was quite dark, I had no idea what time it was. A ray of moonlight silvered one edge of the old spinet, and the polished wood seemed to exhale the sounds as perfume floats above a box of sandal wood. Someone rose in the darkness, and came away weeping quietly, and I was fool enough to cry out 'Geneviève!'

She dropped at my voice, and I had time to curse myself while I made a light and tried to raise her from the floor. She shrank away with a murmur of pain. She was very quiet, and asked for Boris. I carried her to the divan, and went to look for him, but he was not in the house, and the servants were gone to bed.

Perplexed and anxious, I hurried back to Geneviève. She lay where I had left her, looking very white.

'I can't find Boris nor any of the servants,' I said.

'I know,' she answered faintly, 'Boris has gone to Ept with Mr Scott. I did not remember when I sent you for him just now.'

'But he can't get back in that case before to-morrow afternoon, and — are you hurt? Did I frighten you into falling? What an awful fool I am, but I was only half awake.'

'Boris thought you had gone home before dinner. Do please excuse us for letting you stay here all this time.'

'I have had a long nap,' I laughed, 'so sound that I did not know whether I was still asleep or not when I found myself staring at a figure that was moving toward me, and called out your name. Have you been trying the old spinet? You must have played very softly.'

I would tell a thousand more lies worse than that one to see the look of relief that came into her face. She smiled adorably and said in her natural voice: 'Alec, I tripped on that wolf's head, and I think my ankle is sprained. Please call Marie and then go home.'

I did as she bade me and left her there when the maid came in.

III

At noon next day when I called, I found Boris walking restlessly about his studio.

'Geneviève is asleep just now,' he told me, 'the sprain is nothing, but why should she have such a high fever? The doctor can't account for it; or else he will not,' he muttered.

'Geneviève has a fever?' I asked.

'I should say so, and has actually been a little light-headed at intervals all night. The idea! gay little Geneviève, without a care in the world — and she keeps saying her heart's broken, and she wants to die!'

My own heart stood still.

Boris leaned against the door of his studio, looking down, his hands in his pockets, his kind, keen eyes clouded, a new line of trouble drawn 'over the mouth's good mark, that made the smile'. The maid had orders to summon him the instant Geneviève opened her eyes. We waited and waited, and Boris growing restless wandered about, fussing with modelling wax and red clay. Suddenly he started for the next room. 'Come and see my rose-colored bath full of death,' he cried.

'Is it death?' I asked to humor his mood.

'You are not prepared to call it life, I suppose,' he answered. As he spoke he plucked a solitary gold fish squirming and twisting out of its globe. 'We'll send this one after the other — wherever that is,' he said. There was feverish excitement in his voice. A dull weight of fever lay on my limbs and on my brain as I followed him to the fair crystal pool with its pink-tinted sides; and he dropped the creature in. Falling, its scales flashed with a hot orange gleam in its angry twistings and contortions; the moment it struck the liquid it became rigid and sank heavily to the bottom. Then came the milky foam, the splendid hues radiating on the surface and then the shaft of pure serene light broke through from seemingly infinite depths. Boris plunged in his hand and drew out an exquisite marble thing, blue-veined, rose-tinted and glistening with opalescent drops.

'Child's play,' he muttered, and looked wearily, longingly at me — as if I could answer such questions! But Jack Scott came in and entered into the 'game' as he called it with ardor. Nothing would do but to try the experiment on the white rabbit then and there. I was willing that Boris should find distraction from his cares, but I hated to see the life go out of a warm, living creature and I declined to be present. Picking up a book at random I sat down in the studio to read. Alas, I had found *The King in Yellow*. After a few moments which seemed ages, I was putting it away with a nervous shudder, when Boris and Jack came in bringing their marble rabbit. At the same time the bell rang above and a cry came from the sick room. Boris was gone like a flash, and the next moment he called, 'Jack, run for the doctor; bring him back with you. Alec, come here.'

I went and stood at her door. A frightened maid came out in haste and ran away to fetch some remedy. Geneviève, sitting bolt upright, with crimson cheeks and glittering eyes, babbled incessantly and resisted Boris' gentle restraint. He called me to help. At my first touch she sighed and sank back, closing her eyes, and then — then — as we still bent above her, she opened them again, looked straight into Boris' face, poor fever-crazed girl, and told her secret. At the same instant, our three lives turned into new channels; the bond that had held us so long together snapped forever and a new bond was forged in its place, for she had spoken my name, and as the fever tortured her, her heart poured out its load of hidden sorrow. Amazed and dumb I bowed my head, while my face burned like a live coal, and the blood surged in my ears, stupefying me with its clamor. Incapable of movement, incapable of speech, I listened to her feverish words in an agony of shame and sorrow. I could not silence her, I could not look at Boris. Then I felt an arm upon my shoulder, and Boris turned a bloodless face to mine.

'It is not your fault, Alec, don't grieve so if she loves you —' but he could not finish; and as the doctor stepped swiftly into the room saying — 'Ah, the fever!' I seized Jack Scott and hurried him to the street saying, 'Boris would rather be alone.' We crossed the street to our own apartments and that night, seeing I was going to be ill too, he went for the doctor again. The last thing I recollect with any distinctness was hearing Jack say, 'For Heaven's sake, doctor, what ails him, to wear a face like that?' and I thought of *The King in Yellow* and the Pallid Mask.

I was very ill, for the strain of two years which I had endured since that fatal May morning when Geneviève murmured, 'I love you, but I think I love Boris best' told on me at last. I had never imagined that it could become more than I could endure. Outwardly tranquil, I had deceived myself. Although the inward battle raged night after night, and I, lying alone in my room, cursed myself for rebellious thoughts unloyal to Boris and unworthy of Geneviève, the morning always brought relief, and I returned to Geneviève and to my dear Boris with a heart washed clean by the tempests of the night.

Never in word or deed or thought while with them, had I betrayed my sorrow even to myself.

The mask of self-deception was no longer a mask for me, it was a part of me. Night lifted it, laying bare the stifled truth below; but there was no one to see except myself, and when day broke the mask fell back again of its own accord. These thoughts passed through my troubled mind as I lay sick, but they were hopelessly entangled with visions of white creatures, heavy as stone, crawling about in Boris' basin — of the wolf's head on the rug, foaming and snapping at Geneviève, who lay smiling beside it. I thought, too, of *The King in Yellow* wrapt in the fantastic colors of his tattered mantle, and that bitter cry of Cassilda, 'Not upon us, oh King, not upon us!' Feverishly I struggled to put it from me, but I saw the lake of Hali, thin and blank, without a ripple or wind to stir it, and I saw the towers of Carcosa behind the moon. Aldebaran, The Hyades, Alar, Hastur, glided through the cloud rifts which fluttered and flapped as they passed like the scolloped tatters of *The King in Yellow*. Among all these, one sane thought persisted. It never wavered, no matter what else was going on in my disordered mind, that my chief reason for existing, was to meet some requirement of Boris and Geneviève. What this obligation was, its nature, was never clear; sometimes it seemed to be protection, sometimes support, through a great crisis. Whatever it seemed to be for the time, its weight rested only on me, and I was never so ill or so weak that I did not respond with my whole soul. There were always crowds of faces about me, mostly strange, but a few I recognized, Boris among them. Afterward they told me that this could not have been, but I know that once at least he bent over me. It was only a touch, a faint echo of his voice, then the clouds settled back on my senses, and I lost him, but he *did* stand there and bend over me *once* at least.

At last, one morning I awoke to find the sunlight falling across my bed, and Jack Scott reading beside me. I had not strength enough to speak aloud, neither could I think, much less remember, but I could smile feebly, as Jack's eye met mine, and when he jumped up and asked eagerly if I wanted anything, I could whisper, 'Yes, Boris.' Jack moved to the head of my bed, and leaned down to arrange my pillow: I did not see his face, but he answered heartily, 'You must wait Alec, you are too weak to see even Boris.'

I waited and I grew strong; in a few days I was able to see whom I would, but meanwhile I had thought and remembered. From the moment when all the past grew clear again in my mind, I never doubted what I should do when the time came, and I felt sure that Boris would have resolved upon the same course so far as he was concerned; as for what pertained to me alone, I knew he would see that also as I did. I no longer asked for anyone. I never inquired why no message came from them; why during the week I lay there, waiting and growing stronger, I never heard their name spoken. Preoccupied with my own searchings for the right way, and with my feeble but determined fight against despair, I simply acquiesced in Jack's reticence, taking for granted that he was afraid to speak of them, lest I should turn unruly and insist on seeing them. Meanwhile I said over and over to myself, how it would be when life began again for us all. We would take up our relations exactly as they were before Geneviève fell ill. Boris and I would look into each other's eyes and there would be neither rancor nor cowardice nor mistrust in that glance. I would be with them again for a little while in the dear intimacy of their home, and then, without pretext or explanation, I would disappear from their lives forever. Boris would know, Geneviève — the only comfort was that she would never know. It seemed, as I thought it over, that I had found the meaning of that sense of obligation which had persisted all through my delirium, and the only possible answer to it. So, when I was quite ready, I beckoned Jack to me one day, and said,

'Jack, I want Boris at once; and take my dearest greeting to Geneviève ... '

When at last he made me understand that they were both dead, I fell into a wild rage that tore all my little convalescent strength to atoms. I raved and cursed myself into a relapse, from which I crawled forth some weeks afterward a boy of twenty-one who believed that his youth was gone forever. I seemed to be past the capability of further suffering, and one day when Jack handed me a letter and the keys to Boris' house, I took them without a tremor and asked him to tell me all. It was cruel of me to ask him, but there was no help for it, and he leaned wearily on his thin hands, to reopen the wound which could never entirely heal. He began very quietly.

'Alec, unless you have a clue that I know nothing about, you will not be able to explain any more than I, what has happened. I suspect that you would rather not hear these details, but you must learn them, else I would spare you the relation. God knows I wish I could be spared the telling. I shall use few words.

'That day when I left you in the doctor's care and came back to Boris, I found him working on the "Fates". Geneviève, he said, was sleeping under the influence of drugs. She had been quite out of her mind, he said. He kept on working, not talking any more, and I watched him. Before long, I saw that the third figure of the group — the one looking straight ahead, out over the world — bore his face; not as you ever saw it, but as it looked then and to the end. This is one thing for which I should like to find an explanation, but I never shall.

'Well, he worked and I watched him in silence, and we went on that way until nearly midnight. Then we heard a door open and shut sharply, and a swift rush in the next room. Boris sprang through the doorway and I followed; but we were too late. She lay at the bottom of the pool, her hands across her breast. Then Boris shot himself through the heart.' Jack stopped speaking, drops of sweat stood under his eyes, and his thin cheeks twitched. 'I carried Boris to his room. Then I went back and let that hellish fluid out of the pool, and turning on all the water, washed the marble clean of every drop. When at length I dared descend the steps, I found her lying there as white as snow. At last, when I had decided what was best to do, I went into the laboratory, and first emptied the solution in the basin into the waste-pipe; then I poured the contents of every jar and bottle after it. There was wood in the fireplace, so I built a fire, and breaking the locks of Boris' cabinet I burnt every paper, notebook and letter that I found there. With a mallet from the studio I smashed to pieces all the empty bottles, then loading them into a coal scuttle, I carried them to the cellar and threw them over the red-hot bed of the furnace. Six times I made the journey, and at last, not a vestige remained of anything which might again aid in seeking for the formula which Boris had found. Then at last I dared call the doctor. He is a good man, and together we struggled to keep it from the public. Without him I never could have succeeded. At last we got the servants paid and sent away into the country, where old Rosier keeps them quiet with stories of Boris' and Geneviève's travels in distant lands, from whence they will not return for years. We buried Boris in the little cemetery of Sèvres. The doctor is a good creature and knows when to pity a man who can bear no more. He gave his certificate of heart disease and asked no questions of me.'

Then lifting his head from his hands, he said, 'Open the letter, Alec; it is for us both.'

I tore it open. It was Boris' will dated a year before. He left everything to Geneviève, and in case of her dying childless, I was to take control of the house in the Rue Sainte-Cécile, and Jack Scott, the management at Ept. On our deaths the property reverted to his mother's family in Russia, with the exception of the sculptured marbles executed by himself. These he left to me.

The page blurred under our eyes, and Jack got up and walked to the window. Presently he returned and sat down again. I dreaded to hear what he was going to say, but he spoke with the same simplicity and gentleness.

'Geneviève lies before the Madonna in the marble room. The Madonna bends tenderly above her, and Geneviève smiles back into that calm face that never would have been except for her.'

His voice broke, but he grasped my hand, saying, 'Courage, Alec.' Next morning he left for Ept to fulfil his trust.

IV

The same evening I took the keys and went into the house I had known so well. Everything was in order, but the silence was terrible. Though I went twice to the door of the marble room, I could not force myself to enter. It was beyond my strength. I went into the smoking-room and sat down before the spinet. A small lace handkerchief lay on the keys, and I turned away, choking. It was plain I could not stay, so I locked every door, every window, and the three front and back gates, and went away. Next morning Alcide packed my valise, and leaving him in charge of my apartments I took the Orient express for Constantinople. During the two years that I wandered through the East, at first, in our letters, we never mentioned Geneviève and Boris, but gradually their names crept in. I recollect particularly a passage in one of Jack's letters replying to one of mine.

'What you tell me of seeing Boris bending over you while you lay ill, and feeling his touch on your face, and hearing his voice of course troubles me. This that you describe must have happened a fortnight after he died. I say to myself that you were dreaming, that it was part of your delirium, but the explanation does not satisfy me, nor would it you.'

Toward the end of the second year a letter came from Jack to me in India so unlike anything that I had ever known of him that I decided to return at once to Paris. He wrote, 'I am well and sell all my pictures as artists do, who have no need of money. I have not a care of my own, but I am more restless than if I had. I am unable to shake off a strange anxiety about you. It is not apprehension, it is rather a breathless expectancy, of what, God knows! I can only say it is wearing me out. Nights I dream always of you and Boris. I can never recall anything afterward, but I wake in the morning with my heart beating, and all day the excitement increases until I fall asleep at night to recall the same experience. I am quite exhausted by it, and have determined to break up this morbid condition. I must see you. Shall I go to Bombay or will you come to Paris?'

I telegraphed him to expect me by the next steamer.

When we met I thought he had changed very little. I, he insisted, looked in splendid health. It was good to hear his voice again, and as we sat and chatted about what life still held for us, we felt that it was pleasant to be alive in the bright spring weather.

We stayed in Paris together a week, and then I went for a week to Ept with him, but first of all we went to the cemetery at Sèvres, where Boris lay.

'Shall we place the "Fates" in the little grove above him?' Jack asked, and I answered, 'I think only the "Madonna" should watch over Boris' grave.' But Jack was none the better for my home-coming. The dreams of which he could not retain even the least definite outline continued, and he said that at times the sense of breathless expectancy was suffocating.

'You see I do you harm and not good,' I said. 'Try a change without me.' So he started alone for a ramble among the Channel Islands and I went back to Paris. I had not yet entered Boris' house, now mine, since my return, but I knew it must be done. It had been kept in order by Jack; there were servants there, so I gave up my own apartment and went there to live. Instead of the agitation I had feared, I found myself able to paint there tranquilly. I visited all the rooms — all but one. I could not bring myself to enter the marble room where Geneviève lay, and yet I felt the longing growing daily to look upon her face, to kneel beside her.

One April afternoon, I lay dreaming in the smoking-room, just as I had lain two years before, and mechanically I looked among the tawny Eastern rugs for the wolf-skin. At last I distinguished the pointed ears and flat cruel head, and I thought of my dream where I saw Geneviève lying beside it. The helmets still hung against the threadbare tapestry, among them the old Spanish morion which I remembered Geneviève had once put on when we were amusing ourselves with the ancient bits of mail. I turned my eyes to the spinet; every yellow key seemed eloquent of her caressing hand, and I rose, drawn by the strength of my life's passion to the sealed door of the marble room. The heavy doors swung inward under my trembling hands. Sunlight poured through the window, tipping with gold the wings of Cupid, and lingered like a nimbus over the brows of the Madonna. Her tender face bent in compassion over a marble form so exquisitely pure that I knelt and signed myself.

Geneviève lay in the shadow under the Madonna, and yet, through her white arms, I saw the pale azure vein, and beneath her softly clasped hands the folds of her dress were tinged with rose, as if from some faint warm light within her breast.

Bending with a breaking heart I touched the marble drapery with my lips, then crept back into the silent house.

A maid came and brought me a letter, and I sat down in the little conservatory to read it; but as I was about to break the seal, seeing the girl lingering, I asked her what she wanted.

She stammered something about a white rabbit that had been caught in the house and asked what should be done with it. I told her to let it loose in the walled garden behind the house and opened my letter. It was from Jack, but so incoherent that I thought he must have lost his reason. It was nothing but a series of prayers to me not to leave the house until he could get back; he could not tell me why, there were the dreams, he said — he could explain nothing, but he was sure that I must not leave the house in the Rue Sainte-Cécile.

As I finished reading I raised my eyes and saw the same maid-servant standing in the doorway holding a glass dish in which two gold fish were swimming: 'Put them back into the tank and tell me what you mean by interrupting me,' I said.

With a half suppressed whimper she emptied water and fish into an aquarium at the end of the conservatory, and turning to me asked my permission to leave my service. She said people were playing tricks on her, evidently with a design of getting her into trouble; the marble rabbit had been stolen and a live one had been brought into the house; the two beautiful marble fish were gone and she had just found those common live things flopping on the dining-room floor. I reassured her and sent her away saying I would look about myself. I went into the studio; there was nothing there but my canvasses and some casts, except the marble of the Easter Lily. I saw it on a table across the room. Then I strode angrily over to it. But the flower I lifted from the table was fresh and fragile and filled the air with perfume.

Then suddenly I comprehended and sprang through the hallway to the marble room. The doors flew open, the sunlight streamed into my face and through it, in a heavenly glory, the Madonna smiled, as Geneviève lifted her flushed face from her marble couch, and opened her sleepy eyes.

4 The Stone Rider! A Short Story of the Weird (1898)

NELLIE K BLISSETT

It was a dull day in early spring, and the wind in the pine forest behind the Castle of Salitz was making a melancholy moaning. In one of the deep window-seats of the castle I sat, with a book in my hand, looking down at the drowned landscape and the swollen river. I had come to visit that mysterious personage, Count Siebach von Salitz, whose extraordinary powers of thought-reading and prophecy would have brought him in several fortunes had he chosen to use them professionally. As it was, he was the object of much interest, and not a little awe, in half the capitals of Europe; and it was with some curiosity that I accepted his invitation to his Hungarian estate.

So far nothing in the least peculiar had occurred to me — a disappointment I was rather inclined to resent.

Siebach's step disturbed my meditations. I turned and saw him coming down the passage — a tall, gaunt man, with a haggard face and evil eyes. But if Siebach's personal appearance was not prepossessing, his charm of manner was so great that when you knew him well you forgot the small, cruel eyes, the sneering mouth, the curious mixture of power and cunning which characterized his countenance. His voice, too, was singularly beautiful, and atoned for many things.

He smiled as he came up and seated himself beside me.

'If you admire the view, you shouldn't look so solemn, Bazarac,' he said; 'and if you don't, and are bored, shall we go for a ride? Or will you come and look at my study? — you haven't seen it yet, and it is worth seeing.'

'Everything here is,' I answered, as I rose and followed him downstairs.

He laughed. 'That is the disadvantage of being born a Siebach of Salitz — there is no merit in possessing perfection. It is merely inherited property. Don't knock your head against this doorway — it is low. That's right!'

We had passed under a low archway into a long room panelled with black oak. There was a table, littered with papers, near the window, and over the hearth hung the portrait of a young man whose countenance, particularly about the mouth, distinctly resembled that of Siebach.

'How like you that portrait is!' I exclaimed.

He looked at it for a moment as though weighing my remark carefully in his mind.

'Do you think so?' he said at last. 'It is my poor cousin Franz.'

'I didn't know you had one.'

'He is dead. He was drowned whilst we were bathing in the river beneath. I was with him at the time, but I could not save him. His body was never recovered — it was an awful affair. He was only seven and twenty.'

'Younger than you?'

'Oh, no — older. He was the heir. Poor Franz!'

I looked at the portrait with increased interest, and Siebach gazed at it too. There was a disagreeable expression on his face.

'It is a fine portrait,' I said.

'Very — an Auberthal. You know Auberthal, of course? A splendid painter. Singular, now, I forgot that he will arrive here today. He has a long-standing engagement to visit me.'

I was very glad to hear it, for I had known Auberthal when he was a mere boy, studying in Garcia's 'Atelier Espagnol'. We had seen a great deal of each other, and I had liked him exceedingly. Although Siebach was very entertaining, I did not altogether *trust* him; a solitude only relieved by his presence did not at the moment appear alluring.

I expressed my pleasure, and began to walk about the study, admiring the family portraits, of which there were a great number. Under one of them I noticed a curtain drawn across the wall, and, supposing it to conceal a picture or a cabinet, I very innocently put out my hand as if to draw it on one side.

A sharp exclamation from Siebach stopped me. I dropped the curtain and turned to him.

'What is the matter?'

He recovered his self-possession immediately.

'Nothing. I was cutting a pencil and the knife slipped. Oh, it is only a scratch!'

'What is behind this curtain?' I asked, returning to my former occupation.

He did not answer at once. Then he laughed, a trifle uneasily.

'A family superstition — nonsense if you like. You can look.'

I drew it accordingly. The curtain covered a large recess, and in this recess stood the life-sized statue of a horse in white marble, bearing a man in armour upon his back. The singular part about this equestrian group was, that whilst the horse was stone, the trappings and the man's armour were real.

'That is an odd idea,' I remarked.

'What, the armour? Oh, it belonged to an ancestor of mine. Of course there is a stone figure underneath to match the horse.'

'The vizor of his helmet is down. Why don't you raise it? It would be far more effective.'

He laughed again more uneasily than ever.

'My dear Bazarac, "let sleeping men lie" is an excellent transposition of the old proverb. This gentleman is supposed to "walk" — or rather ride. In other words, he is the family apparition. He is supposed to ride about the castle at night.'

'What a very unpleasant idea!'

'Do you think so? Well, it is sufficiently ghastly, I admit.'

'Have you ever seen him?'

'No, but I have often fancied I heard a horse snorting and trampling about the passages. At this time of year he is often heard. The servants tell odd stories about him, but I have never encountered him myself.'

'It would be an interesting encounter.'

Siebach shuddered visibly.

'I think not,' he said, in an altered tone.

I looked up at him. His face was very pale, and his shifty glance avoided mine.

'You are afraid of him,' I said, laughing.

An odd light blazed for a second in his eyes. He had a pair of gloves in his hand, having just come in from a walk. Suddenly, without any warning, he flung one glove full at the mailed face of the Stone Rider. The armour rattled, and the glove fell back at Siebach's feet. He picked it up and looked me in the face.

'You see whether I am afraid,' he said, haughtily.

I did not understand his manner, but I saw that it would be better to change the subject at once, and avoid it for the future. So I asked him at what time Auberthal would arrive, and we talked of other things.

Auberthal came in time for dinner — a little round man with a face all brown skin and black beard, and extraordinarily bright eyes. I should never have recognized in him the slip of a boy whose genius had electrified the 'Atelier Espagnol', but he was as pleasant as ever. We passed a very enjoyable evening, and retired in due course to bed.

From the moment I had dropped the curtain across the recess in the study, I had never given another thought to the Stone Rider. Auberthal's arrival had successfully banished reflection on that somewhat peculiar incident. I undressed, and got into bed, and, as I was not sleepy, began to read. I suppose this was at about half-past eleven, and I went on reading steadily for over half an hour, at the end of which period I laid down my book and prepared to blow out my candles, when a sound arrested my attention, and I paused to listen. The castle had long been silent, and everyone had retired to rest. Yet there was a distinct sound as of someone moving about the corridors under me.

My room was in the second story of the building, at the head of the grand staircase — an immensely broad and imposing affair of beautifully inlaid marble. The corridors, too, were all marble paved, so that the slightest sound was noticeable in them. I listened, and distinctly heard the noise, whatever its cause, approach the foot of the staircase. Then it paused for a moment, and there followed a curious sound of scrambling, as of a large and somewhat unwieldy object coming up the stairs.

By this time my curiosity was thoroughly excited. I got out of bed and went to the door. As the room was very long, and the door at the farther end of it, this was a decidedly better post for listening purposes. I had not been there a second before I heard the unmistakable rattle of armour, and the snuffling sound a horse would make after any unusual exertion. A wild idea flashed across my mind, and I pressed closer to the door.

This was the Stone Rider!

The sounds came nearer and nearer until they were just outside. Then came another pause, and a heavy sigh — almost a groan — but whether from horse, or rider, I could not decide. Then the horse was turned round, and clattered and rattled down the shallow steps of the staircase, and away down the corridors, until all was silent once more.

All this time, though greatly excited, I had not felt the slightest sensation of fear; but now that all was still such a feeling of terror came over me that I lay awake for hours scarcely able to breathe, listening for the return of this midnight visitant. But he did not come, and towards morning I fell asleep.

At breakfast I observed that Auberthal, who had been very lively the previous evening, seemed silent and depressed. Siebach, too, looked rather yellower and thinner than usual. I enquired if they had not slept well.

'Oh, yes,' answered Siebach, hastily, 'I have slept very well indeed, thank you.'

Auberthal said nothing for a moment.

'You don't look particularly brilliant yourself, Bazarac,' he remarked presently.

'Somebody was racketing about the staircase last night and disturbed me,' I replied carelessly. 'Didn't you hear it, Auberthal? Your room is next to mine. I wondered whether the noise would keep you awake.'

Siebach looked up at me sharply and seemed about to speak. But he thought better of it, and returned to his breakfast.

'Yes,' said Auberthal, quietly. 'Something certainly kept me awake. That family ghost of yours, Siebach, I expect — the Stone Rider.'

'I heard nothing,' returned the Count, stolidly.

But Auberthal was not to be silenced.

'No? That is odd. I heard him distinctly. He stopped outside my door; and something groaned. It gave me a peculiar sensation. What makes him walk, Siebach — I suppose there's a legend?'

'Oh, there are lots of legends,' answered Siebach, offhandedly. 'One says that the Ritter von Salitz in the thirteenth century caused a statue of himself, on his favourite charger, to be set up in the courtyard of the castle, and when he took prisoners of war, he chained them to the Stone Rider and flogged them to death. When he was about sixty he married for the second time. His wife was very young and very beautiful, and had been betrothed to his eldest son, whom he hated, and banished from the castle. One day he found his son and his wife talking together in the forest. He seized them, had them lashed to the statue, and directed his men to flog them to death, whilst he himself stood by and derided them. However, that was the last atrocity he perpetrated, for he soon after went mad, and died. And his spirit is doomed to ride the stone horse for ever.'

'A sufficiently horrible story, at any rate,' remarked Auberthal, composedly. 'Is the horse in your study the original of the courtyard?'

'Yes. It has been most carefully preserved, and handed down from generation to generation.'

'No wonder it roams about the castle at night,' I said.

'That is mere nonsense,' returned Siebach, irritably.

I said nothing more; but after breakfast I found an opportunity of speaking to Auberthal alone.

'I should like to investigate this matter,' I said. 'Will you help me, Auberthal?'

He laughed. 'Certainly; but I don't believe in ghosts, you know, Bazarac. I trust you don't?'

'I have seen some very strange things in connection with ghosts; at all events, will you keep up tonight, and follow the Stone Rider with me?'

'If it will afford you any amusement.'

'Don't speak to Siebach about it, then. He evidently does not care for the subject,' and I related to him the incident of the glove.

He looked rather grave.

'I am sorry to hear it,' he said, when I had finished. 'There is insanity in his family, you know — I don't think his brain is what it was. And once he went off his head altogether.'

'When?'

'Soon after his cousin was drowned. He saw it happen. That was enough to drive anyone mad, perhaps. But he was always queer.'

'Then, tonight —?'

'Yes. When he gets to the bottom of the staircase again we will follow him.'

The day passed off very quietly, and nothing more was said about the statue. We went to our rooms at the usual time, and I sat down to wait. At a few minutes past twelve I heard the noise beginning. It came up the staircase as it had done before, and paused for a moment outside the door. Then I again heard the sigh, or groan, and the clattering down the stairs. I opened my door and found Auberthal already on the landing.

'Make haste,' he said. 'It is going down the corridor towards the study.'

We rushed down, and along the passage, the rattling going in front of us. But we were too slow. When we reached the study, the green baize curtain was drawn, and everything was perfectly still. After a moment's hesitation I pushed back the curtain. There sat the Stone Rider, immovable as ever, mailed and erect.

'He looks quite harmless,' I said, doubtfully.

Auberthal bent down and held the candle closer. On the side of the horse were great dark stains, and the armour glimmered redly in the flame. The painter put his hand on one big patch, and drew back quickly.

'I could swear it was wet,' he whispered. 'Let us go!'

We returned, and I drew him into my room.

'It's very odd!'

'Very!' He held up his hand. 'Do you see?'

'Good Heavens!' I gasped, 'it's all red!'

'With blood,' he said, solemnly.

×

For some days neither Auberthal nor I spoke of our adventure with the Stone Rider. But at last, one evening before dinner he came to me in my room.

'I shall go down into the study tonight,' he said, 'and see what really happens. Will you come too?'

'Yes. The noise at night still goes on?'

'Regularly every night. Bazarac, I mean to get to the bottom of this mystery.'

'All right. I shall be charmed if you can prove the whole thing a hoax, but —'

'But what?'

'I don't think you will.'

He considered for a moment.

'I don't think I shall either,' he said, as he left me.

Siebach was unusually brilliant and amusing at dinner. He kept us at table long after our usual hour, and when we at last got away to our rooms there was barely time to let the castle become quiet, and get back to the study, before twelve o'clock. However, we accomplished the feat, seated ourselves near together, blew out the candle, and waited for the ghost to move.

For some time everything was silent. Then, all at once, the room became strangely illuminated. One after another the chairs, and tables, and pictures grew out of the gloom, lit up with a pale, peculiar light. And at last the curtain was drawn aside — the horse shook himself, and snorted — the armour rattled — and the Stone Rider rode slowly out into the middle of the room.

The supernatural radiance streamed from him — it issued from the closed bars of his helmet, from the steel breastplate, from the joints of the rusted gorget. It seemed to grow brighter every moment, till, almost dazzled, I turned my attention to the horse.

I did not at first notice the stain on his side which Auberthal had observed. But as I looked at him, I saw that a dark stream began to trickle down the whiteness of the marble. It dripped from a great dent in the breastplate of the Rider — dripped slowly and steadily over the horse's neck, and rolled down to the floor.

For a few moments the rider remained motionless; then struck his spurs into the marble flanks of his steed, and they moved away. The light went with them through the open door, and Auberthal sprang up and rushed after them.

I saw the Stone Rider turn in his saddle and look back as we raced after him; and a flash of flame seemed to shoot out from between the helmet-bars. On they went — clattering, clashing, rattling through the stone passages, and we after them. They reached the staircase — the Rider rose in his stirrups and urged the horse up. The pace was too fast — the horse slipped, plunged — and finally recovered himself, just as an ordinary horse might do, and halted.

But the Rider's balance was destroyed. He swayed in the high saddle — his arms went wildly into the air — and he crashed forward, and fell, with a horrible rattling sound, at our feet. The clasps that fastened the gorget and breastplate burst — the helmet rolled away — and on the pavement before us lay a skeleton!

For a time we were too stunned to speak. Then Auberthal uttered an exclamation of horror and looked up.

Half way up the staircase stood Siebach von Salitz. His face was ghastly white — his eyes were widened with an expression of awful terror — his hands were stretched out as though grasping the air. He stood motionless for some moments, staring into vacancy; then his rigid expression relaxed, his arms dropped to his sides, and he came down the stairs.

'What has happened?' he enquired.

'That!' said Auberthal, bluntly, pointing to the skeleton.

Siebach bent over it for a moment. Then he kicked it contemptuously aside.

'Somebody has been playing a practical joke,' he remarked.

Auberthal coughed.

'I have not, nor has Bazarac. Who could have done it?'

'Do you suppose I have?'

Siebach seemed indignant. Auberthal looked at him very quietly.

'I do not suppose anything,' he said, 'but there is the skeleton, and there is —'

He turned to look for the horse, but it was gone.

'There was the horse,' he concluded, 'and to-morrow morning I leave for Paris. Good-night!'

He disappeared up the staircase, leaving me face to face with Siebach.

'What does he mean?'

'I really don't know, Siebach.'

'Do you intend to leave for Paris, too?'

'I am very sorry,' I said, 'but my nerves are really not equal to this sort of thing. Good-night, Siebach!'

He surveyed me with an odd expression; then, suddenly, he gripped my arm.

'Do you think —' he almost gasped in my ear — 'do you think that he suspects anything?'

I shook him off.

'Good heavens, Siebach! What should he suspect? Can't you explain this horrible thing?'

He recovered his self-command almost immediately, and smiled feebly.

'No. I can't,' he said. 'Am I to explain all my family skeletons, Bazarac?'

'Not if you do not wish.'

And I left him standing by the skeleton of the Stone Rider.

⚹

For some years I did not come across Count Siebach von Salitz — neither, I am afraid, did I wish to do so. Of the Stone Rider — who had proved to be no stone at all — I often thought, but at last I hardly regarded the incident as anything more than the recollection of a bad dream. Auberthal and I met frequently, and often discussed our adventure; and I believed that he had suspicions concerning Siebach which I did not care to share. But one evening as we sat in the 'Atelier Espagnol' — Auberthal and myself — someone knocked at the door and came hastily in. I recognised one of Siebach's servants.

'What is it?' I asked.

'Will M Bazarac or M Auberthal come to my master at once? He is very ill at the Hôtel ——.'

We both rose and looked at each other, and Auberthal slipped his arm through mine.

'We had better go together.'

So we went. The Hôtel —— was close by. In ten minutes we were in Siebach's bedroom.

He lay in bed, looking thinner and more haggard than ever. His eyes blazed with feverish light, and he beckoned us eagerly to approach.

'There is not much time,' he said, speaking in a weak, strained voice; 'I sent for you to tell you — what is that?'

His eyes dilated with fear, and he glanced round the room.

'It is nothing,' said Auberthal, gently.

He laughed — a short, bitter laugh.

'He is not far off — he never is. Don't you hear the horse breathing outside the door? I can. I always hear it now. Don't let it come in — don't — don't, Auberthal!'

His voice rose to a shriek.

'Nothing shall come in.'

'Thank you. I am so foolish to mind! I — I wanted to tell you. I — I murdered him.'

He fell back exhausted.

'Whom?' asked Auberthal, aghast.

'My cousin Franz. He was the heir.'

'But he was drowned.'

Siebach struggled up on his elbow.

'No, I told them that. I shot him; and I knew if they found the body they would accuse me, so I hid it. And when his father died, and I got the castle, I dug him up — and — you know. I could not hide the skeleton, so I put it on the horse. Don't you think that was a good idea?'

He laughed, and Auberthal looked at me with a shudder.

'The armour hid it,' went on Siebach, 'and I knew they were all so superstitious they wouldn't touch it. And then you came — you and Auberthal.'

At that moment the doctor came in. When he left the room he called me out.

'Count Siebach is mad?' I questioned,

'He is not responsible for what he says. Are you a friend of his?'

'In a way.'

'Then you had better stay with him. Send for me if he gets worse. I shall do no good by stopping.'

I went back to Auberthal. Siebach was obviously too ill to be left. I agreed to sit up with him half the night, whilst Auberthal rested.

Siebach was exhausted, and for some hours lay quite still. I think he was insensible. But about 12 o'clock I heard a sound from the bed, and went to him. He was sitting up, looking straight before him into space.

'Don't you hear it?' he asked.

I listened, to appease him. 'No.'

'Not the horse?'

I listened more attentively.

Yes — the old rattle — the old sound of a horse's hoofs. It was coming up the stairs.

Slowly the door opened — slowly the light I had seen before grew in the darkened air — and into the room rode the Stone Rider, rigid, erect, with the unearthly radiance all around him.

He came up to the foot of the bed, and slowly lifted the vizor of his helmet, disclosing a glistening skull — and, as I looked, the skull became the face in the portrait over the mantelpiece of the study at Salitz. It was too evident that Siebach recognised it. His eyes were fixed on the apparition; his thin features were grey, and drawn with fear. For a moment he remained motionless, staring at it; then he threw up his arms with an awful cry, and fell back.

Slowly the Stone Rider drew the mailed gauntlet from his right hand. For a moment he poised it deliberately in the air, then flung it full in Siebach's face.

A shudder ran through the prostrate figure, but it did not move again; and the Stone Rider turned his horse and rode from the room. The light followed him, and we were again in semi-darkness.

Then I lit a candle and rang for Auberthal and the servants.

×

Whether the story of the murder was correct or not, I cannot say. It may have been the madness of a diseased imagination, or it may have been the late remorse of a criminal. At any rate, it is not for me to throw suspicion on the name of a dead man. I can only relate what I myself saw and heard. The doctor declared, and maintains to this day, that his patient was insane; and, being a doctor, he very naturally has the world on his side. But, say what he will, there is one thing he can never explain. When I lit the candle that night, and found Count Siebach von Salitz lying dead, I found also that on his forehead was the distinct print — purple and bruised — of a clenched fist. The doctor cannot explain this; perhaps I can. For what could it be if it was not left by the gauntlet of the Stone Rider?

5 A Marble Woman (1899)

W C MORROW

Only once in my life have I seen Dr Entrefort not in full possession of all his wonderful faculties. How it really came about that he lost himself would make a very interesting story, revealing in a singular light one of the many sides of this extraordinary man, but the purpose of this narrative is to relate merely the consequences of his condition.

His confidential servant came to me one night in great distress and perplexity and informed me that the physician desired my presence immediately.

I found Entrefort reeling and plunging about his bedroom in complete nervous disorganisation. He was arrayed in a dressing-gown thrown over his sleeping clothes, and his bed showed that he had been occupying it that night. His face was flushed, his eyes danced and glistened, and the erratic conduct of his muscular system plainly indicated a serious mental disorder.

He seemed greatly relieved to see me.

'I thought you would never come!' he greeted me breathlessly, as though he might have been running a long distance. Then he dismissed the servant for the night, locked the door, and threw himself tumultuously upon his couch, where he lay for some moments panting and making a masterly effort to bring himself under control. I was so alarmed at seeing my friend in this condition that I asked him if he was ill, for if so he should have a physician at once.

'No!' he cried in alarm. 'For heaven's sake, no! Something is the matter with me — I don't know what. It would be impossible to frighten me under ordinary circumstances. You have seen me in all sorts of trying positions, and you never saw my nerve fail. In all my life I have never had the strange and terrible sensations that now seem to be straining me to bursting. I am mad for the time — that is all. I need your kind, gentle presence, your sympathy, your companionship. I was sane enough to send for you in time. No; I don't need a physician. Why should I?' he asked, shooting a suspicious look at me.

I suggested that he return to bed and make himself comfortable, but he vehemently refused. His whole manner was so wild and distraught that I could only await results to determine my procedure.

Entrefort, cautiously listening for any sound in the corridor, sat up on the couch and whispered: 'A terrible accident has happened — my statue toppled over this evening while I was dusting it, and the left arm broke off just above the elbow.'

A tug at the seal of this mystery at last. For the first time in all these years of our intimacy, Entrefort seemingly was going to break the silence. I held my breath and tried to conceal my eagerness. Well I remembered that wonderful piece of chiselled marble. I had already had a glimpse of the history of the strange and beautiful girl whom it represented, but it was all shadowy and intangible, and Entrefort had never proffered an explanation. I knew that after a rumour of her death Entrefort kept in the strictest seclusion for a long time, that when he emerged he looked for a while singularly old, withered and decrepit, and that he returned but gradually to his normal condition of boundless enthusiasm and irrepressible energy; and I knew that he then had with him a marble statue of the girl, and that it was a surpassingly beautiful and startling production. I knew that he took the most exquisite care of it, permitting no one but himself to go near it or touch it, and that in his travels he invariably took it with him, tending it as though it might have been a sentient thing, packing and unpacking it with incredible patience and unfailing skill, and keeping it always locked securely in a closet or, if he could, a special room. I was aware that he kept fresh flowers daily on a table at its side, and that he would sometimes spend hours alone with it, emerging in the deepest melancholy.

The figure was that of a young woman in whose features appeared strong traces of Oriental blood. It showed a woman of medium size, perfectly modelled and adorned with all the finer graces of configuration peculiar to the sex. The attitude was the most striking feature of the work. The sculptor had chosen a pose showing the right arm upraised in a gesture of agonised pleading, which the expression of the wide-open eyes, the parted lips and the head thrust forward emphasised to a marvellous extent. The left arm seemed to be arrested as it was being raised from the side, and was the one awkward feature of the sculpture. That it, the one best protected against injury, should have been the one to suffer fracture, appeared to me to be a very puzzling circumstance. I could find in the work not the slightest trace of skill of any of the great sculptors, for it seemed vastly finer than any of them could produce. Entrefort had never enlightened me on the subject.

'Yes,' repeated Entrefort, 'the left arm is broken off at the elbow. Do you know what that means to me?'

I shook my head.

'It means despair, it means —' He threw himself again on his couch and writhed and ground his teeth.

I drew my chair close to him, took his hand, and began to speak soothingly. Presently I suggested: 'I can't see how that should be a serious matter. There are artisans who are skilled in mending fractured marbles.'

'None but God could mend this fracture!' he passionately exclaimed.

'Entrefort,' said I, for the first time speaking firmly and threateningly, 'unless you make an effort to control yourself you will become a madman in an hour.'

He shivered under the thrust.

'Am I not already a madman?' he asked, his eyes opening wide in terror. 'Is anyone of us ever safe from that frightful malady? But I am sane — it is only an unspeakable dread that unmans me. Let me explain, and then you will understand; for, man, I need your sympathy, the consolation of your friendship.

'I loved her, living, as a man of my ardent temperament must love the one woman in the world who was created for him to live with all his soul. She was heart of my heart, soul of my soul. There enwrapped us in one enfolding a great encompassing spirit of infinite power and sweetness. My friend, there are degrees of affinities between men and woman. The more nearly perfect the affinity, the purer their love. What is affinity? Merely mutual adaptability. It is as true of love as of chemistry. Two molecules with totally different elements combine and form a third, more complex than either, but with properties and functions none the less stable. Thenceforward they work for ever as one. That also is love, perfect love.

'Such was the love between her and me. It was as perfect and pure on her side as on mine. But was mine really perfect? If so, how came it that I brought her to that terrible end? Was it perfect indeed, and was the inconceivable evil that I brought upon her and myself but a part of the divine plan? Who can know?

'Listen. She was so surpassingly beautiful that I longed with all the intensity of my nature to perpetuate her heaven-sent charms. I knew that I should in time grow old and die, but I wanted the world to keep her glorious beauty for ever. As God is my witness, I had no selfish design in all that I did. You know that there never has been a limit to my insane ambition. You have understood me well.

'I was frank with her, for without frankness there can be no love. I told her what I desired to do. I can never forget the look of amused astonishment that lighted up her face. She chided me for hunting will-o'-the-wisps, and said that it was all impossible — impossible, mind you — to me! And then she said she would infinitely prefer that we grew old together, so that the harmony between us should remain unshaken.

'But I could not bear to think of her slowly passing into decay and death, and I frankly told her that I would adhere to my purpose. At this she laughingly replied that if I was so determined she would yield. I did not realise, in the exuberance of my self-confidence, that she had no faith in the plans which I intended to follow. She submitted cheerfully to the régime that I imposed upon her — not a hard one, understand; that would have been impossible with me. It was all pleasant enough, and she went singing through it without the slightest mar to our happiness.

'A curious feature of the regime was that while she was utterly unconscious of the effect that it was having upon her, I could see clearly the signs of progress. Had I not given the best thought of my life to the subject? Had I not delved sufficiently into the mysteries of life to learn how the ravages of years may be checked? This, you will understand, is a thing not for the world to know. The laws of nature are of divine institution; to set them aside, to violate them — that is a crime. These secrets will be learned in time, but that time has not yet come. Evolution must be shown in order to be permanent and beneficial. I told her plainly that I could see the changes taking place, but she only laughed and called me a darling idiot!

'There came at last some symptoms that puzzled me exceedingly — a marble-like appearance of the skin, a coldness to the touch, a remarkable increase in weight, a disappearance of the usual elasticity of movement, and an unaccountable languor. Some of these I could not understand, but I went over my studies carefully, I analysed my formula, I made exhaustive tests of the ingredients composing the preparation that I was administering to her. She had perfect health and content, but an alarming tendency to sleep. Then her muscles became indurated. Instead of all this there should have been nothing but a heightening and fixing of her charms. Still I could find nothing wrong either with the theory or the formula.

'One day, after having been out, I returned to find a most distressing condition of affairs. She was sitting on a chair asleep and, as I entered, the death-like appearance that sat upon her face startled me. I ran to her, caught her by the arm, called loudly to her, and tried to raise her to her feet. I suddenly found that her weight had become so great that this was nearly impossible. Presently she stood erect, her eyes still closed. She was terribly white, and her skin had the clarity of the finest marble, and she was very cold. I called loudly, I shook her, I kissed her, I tried to breathe into her some of the intense vitality that filled me. She opened her eyes slowly and stared straight ahead. I called the more urgently, a torrent of agonised anxiety pouring forth in my words.

'She trembled, breathed faintly, and turned her glance upon me. Gradually there began to well up in them the flood of the old love that had filled them for so long. A faint smile played upon her lips. I stepped back, and, holding out my arms, asked her to come to me. She made an effort and failed. Then a great and awful fear came into her face. Her eyes stared, she thrust out her head toward me, her lips parted, her right arm was slowly raised in an attitude of desperate supplication. Faintly there came from her lips the cry, "Save me!" I still pleaded with her to come, but there she stood immovable. Then, with a feeling of unspeakable dread, I went close and touched her. She was perfectly rigid — she was a marble statue! Do you wonder that I have kept this lifeless stone with me and tended it so carefully? It is she herself, not a carved image of her. And do you understand what the fearful calamity of the broken arm means when I tell you that all my hopes, all my efforts, are directed to her restoration to life?'

Entrefort's breathless, passionate delivery of this history had a strangely impressive effect upon me. At the close he was in a transport of nervous exaltation.

'I have said it was marble!' he cried. 'You have thought it was. Wait.'

He strode into the small room in which the statue stood, took the separated arm from the table, and brought it to me.

'Look at this section,' he exclaimed, holding up the fractured surface to my inspection.

It is with great hesitancy that I now relate what I saw. Up to this time, in spite of the vivid account that Entrefort had given, there still had remained with me unconsciously a rational explanation of the whole wonderful thing. But now, when I examined the fracture and saw what it revealed — After all, what do I care? It is incumbent on no one to believe — it is best that none should. And as I lay greater store by my veracity than by my reputation, I will out with it, and the wise ones — there is always an abundance of such in the world — may think what they please. In the centre was a spot of delicate, cream-tinted stone; surrounding it was a zone of denser, coarser and whiter stone; outside of this a thicker one of pure white stone of the finest and most delicate structure. That is to say, I saw the marrow, bone, and flesh of a human arm, all turned to stone.

Entrefort, gazing at me triumphantly, returned the arm to its table in the inner room, and came back. I was looking at him stupidly, amazed. The strain under which he had laboured thus far suddenly relaxed. He swept his hand across his forehead in a bewildered manner and began to totter. I caught him and laid him on his bed, and there he at once fell into a profound slumber.

I watched at his bedside all night and till late the next day, when he awoke. He seemed surprised and gratified to see me.

'When did you come?' he faintly asked.

'Last night, when you sent for me.'

'Sent for you? I don't remember.'

'You don't remember — all that you told me last night of the history of the statue?'

It was as though I had dealt him a heavy physical blow.

'Did I tell you a fantastic story about its having been once a woman, and about my changing her to stone while trying to render her immune to age and death?'

I nodded, wondering at the sneering bitterness with which he spoke.

'Well, of course a man of your sense will understand that it was a lie from beginning to end.'

I made no response.

'Do you not?' he asked, with angry petulance.

But I merely turned my head and looked another way, and my gentle pressure of his hand calmed him into silence.

6 The Duchess at Prayer (1900)

EDITH WHARTON

I

Have you ever questioned the long shuttered front of an old Italian house, that motionless mask, smooth, mute, equivocal as the face of a priest behind which buzz the secrets of the confessional? Other houses declare the activities they shelter; they are the clear expressive cuticle of a life flowing close to the surface; but the old palace in its narrow street, the villa on its cypress-hooded hill, are as impenetrable as death. The tall windows are like blind eyes, the great door is a shut mouth. Inside there may be sunshine, the scent of myrtles, and a pulse of life through all the arteries of the huge frame; or a mortal solitude where bats lodge in the disjointed stones, and the keys rust in unused doors ...

II

From the loggia, with its vanishing frescoes, I looked down an avenue barred by a ladder of cypress-shadows to the ducal escutcheon and mutilated vases of the gate. Flat noon lay on the gardens, on fountains, porticoes and grottoes. Below the terrace, where a chrome-colored lichen had sheeted the balustrade as with fine *laminæ* of gold, vineyards stooped to the rich valley clasped in hills. The lower slopes were strewn with white villages like stars spangling a summer dusk; and beyond these, fold on fold of blue mountain, clear as gauze against the sky. The August air was lifeless, but it seemed light and vivifying after the atmosphere of the shrouded rooms through which I had been led. Their chill was on me and I hugged the sunshine.

'The Duchess's apartments are beyond,' said the old man.

He was the oldest man I had ever seen; so sucked back into

the past that he seemed more like a memory than a living being. The one trait linking him with the actual was the fixity with which his small saurian eye held the pocket that, as I entered, had yielded a *lira* to the gate-keeper's child. He went on, without removing his eye:

'For two hundred years nothing has been changed in the apartments of the Duchess.'

'And no one lives here now?'

'No one, sir. The Duke goes to Como for the summer season.'

I had moved to the other end of the loggia. Below me, through hanging groves, white roofs and domes flashed like a smile.

'And that's Vicenza?'

'*Proprio!*' The old man extended fingers as lean as the hands fading from the walls behind us. 'You see the palace roof over there, just to the left of the Basilica? The one with the row of statues like birds taking flight? That's the Duke's town palace, built by Palladio.'

'And does the Duke come there?'

'Never. In winter he goes to Rome.'

'And the palace and the villa are always closed?'

'As you see — always.'

'How long has this been?'

'Since I can remember.'

I looked into his eyes: they were like tarnished metal mirrors reflecting nothing. 'That must be a long time,' I said, involuntarily.

'A long time,' he assented.

I looked down on the gardens. An opulence of dahlias overran the box-borders, between cypresses that cut the sunshine like basalt shafts. Bees hung above the lavender; lizards sunned themselves on the benches and slipped through the cracks of the dry basins. Everywhere were vanishing traces of that fantastic horticulture of which our dull age has lost the art. Down the alleys maimed statues stretched their arms like rows of whining beggars; faun-eared terms grinned in the thicket, and above the laurustinus walls rose the mock ruin of a temple, falling into real ruin in the bright disintegrating air. The glare was blinding.

'Let us go in,' I said.

The old man pushed open a heavy door, behind which the cold lurked like a knife.

'The Duchess's apartments,' he said.

Overhead and around us the same evanescent frescoes, underfoot the same scagliola volutes, unrolled themselves interminably. Ebony cabinets, with colonnades of precious marbles in cunning perspective, alternated down the room with the tarnished efflorescence of gilt consoles supporting Chinese monsters; and from the chimney-panel a gentleman in the Spanish habit haughtily ignored us.

'Duke Ercole II,' the old man explained, 'by the Genoese Priest.'

It was a narrow-browed face, sallow as a wax effigy, high-nosed and cautious-lidded, as though modelled by priestly hands; the lips weak and vain rather than cruel; a quibbling mouth that would have snapped at verbal errors like a lizard catching flies, but had never learned the shape of a round yes or no. One of the Duke's hands rested on the head of a dwarf with pearl earrings and fantastic dress; the other turned the pages of a folio propped on a skull.

'Beyond is the Duchess's bedroom,' the old man reminded me.

Here the shutters admitted but two narrow shafts of light, gold bars deepening the subaqueous gloom. On a dais, the bedstead, grim, nuptial, official, lifted its baldachin; a yellow Christ agonized between the curtains, and across the room a lady smiled at us from the chimney-breast.

The old man unbarred a shutter and the light touched her face. Such a face it was, with a flicker of laughter over it like the wind on a June meadow, and a singular tender pliancy of mien, as though one of Tiepolo's lenient goddesses had been busked into the stiff sheath of a seventeenth century dress!

'No one has slept here,' said the old man, 'since the Duchess Violante.'

'And she was —?'

'The lady there — first Duchess of Duke Ercole II.'

He drew a key from his pocket and unlocked a door at the

farther end of the room. 'The chapel,' he said. 'This is the Duchess's balcony.' As I turned to follow him the Duchess tossed me a side-long smile.

I stepped into a grated tribune above a chapel festooned with stucco. Pictures of bituminous saints mouldered between the pilasters; the artificial roses in the altar-vases were gray with dust and age, and under the cobwebby rosettes of the vaulting a bird's nest clung. Before the altar stood a row of tattered arm-chairs, and I drew back at sight of a figure kneeling near them. 'The Duchess,' the old man whispered. 'By the Cavaliere Bernini.'

It was the image of a woman in furred robes and spreading *fraise*, her hands lifted, her face addressed to the tabernacle. There was a strangeness in the sight of that immovable presence locked in prayer before an abandoned shrine. Her face was hidden, and I wondered whether it were grief or gratitude that raised her hands and drew her eyes to the altar, where no living prayer joined her marble invocation. I followed my guide down the tribune steps, impatient to see what mystic version of such terrestrial graces the ingenious artist had found — the Cavaliere was master of such arts. The Duchess's attitude was one of transport, as though heavenly airs fluttered her laces and the love-locks escaping from her coif. I saw how admirably the sculptor had caught the poise of her head, the tender slope of the shoulder; then I crossed over and looked into her face — it was a frozen horror. Never have hate, revolt, and agony so possessed a human countenance ...

The old man crossed himself and shuffled his feet on the marble.

'The Duchess Violante,' he repeated.

'The same as in the picture?'

'Eh — the same.'

'But the face — what does it mean?'

He shrugged his shoulders and turned deaf eyes on me. Then he shot a glance round the sepulchral place, clutched my sleeve and said, close to my ear: 'It was not always so.'

'What was not?'

'The face — so terrible.'

'The Duchess's face?'

'The statue's. It changed after—'

'After?'

'It was put here.'

'The statue's face *changed* —?'

He mistook my bewilderment for incredulity and his confidential finger dropped from my sleeve. 'Eh, that's the story. I tell what I've heard. What do I know?' He resumed his senile shuffle across the marble. 'This is a bad place to stay in — no one comes here. It's too cold. But the gentleman said, *I must see everything!*'

I let the *lire* sound. 'So I must — and hear everything. This story, now — from whom did you have it?'

His hand stole back. 'One that saw it, by God!'

'That saw it?'

'My grandmother, then. I'm a very old man.'

'Your grandmother? Your grandmother was —?'

'The Duchess's serving girl, with respect to you.'

'Your grandmother? Two hundred years ago?'

'Is it too long ago? That's as God pleases. I am a very old man and she was a very old woman when I was born. When she died she was as black as a miraculous Virgin and her breath whistled like the wind in a keyhole. She told me the story when I was a little boy. She told it to me out there in the garden, on a bench by the fish-pond, one summer night of the year she died. It must be true, for I can show you the very bench we sat on ...'

III

Noon lay heavier on the gardens; not our live humming warmth, but the stale exhalation of dead summers. The very statues seemed to drowse like watchers by a death-bed. Lizards shot out of the cracked soil like flames and the bench in the laurustinus niche was strewn with the blue varnished bodies of dead flies. Before us lay the fish-pond, a yellow marble slab above rotting secrets. The villa looked across it, composed as a dead face, with the cypresses flanking it for candles ...

IV

'... Impossible, you say, that my mother's mother should have been the Duchess's maid? What do I know? It is so long since anything has happened here that the old things seem nearer, perhaps, than to those who live in cities ... But how else did she know about the statue then? Answer me that, sir! That she saw with her eyes, I can swear to, and never smiled again, so she told me, till they put her first child in her arms ... for she was taken to wife by the steward's son, Antonio, the same who had carried the letters ... But where am I? Ah, well ... she was a mere slip, you understand, my grandmother, when the Duchess died, a niece of the upper maid, Nencia, and suffered about the Duchess because of her pranks and the funny songs she knew. It's possible, you think, she may have heard from others what she afterward fancied she had seen herself? How that is, it's not for an unlettered man to say; though indeed I myself seem to have seen many of the things she told me. This is a strange place. No one comes here, nothing changes, and the old memories stand up as distinct as the statues in the garden ...

'It began the summer after they came back from the Brenta. Duke Ercole had married the lady from Venice, you must know; it was a gay city, then, I'm told, with laughter and music on the water, and the days slipped by like boats running with the tide. Well, to humor her he took her back the first autumn to the Brenta. Her father, it appears, had a grand palace there, with such gardens, bowling-alleys, grottoes and casinos as never were; gondolas bobbing at the water-gates, a stable full of gilt coaches, a theatre full of players, and kitchens and offices full of cooks and lackeys to serve up chocolate all day long to the fine ladies in masks and furbelows, with their pet dogs and their blackamoors and their *abates*. Eh! I know it all as if I'd been there, for Nencia, you see, my grandmother's aunt, travelled with the Duchess, and came back with her eyes round as platters, and not a word to say for the rest of the year to any of the lads who'd courted her here in Vicenza.

'What happened there I don't know — my grandmother could never get at the rights of it, for Nencia was mute as a fish where her lady was concerned — but when they came back to Vicenza the Duke ordered the villa set in order; and in the spring he brought the Duchess here and left her. She looked happy enough, my grandmother said, and seemed no object for pity. Perhaps, after all, it was better than being shut up in Vicenza, in the tall painted rooms where priests came and went as softly as cats prowling for birds, and the Duke was forever closeted in his library, talking with learned men. The Duke was a scholar; you noticed he was painted with a book? Well, those that can read 'em make out that they're full of wonderful things; as a man that's been to a fair across the mountains will always tell his people at home it was beyond anything *they'll* ever see. As for the Duchess, she was all for music, play-acting, and young company. The Duke was a silent man, stepping quietly, with his eyes down, as though he'd just come from confession; when the Duchess's lap-dog yapped at his heels he danced like a man in a swarm of hornets; when the Duchess laughed he winced as if you'd drawn a diamond across a window-pane. And the Duchess was always laughing.

'When she first came to the villa she was very busy laying out the gardens, designing grottoes, planting groves, and planning all manner of agreeable surprises in the way of water-jets that drenched you unexpectedly, and hermits in caves, and wild men that jumped at you out of thickets. She had a very pretty taste in such matters, but after awhile she tired of it, and there being no one for her to talk to but her maids and the chaplain — a clumsy man deep in his books — why, she would have strolling players out from Vicenza, mountebanks and fortune-tellers from the market-place, travelling doctors and astrologers, and all manner of trained animals. Still it could be seen that the poor lady pined for company, and her waiting women, who loved her, were glad when the Cavaliere Ascanio, the Duke's cousin, came to live at the vineyard across the valley — you see the pinkish house over there in the mulberries, with a red roof and a pigeon-cote?

'The Cavaliere Ascanio was a cadet of one of the great Venetian houses, *pezzi grossi* of the Golden Book. He had been meant for the Church, I believe, but what! he set fighting above praying and cast in his lot with the captain of the Duke of Mantua's *bravi*, himself a Venetian of good standing, but a little at odds with the law. Well, the next I knew, the Cavaliere was in Venice again, perhaps not in good odor on account of his connection with the gentleman I speak of. Some say he tried to carry off a nun from the convent of Santa Croce; how that may be I can't say; but my grandmother declared he had enemies there, and the end of it was that on some pretext or other the Ten banished him to Vicenza. There, of course, the Duke, being his kinsman, had to show him a civil face; and that was how he first came to the villa.

'He was a fine young man, beautiful as a Saint Sebastian, a rare musician, who sang his own songs to the lute in a way that used to make my grandmother's heart melt and run through her body like mulled wine. He had a good word for everybody, too, and was always dressed in the French fashion, and smelt as sweet as a bean-field; and every soul about the place welcomed the sight of him.

'Well, the Duchess, it seemed, welcomed it too; youth will have youth, and laughter turns to laughter; and the two matched each other like the candlesticks on an altar. The Duchess — you've seen her portrait — but to hear my grandmother, sir, it no more approached her than a weed comes up to a rose. The Cavaliere, indeed, as became a poet, paragoned her in his song to all the pagan goddesses of antiquity; and doubtless these were finer to look at than mere women; but so, it seemed, was she; for, to believe my grandmother, she made other women look no more than the big French fashion-doll that used to be shown on Ascension days in the Piazza. She was one, at any rate, that needed no outlandish finery to beautify her; whatever dress she wore became her as feathers fit the bird; and her hair didn't get its color by bleaching on the housetop. It glittered of itself like the threads in an Easter chasuble, and her skin was whiter than fine wheaten bread, and her mouth as sweet as a ripe fig.

'Well, sir, you could no more keep them apart than the bees and the lavender. They were always together, singing, bowling, playing cup and ball, walking in the gardens, visiting the aviaries and petting her grace's trick-dogs and monkeys. The Duchess was as gay as a foal, always playing pranks and laughing, tricking out her animals like comedians, disguising herself as a peasant or a nun (you should have seen her one day pass herself off to the chaplain as a mendicant sister), or teaching the lads and girls of the vineyards to dance and sing madrigals together. The Cavaliere had a singular ingenuity in planning such entertainments, and the days were hardly long enough for their diversions. But toward the end of the summer the Duchess fell quiet and would hear only sad music, and the two sat much together in the gazebo at the end of the garden. It was there the Duke found them one day when he drove out from Vicenza in his gilt coach. He came but once or twice a year to the villa, and it was, as my grandmother said, just a part of her poor lady's ill-luck to be wearing that day the Venetian habit, which uncovered the shoulders in a way the Duke always scowled at, and her curls loose and powdered with gold. Well, the three drank chocolate in the gazebo, and what happened no one knew, except that the Duke, on taking leave, gave his cousin a seat in his carriage; but the Cavaliere never returned.

'Winter approaching, and the poor lady thus finding herself once more alone, it was surmised among her women that she must fall into a deeper depression of spirits. But far from this being the case, she displayed such cheerfulness and equanimity of humor that my grandmother, for one, was half-vexed with her for giving no more thought to the poor young man who, all this time, was eating his heart out in the house across the valley. It is true she quitted her gold-laced gowns and wore a veil over her head; but Nencia would have it she looked the lovelier for the change, and so gave the Duke greater displeasure. Certain it is that the Duke drove out oftener to the villa, and though he found his lady always engaged in some innocent pursuit, such as embroidery or music, or playing games with her young women, yet he always went away with a sour look and a whispered word to the chaplain. Now as to the chaplain, my grandmother owned there had been a time when her grace had not handled him over-wisely. For, according to Nencia, it seems that his reverence, who seldom approached the Duchess, being buried in his library like a mouse in a cheese — well, one day he made bold to appeal to her for a sum of money, a large sum, Nencia said, to buy certain tall books, a chest full of them, that a foreign pedler had brought him; whereupon the Duchess, who could never abide a book, breaks out at him with a laugh and a flash of her old spirit — "Holy Mother of God, must I have more books about me? I was nearly smothered with them in the first year of my marriage," and the chaplain turning red at the affront, she added: "You may buy them and welcome, my good chaplain, if you can find the money; but as for me, I am yet seeking a way to pay for my turquoise necklace, and the statue of Daphne at the end of the bowling-green, and the Indian parrot that my black boy brought me last Michaelmas from the Bohemians — so you see I've no money to waste on trifles," and as he backs out awkwardly she tosses at him, over her shoulder: "You should pray to Saint Blandina to open the Duke's pocket!" to which he returned, very quietly, "Your excellency's suggestion is an admirable one, and I have already entreated that blessed martyr to open the Duke's understanding."

'Thereat, Nencia said (who was standing by), the Duchess flushed wonderfully red and waved him out of the room; and then "Quick!" she cried to my grandmother (who was too glad to run on such errands), "Call me Antonio, the gardener's boy, to the box-garden; I've a word to say to him about the new clove-carnations ..."

'Now, I may not have told you, sir, that in the crypt under the chapel there has stood, for more generations than a man can count, a stone coffin containing a thigh-bone of the blessed Saint Blandina of Lyons, a relic offered, I've been told, by some great Duke of France to one of our own dukes when they fought the Turk together; and the object, ever since, of particular veneration in this illustrious family. Now, since the Duchess had been left to herself, it was observed she affected a fervent devotion to this relic, praying often in the chapel and even causing the stone slab that covered the entrance to the crypt to be replaced by a wooden one, that she might at will descend and kneel by the coffin. This was matter of edification to all the household, and should have been peculiarly pleasing to the chaplain; but, with respect to you, he was the kind of man who brings a sour mouth to the eating of the sweetest apple.

'However that may be, the Duchess, when she dismissed him, was seen running to the garden, where she talked earnestly with the boy Antonio about the new clove-carnations; and the rest of the day she sat indoors and played sweetly on the virginal. Now Nencia always had it in mind that her Grace had made a mistake in refusing that request of the chaplain's; but she said nothing, for to talk reason to the Duchess was of no more use than praying for rain in a drought.

'Winter came early that year, there was snow on the hills by All Souls, the wind stripped the gardens, and the lemon-trees were nipped in the lemon-house. The Duchess kept her room in this black season, sitting over the fire, embroidering, reading books of devotion (which was a thing she had never done), and praying frequently in the chapel. As for the chaplain, it was a place he never set foot in but to say mass in the morning, with the Duchess overhead in the tribune, and the servants aching with rheumatism on the marble floor. The chaplain himself hated the cold, and galloped through the mass like a man with witches after him. The rest of the day he spent in his library, over a brazier, with his eternal books ...

'You'll wonder, sir, if I'm ever to get to the gist of the story; and I've gone slowly, I own, for fear of what's coming. Well, the winter was long and hard. When it fell cold the Duke ceased to come out from Vicenza, and not a soul had the Duchess to speak to but her maid-servants and the gardeners about the place. Yet it was wonderful, my grandmother said, how she kept her brave colors and her spirits; only it was remarked that she prayed longer in the chapel, where a brazier was kept burning for her all day.

When the young are denied their natural pleasures, they turn often enough to religion; and it was a mercy, as my grandmother said, that she, who had scarce a live sinner to speak to, should take such comfort in a dead saint.

'My grandmother seldom saw her that winter, for though she showed a brave front to all, she kept more and more to herself, choosing to have only Nencia about her, and dismissing even her when she went to pray. For her devotion had that mark of true piety, that she wished it not to be observed; so that Nencia had strict orders, on the chaplain's approach, to warn her mistress if she happened to be in prayer.

'Well, the winter passed, and spring was well forward, when my grandmother one evening had a bad fright. That it was her own fault I won't deny, for she'd been down the lime-walk with Antonio when her aunt fancied her to be stitching in her chamber; and seeing a sudden light in Nencia's window, she took fright lest her disobedience be found out, and ran up quickly through the laurel-grove to the house. Her way lay by the chapel, and as she crept past it, meaning to slip in through the scullery, and groping her way, for the dark had fallen and the moon was scarce up, she heard a crash close behind her, as though someone had dropped from a window of the chapel. The young fool's heart turned over, but she looked round as she ran, and there, sure enough, was a man scuttling across the terrace; and as he doubled the corner of the house my grandmother swore she caught the whisk of the chaplain's skirts. Now that was a strange thing, certainly; for why should the chaplain be getting out of the chapel window when he might have passed through the door? For you may have noticed, sir, there's a door leads from the chapel into the saloon on the ground floor; the only other way out being through the Duchess's tribune.

'Well, my grandmother turned the matter over, and next time she met Antonio in the lime-walk (which, by reason of her fright, was not for some days) she laid before him what had happened; but to her surprise he only laughed, and said, "You little simpleton, he wasn't getting out of the window, he was trying to look in," and not another word could she get from him.

'So the season moved on to Easter, and news came the Duke had gone to Rome for that holy festivity. His comings and goings made no change at the villa, and yet there was no one there but felt easier to think his yellow face was on the far side of the Apennines, unless, perhaps, it was the chaplain.

'Well, it was one day in May that the Duchess, who had walked long with Nencia on the terrace, rejoicing at the sweetness of the prospect and the pleasant scent of the gilly-flowers in the stone vases, the Duchess toward midday withdrew to her rooms, giving orders that her dinner should be served in her bed-chamber. My grandmother helped to carry in the dishes, and observed, she said, the singular beauty of the Duchess, who, in honor of the fine weather, had put on a gown of shot-silver and hung her bare shoulders with pearls, so that she looked fit to dance at court with an emperor. She had ordered, too, a rare repast for a lady that heeded so little what she ate — jellies, game-pastries, fruits in syrup, spiced cakes, and a flagon of Greek wine; and she nodded and clapped her hands as the women set it before her, saying, again and again, "I shall eat well today."

'But presently another mood seized her; she turned from the table, called for her rosary, and said to Nencia: "The fine weather has made me neglect my devotions. I must say a litany before I dine."

'She ordered the women out and barred the door, as her custom was; and Nencia and my grandmother went downstairs to work in the linen-room.

'Now the linen-room gives on the court-yard, and suddenly my grandmother saw a strange sight approaching. First up the avenue came the Duke's carriage (whom all thought to be in Rome), and after it, drawn by a long string of mules and oxen, a cart carrying what looked like a kneeling figure wrapped in death-clothes. The strangeness of it struck the girl dumb and the Duke's coach was at the door before she had the wit to cry out that it was coming. Nencia, when she saw it, went white and ran out of the room. My grandmother followed, scared by her face, and the two fled along the corridor to the chapel. On the way they met the chaplain, deep in a book, who asked in surprise where they were running, and when they said, to announce the Duke's arrival, he fell into such astonishment, and asked them so many questions and uttered such ohs and ahs that by the time he let them by the Duke was at their heels. Nencia reached the chapel-door first and cried out that the Duke was coming; and before she had a reply he was at her side, with the chaplain following.

'A moment later the door opened and there stood the Duchess. She held her rosary in one hand and had drawn a scarf over her shoulders; but they shone through it like the moon in a mist, and her countenance sparkled with beauty.

'The Duke took her hand with a bow. "Madam," he said, "I could have had no greater happiness than thus to surprise you at your devotions."

'"My own happiness," she replied, "would have been greater had your excellency prolonged it by giving me notice of your arrival."

'"Had you expected me, Madam," said he, "your appearance could scarcely have been more fitted to the occasion. Few ladies of your youth and beauty array themselves to venerate a saint as they would to welcome a lover."

'"Sir," she answered, "having never enjoyed the latter opportunity, I am constrained to make the most of the former — What's that?" she cried, falling back, and the rosary dropped from her hand.

'There was a loud noise at the other end of the saloon, as of a heavy object being dragged down the passage; and presently a dozen men were seen haling across the threshold the shrouded thing from the ox-cart. The Duke waved his hand toward it. "That," said he, "Madam, is a tribute to your extraordinary piety. I have heard with peculiar satisfaction of your devotion to the blessed relics in this chapel, and to commemorate a zeal which neither the rigors of winter nor the sultriness of summer could abate, I have ordered a sculptured image of you, marvellously executed by the Cavaliere Bernini, to be placed before the altar over the entrance to the crypt."

'The Duchess, who had grown pale, nevertheless smiled

playfully at this. "As to commemorating my piety," she said. "I recognize there one of your excellency's pleasantries —"

"A pleasantry?" the Duke interrupted; and he made a sign to the men, who had now reached the threshold of the chapel. In an instant the wrappings fell from the figure, and there knelt the Duchess to the life. A cry of wonder rose from all, but the Duchess herself stood whiter than the marble.

"You will see," says the Duke, "this is no pleasantry, but a triumph of the incomparable Bernini's chisel. The likeness was done from your miniature portrait by the divine Elisabetta Sirani, which I sent to the master some six months ago, with what results all must admire."

"Six months!" cried the Duchess, and seemed about to fall; but his excellency caught her by the hand.

"Nothing," he said, "could better please me than the excessive emotion you display, for true piety is ever modest, and your thanks could not take a form that better became you. And now," says he to the men, "let the image be put in place."

'By this, life seemed to have returned to the Duchess, and she answered him with a deep reverence. "That I should be overcome by so unexpected a grace, your excellency admits to be natural; but what honors you accord it is my privilege to accept, and I entreat only that in mercy to my modesty the image be placed in the remotest part of the chapel."

'At that the Duke darkened. "What! You would have this masterpiece of a renowned chisel, which, I disguise not, cost me the price of a good vineyard in gold pieces, you would have it thrust out of sight like the work of a village stone-cutter?"

"It is my semblance, not the sculptor's work, I desire to conceal"

"If you are fit for my house, Madam, you are fit for God's, and entitled to the place of honor in both. Bring the statue forward, you dawdlers!" he called out to the men.

'The Duchess fell back submissively. "You are right, sir, as always; but I would at least have the image stand on the left of the altar, that, looking up, it may behold your excellency's seat in the tribune."

"'A pretty thought, Madam, for which I thank you; but I design before long to put my companion image on the other side of the altar; and the wife's place, as you know, is at her husband's right hand."

"'True, my lord — but, again, if my poor presentment is to have the unmerited honor of kneeling beside yours, why not place both before the altar, where it is our habit to pray in life?"

"'And where, Madam, should we kneel if they took our places? Besides," says the Duke, still speaking very blandly, "I have a more particular purpose in placing your image over the entrance to the crypt; for not only would I thereby mark your special devotion to the blessed saint who rests there, but, by sealing up the opening in the pavement, would assure the perpetual preservation of that holy martyr's bones, which hitherto have been too thoughtlessly exposed to sacrilegious attempts."

"'What attempts, my lord?" cries the Duchess. "No one enters this chapel without my leave."

"'So I have understood, and can well believe from what I have learned of your piety; yet at night a malefactor might break in through a window, Madam, and your excellency not know it."

"'I'm a light sleeper," said the Duchess.

'The Duke looked at her gravely. "Indeed?" said he. "A bad sign at your age. I must see that you are provided with a sleeping-draught."

'The Duchess's eyes filled. "You would deprive me, then, of the consolation of visiting those venerable relics?"

"'I would have you keep eternal guard over them, knowing no one to whose care they may more fittingly be entrusted."

'By this the image was brought close to the wooden slab that covered the entrance to the crypt, when the Duchess, springing forward, placed herself in the way.

"'Sir, let the statue be put in place to-morrow, and suffer me, tonight, to say a last prayer beside those holy bones."

'The Duke stepped instantly to her side. "Well thought, Madam; I will go down with you now, and we will pray together."

"'Sir, your long absences have, alas! given me the habit of solitary devotion, and I confess that any presence is distracting."

"'Madam, I accept your rebuke. Hitherto, it is true, the duties of my station have constrained me to long absences; but henceforward I remain with you while you live. Shall we go down into the crypt together?"

"'No; for I fear for your excellency's ague. The air there is excessively damp."

"'The more reason you should no longer be exposed to it; and to prevent the intemperance of your zeal I will at once make the place inaccessible."

'The Duchess at this fell on her knees on the slab, weeping excessively and lifting her hands to heaven.

"'Oh," she cried, "you are cruel, sir, to deprive me of access to the sacred relics that have enabled me to support with resignation the solitude to which your excellency's duties have condemned me; and if prayer and meditation give me any authority to pronounce on such matters, suffer me to warn you, sir, that I fear the blessed Saint Blandina will punish us for thus abandoning her venerable remains!"

'The Duke at this seemed to pause, for he was a pious man, and my grandmother thought she saw him exchange a glance with the chaplain; who, stepping timidly forward, with his eyes on the ground, said, "There is, indeed, much wisdom in her excellency's words, but I would suggest, sir, that her pious wish might be met, and the saint more conspicuously honored, by transferring the relics from the crypt to a place beneath the altar."

"'True!" cried the Duke, "and it shall be done at once."

'But thereat the Duchess rose to her feet with a terrible look.

"'No," she cried, "by the body of God! For it shall not be said that, after your excellency has chosen to deny every request I addressed to him, I owe his consent to the solicitation of another!"

'The chaplain turned red and the Duke yellow, and for a moment neither spoke.

'Then the Duke said, "Here are words enough, Madam. Do you wish the relics brought up from the crypt?"

"'I wish nothing that I owe to another's intervention!"

"'Put the image in place then," says the Duke, furiously; and handed her grace to a chair.

'She sat there, my grandmother said, straight as an arrow, her hands locked, her head high, her eyes on the Duke, while the statue was dragged to its place; then she stood up and turned away. As she passed by Nencia, "Call me Antonio," she whispered; but before the words were out of her mouth the Duke stepped between them.

"'Madam," says he, all smiles now, "I have travelled straight from Rome to bring you the sooner this proof of my esteem. I lay last night at Monselice and have been on the road since daybreak. Will you not invite me to sup?"

"'Surely, my lord," said the Duchess. "It shall be laid in the dining-parlor within the hour."

"'Why not in your chamber and at once. Madam? Since I believe it is your custom to sup there."

"'In my chamber?" says the Duchess, in disorder.

"'Have you anything against it?" he asked.

"'Assuredly not, sir, if you will give me time to prepare myself."

"'I will wait in your cabinet," said the Duke.

'At that, said my grandmother, the Duchess gave one look, as the souls in hell may have looked when the gates closed on our Lord; then she called Nencia and passed to her chamber.

'What happened there my grandmother could never learn, but that the Duchess, in great haste, dressed herself with extraordinary splendor, powdering her hair with gold, painting her face and bosom, and covering herself with jewels till she shone like our Lady of Loreto; and hardly were these preparations complete when the Duke entered from the cabinet, followed by the servants, carrying supper. Thereupon the Duchess dismissed Nencia, and what follows my grandmother learned from a pantry-lad who brought up the dishes and waited in the cabinet; for only the Duke's body-servant entered the bed-chamber.

'Well, according to this boy, sir, who was looking and listening with his whole body, as it were, because he had never before been suffered so near the Duchess, it appears that the noble couple sat down in great good humor, the Duchess playfully reproving her husband for his long absence, while the Duke swore that to look so beautiful was the best way of punishing him. In this tone the talk continued, with such gay sallies on the part of the Duchess, such tender advances on the Duke's, that the lad declared they were for all the world like a pair of lovers courting on a summer's night in the vine-yard; and so it went till the servant brought in the mulled wine.

"'Ah," the Duke was saying at that moment, "this agreeable evening repays me for the many dull ones I have spent away from you; nor do I remember to have enjoyed such laughter since the afternoon last year when we drank chocolate in the gazebo with my cousin Ascanio. And that reminds me," he said, "is my cousin in good health?"

"'I have no reports of it," says the Duchess. "But your excellency should taste these figs stewed in malmsey —"

"'I am in the mood to taste whatever you offer," said he; and as she helped him to the figs he added, "If my enjoyment were not complete as it is, I could almost wish my cousin Ascanio were with us. The fellow is rare good company at supper. What do you say, Madam? I hear he's still in the country; shall we send for him to join us?"

"'Ah," said the Duchess, with a sigh and a languishing look, "I see your excellency wearies of me already."

"'I, Madam? Ascanio is a capital good fellow, but to my mind his chief merit at this moment is his absence. It inclines me so tenderly to him, that, by God, I could empty a glass to his good health."

'With that the Duke caught up his goblet and signed to the servant to fill the Duchess's.

"'Here's to the cousin," he cried, standing, "who has the good taste to stay away when he's not wanted. I drink to his very long life — and you, Madam?"

'At this the Duchess, who had sat staring at him with a changed face, rose also and lifted her glass to her lips.

"'And I to his happy death," says she in a wild voice; and as she spoke the empty goblet dropped from her hand and she fell face down on the floor.

'The Duke shouted to her women that she had swooned, and they came and lifted her to the bed … She suffered horribly all night, Nencia said, twisting herself like a heretic at the stake, but without a word escaping her. The Duke watched by her, and toward daylight sent for the chaplain; but by this she was unconscious and, her teeth being locked, our Lord's body could not be passed through them.'

×

'The Duke announced to his relations that his lady had died after partaking too freely of spiced wine and an omelet of carp's roe, at a supper she had prepared in honor of his return; and the next year he brought home a new Duchess, who gave him a son and five daughters …'

V

The sky had turned to a steel gray, against which the villa stood out sallow and inscrutable. A wind strayed through the gardens, loosening here and there a yellow leaf from the sycamores; and the hills across the valley were purple as thunder-clouds.

×

'And the statue —?' I asked.

'Ah, the statue. Well, sir, this is what my grandmother told me, here on this very bench where we're sitting. The poor child, who worshipped the Duchess as a girl of her years will worship a beautiful kind mistress, spent a night of horror, you may fancy, shut out from her lady's room, hearing the cries that came from it, and seeing, as she crouched in her corner, the women rush to and fro with wild looks, the Duke's lean face in the door, and the chaplain skulking in the antechamber with his eyes on his breviary. No one minded her that night or the next morning; and toward dusk, when it became known the Duchess was no more, the poor girl felt the pious wish to say a prayer for her dead mistress. She crept to the chapel and stole in unobserved.

The place was empty and dim, but as she advanced she heard a low moaning, and coming in front of the statue she saw that its face, the day before so sweet and smiling, had the look on it that you know — and the moaning seemed to come from its lips. My grandmother turned cold, but something, she said afterward, kept her from calling or shrieking out, and she turned and ran from the place. In the passage she fell in a swoon; and when she came to her senses, in her own chamber, she heard that the Duke had locked the chapel door and forbidden any to set foot there ... The place was never opened again till the Duke died, some ten years later; and then it was that the other servants, going in with the new heir, saw for the first time the horror that my grandmother had kept in her bosom ...'

'And the crypt?' I asked. 'Has it never been opened?'

'Heaven forbid, sir!' cried the old man, crossing himself. 'Was it not the Duchess's express wish that the relics should not be disturbed?'

7 Benlian (1911)

OLIVER ONIONS

I

It would be different if you had known Benlian. It would be different if you had had even that glimpse of him that I had the very first time I saw him, standing on the little wooden landing at the top of the flight of steps outside my studio door. I say 'studio'; but really it was just a sort of loft looking out over the timber-yard, and I used it as a studio. The real studio, the big one, was at the other end of the yard, and that was Benlian's.

Scarcely anybody ever came there. I wondered many a time if the timber-merchant was dead or had lost his memory and forgotten all about his business; for his stacks of floorboards, set criss-cross-wise to season (you know how they pile them up) were grimy with soot, and nobody ever disturbed the rows of scaffold-poles that stood like palisades along the walls. The entrance was from the street, through a door in a billposter's hoarding; and on the river not far away the steamboats hooted, and, in windy weather, the floorboards hummed to keep them company.

I suppose some of these real, regular artists wouldn't have called *me* an artist at all; for I only painted miniatures, and it was trade-work at that, copied from photographs and so on. Not that I wasn't jolly good at it, and punctual too (lots of these high-flown artists have simply no idea of punctuality); and the loft was cheap, and suited me very well. But of course a sculptor wants a big place on the ground floor; it's slow work, that with blocks of stone and marble that cost you twenty pounds every time you lift them; so Benlian had the studio. His name was on a plate on the door, but I'd never seen him till this time I'm telling you of.

I was working that evening at one of the prettiest little things I'd ever done: a girl's head on ivory, that I'd stippled up just like … oh, you'd never have thought it was done by hand at all. The daylight had gone, but I knew that 'Prussian' would be about the colour for the eyes and the bunch of flowers at her breast, and I wanted to finish.

I was working at my little table, with a shade over my eyes; and I jumped a bit when somebody knocked at the door — not having heard anybody come up the steps, and not having many visitors anyway. (Letters were always put into the box in the yard door.)

When I opened the door, there he stood on the platform; and I gave a bit of a start, having come straight from my ivory, you see. He was one of these very tall, gaunt chaps, that make us little fellows feel even smaller than we are; and I wondered at first where his eyes were, they were set so deep in the dark caves on either side of his nose. Like a skull, his head was; I could fancy his teeth curving round inside his cheeks; and his zygomatics stuck up under his skin like razor-backs (but if you're not one of us artists you'll not understand that). A bit of smoky, greenish sky showed behind him; and then, as his eyes moved in their big pits, one of them caught the light of my lamp and flashed like a well of lustre.

He spoke abruptly, in a deep, shaky sort of voice.

'I want you to photograph me in the morning,' he said. I supposed he'd seen my printing-frames out on the window-sash some time or other.

'Come in,' I said. 'But I'm afraid, if it's a miniature you want, that I'm retained — my firm retains me — you'd have to do it through them. But come in, and I'll show you the kind of thing I do — though you ought to have come in the daylight —'

He came in. He was wearing a long, grey dressing-gown that came right down to his heels and made him look something like a Noah's-ark figure. Seen in the light, his face seemed more ghastly bony still; and as he glanced for a moment at my little ivory he made a sound of contempt — I know it was contempt. I thought it rather cheek, coming into my place and —

He turned his cavernous eyeholes on me.

'I don't want anything of that sort. I want you to photograph me. I'll be here at ten in the morning.'

So, just to show him that I wasn't to be treated that way, I said, quite shortly, 'I can't. I've an appointment at ten o'clock.'

'What's that?' he said — he'd one of these rich deep voices that always sound consumptive. 'Take that thing off your eyes, and look at me,' he ordered.

Well, I was awfully indignant.

'If you think I'm going to be told to do things like this —' I began.

'Take that thing off,' he just ordered again.

I've got to remember, of course, that you didn't know Benlian. *I* didn't then. And for a chap just to stalk into a fellow's place, and tell him to photograph him, and order him about ... but you'll see in a minute — I took the shade off my eyes, just to show him that *I* could browbeat a bit, too.

I used to have a tall strip of looking-glass leaning against my wall; for though I didn't use models much, it's awfully useful to go to Nature for odd bits now and then, and I've sketched myself in that glass, oh, hundreds of times! We must have been standing in front of it, for all at once I saw the eyes at the bottom of his pits looking rigidly over my shoulder. Without moving his eyes from the glass, and scarcely moving his lips, he muttered:

'Get me a pair of gloves, get me a pair of gloves.'

It was a funny thing to ask for; but I got him a pair of my gloves from a drawer. His hands were shaking so that he could hardly get them on, and there was a little glistening of sweat on his face, that looked like the salt that dries on you when you've been bathing in the sea. Then I turned, to see what it was that he was looking so earnestly and profoundly at in the mirror. I saw nothing except just the pair of us, he with my gloves on.

He stepped aside, and slowly drew the gloves off. I think *I* could have bullied *him* just then. He turned to me.

'Did that look all right to you?' he asked.

'Why, my dear chap, whatever ails you?' I cried.

'I suppose,' he went on, 'you couldn't photograph me tonight
— now?'

I could have done, with magnesium, but I hadn't a scrap in
the place. I told him so. He was looking round my studio. He
saw my camera standing in a corner.

'Ah!' he said.

He made a stride towards it. He unscrewed the lens, brought
it to the lamp, and peered attentively through it, now into the
air, now at his sleeve and hand, as if looking for a flaw in it. Then
he replaced it, and pulled up the collar of his dressing-gown as
if he was cold.

'Well, another night of it,' he muttered; 'but,' he added, facing
suddenly round on me, 'if your appointment was to meet
your God Himself, you must photograph me at ten tomorrow
morning!'

'All right,' I said, giving in (for he seemed horribly ill). 'Draw
up to the stove and have a drink of something and a smoke.'

'I neither drink nor smoke,' he replied, moving towards the
door.

'Sit down and have a chat, then,' I urged; for I always like to be
decent with fellows, and it was a lonely sort of place, that yard.

He shook his head.

'Be ready by ten o'clock in the morning,' he said; and he passed
down my stairs and crossed the yard to his studio without even
having said 'Good-night'.

Well, he was at my door again at ten o'clock in the morning,
and I photographed him. I made three exposures; but the plates
were some that I'd had in the place for some time, and they'd
gone off and fogged in the developing.

'I'm awfully sorry,' I said; 'but I'm going out this afternoon, and
will get some more, and we'll have another shot in the morning.'

One after the other, he was holding the negatives up to the
light and examining them. Presently he put them down quietly,
leaning them methodically up against the edge of the developing
bath.

'Never mind. It doesn't matter. Thank you,' he said; and
left me.

After that, I didn't see him for weeks; but at nights I could see the light of his roof-window, shining through the wreathing river-mists, and sometimes I heard him moving about, and the muffled knock-knocking of his hammer on marble.

II

Of course, I did see him again, or I shouldn't be telling you all this. He came to my door, just as he had done before, and at about the same time in the evening. He hadn't come to be photographed this time, but for all that it was something about a camera — something he wanted to know. He'd brought two books with him, big books, printed in German. They were on Light, he said, and Physics (or else it was Psychics — I always get those two words wrong). They were full of diagrams and equations and figures; and, of course, it was all miles above my head.

He talked a lot about 'hyper-space', whatever that is; and at first I nodded, as if I knew all about it. But he very soon saw that I didn't, and he came down to my level again. What he'd come to ask me was this — Did I know anything, of my own experience, about things 'photographing through'? (You know the kind of thing: a name, that's been painted out on a board, say, comes up in the plate.)

Well, as it happened, I *had* once photographed a drawing for a fellow, and the easel I had stood it on had come up through the picture; and I knew by the way Benlian nodded that that was the kind of thing he meant.

'More,' he said.

I told him I'd once seen a photograph of a man with a bowler hat on, and the shape of his crown had showed through the hat.

'Yes, yes,' he said, musing; and then he asked: 'Have you ever heard of things *not photographing at all*?'

But I couldn't tell him anything about that; and off he started again, about Light and Physics, and so on. Then, as soon as I could get a word in, I said, 'But, of course, the camera isn't Art.'

(Some of my miniatures, you understand, were jolly nice little things.)

'No — no —,' he murmured absently; and then abruptly he said: 'Eh? What's that? — And what the devil do *you* know about it?'

'Well,' said I, in a dignified sort of way, 'considering that for ten years I've been —'

'Chut! ... Hold your tongue,' he said, turning away.

There he was, talking to me again, just as if I'd asked him in to bully me. But you've got to be decent to a fellow when he's in your own place; and by and by I asked him, but in a cold, offhand sort of way, how his own work was going on. He turned to me again.

'Would you like to see it?' he asked.

'Aha!' thought I, 'he's got to a sticking-point with *his* work! It's all very well' (I thought) 'for you to sniff at my miniatures, my friend, but we all get stale on our work sometimes, and the fresh eye, even of a miniature-painter ...'

'I shall be glad if I can be of any help to you,' I answered, still a bit huffish, but bearing no malice.

'Then come,' he said.

We descended and crossed the timber-yard, and he held his door open for me to pass in.

It was an enormous great place, his studio, and all full of mist; and the gallery that was his bedroom was up a little staircase at the farther end. In the middle of the floor was a tall structure of scaffolding, with a stage or two to stand on; and I could see the dim ghostly marble figure in the gloom. It had been jacked up on a heavy base; and as it would have taken three or four men to put it into position, and scarcely a stranger had entered the yard since I had been there, I knew that the figure must have stood for a long time. Sculpture's weary, slow work.

Benlian was pottering about with a taper at the end of a long rod; and suddenly the overhead gas-ring burst into light. I placed myself before the statue — to criticise, you know.

Well, it didn't seem to me that he needed to have turned up his nose at my ivories, for I didn't think much of his statue

— except that it was a great, lumping, extraordinary piece of work. It had an outstretched arm that, I remember thinking, was absolutely misshapen — disproportioned, big enough for a giant, ridiculously out of drawing. And as I looked at the thing this way and that, I knew that his eyes in their deep cellars never left my face for a moment.

'It's a god,' he said by and bye.

Then I began to tell him about that monstrous arm; but he cut me very short.

'I say it's a god,' he interrupted, looking at me as if he would have eaten me. 'Even you, child as you are, have seen the gods men have made for themselves before this. Half-gods they've made, all good or all evil (and then they've called them the Devil). This is *my* god — the god of good and of evil also.'

'Er — I see,' I said, rather taken aback (but quite sure he was off his head for all that). Then I looked at the arm again; a child could have seen how wrong it was ...

But suddenly, to my amazement, he took me by the shoulders and turned me away.

'That'll do,' he said curtly. 'I didn't ask you to come in here with a view to learning anything from you. I wanted to see how it struck you. I shall send for you again — and again —'

Then he began to jabber, half to himself.

'Bah!' he muttered. '"Is that all?" they ask before a stupendous thing! Show them the ocean, the heavens, infinity, and they ask, "Is that all?" If they saw their God face to face they'd ask it! ... There's only one Cause, that works now in good and now in evil, but show It to them and they put their heads on one side and begin to appraise and patronise It! ... I tell you, what's seen at a glance flies away at a glance. Gods come slowly over you, but presently, ah! they begin to grip you, and at the end there's no fleeing from them! You'll tell me more about my statue by and bye! ... What was that you said?' he demanded, facing swiftly round on me. 'That arm? — Ah, yes; but we'll see what you say about that arm six months from now! Yes, the arm ... Now be off!' he ordered me. 'I'll send for you again when I want you!'

He thrust me out.

'An asylum, Mr Benlian' (I thought as I crossed the yard), 'is the place for *you!*' You see, I didn't know him then, and that he wasn't to be judged as an ordinary man is. Just you wait till you see ...

And straight away, I found myself vowing that I'd have nothing more to do with him. I found myself resolving that, as if I were making up my mind not to smoke or drink — and (I don't know why) with a similar sense that I was depriving myself of something. But, somehow, I forgot, and within a month he'd been in several times to see me, and once or twice had fetched me in to see his statue.

In two months I was in an extraordinary state of mind about him. I was familiar with him in a way, but at the same time I didn't know one scrap more about him. Because I'm a fool (oh, yes, I know quite well, now, what I am) you'll think I'm talking folly if I even begin to tell you what sort of a man he was. I don't mean just his knowledge (though I think he knew everything — sciences, languages, and all that), for it was far more than that.

Somehow, when he was there, he had me all restless and uneasy; and when he wasn't there I was (there's only the one word for it) jealous — as jealous as if he'd been a girl! Even yet I can't make it out ...

And he knew how unsettled he'd got me; and I'll tell you how I found that out.

Straight out one night, when he was sitting up in my place, he asked me: 'Do you like me, Pudgie?' (I forgot to say that I'd told him they used to call me Pudgie at home, because I was little and fat; it was odd, the number of things I told him that I wouldn't have told anybody else.)

'Do you like me, Pudgie?' he said.

As for my answer, I don't know how it spirted out. I was much more surprised than he was, for I really didn't intend it. It was for all the world as if somebody else was talking with my mouth.

'*I loathe and adore you!*' it came; and then I looked round, awfully startled to hear myself saying that.

But he didn't look at me. He only nodded.

'Yes. Of good and evil too —,' he muttered to himself. And then all of a sudden he got up and went out.

I didn't sleep for ever so long after that, thinking how odd it was I should have said that.

Well (to get on), after that, something I couldn't account for began to come over me sometimes as I worked. It began to come over me, without any warning, that he was thinking of me down there across the yard. I used to *know* (this must sound awfully silly to you) that he was down yonder, thinking of me and doing something to me. And one night I was so sure that it wasn't fancy that I jumped straight up from my work, and I'm not quite sure what happened then, until I found myself in his studio, just as if I'd walked there in my sleep.

And he seemed to be waiting for me, for there was a chair by his own, in front of the statue.

'What is it, Benlian?' I burst out.

'Ah!' he said ... 'Well, it's about that arm, Pudgie; I want you to tell me about the arm. Does it look so strange as it did?'

'No,' I said.

'I thought it wouldn't,' he observed. 'But I haven't touched it, Pudgie —'

So I stayed the evening there.

But you must not think he was always doing that thing — whatever it was — to me. On the other hand, I sometimes felt the oddest sort of release (I don't know how else to put it) ... like when, on one of these muggy, earthy-smelling days, when everything's melancholy, the wind freshens up suddenly, and you breathe again. And that (I'm trying to take it in order, you see, so that it will be plain to you) brings me to the time I found out that *he* did that too, and knew when he was doing it.

I'd gone into his place one night, to have a look at his statue. It was surprising what a lot I was finding out about that statue. It was still all out of proportion (that is to say, I knew it must be — remembered I'd thought so — though it didn't annoy me now quite so much — I suppose I'd lost *my* fresh eye by that time). Somehow, too, my own miniatures had begun to look a bit kiddish; they made me impatient; and that's horrible, to be discontented with things that once seemed jolly good to you.

Well, he'd been looking at me in the hungriest sort of way, and I looking at the statue, when all at once that feeling of release and lightness came over me. The first I knew of it was that I found myself thinking of some rather important letters my firm had written to me, wanting to know when a job I was doing was going to be finished. I thought myself it was time I got it finished; I thought I'd better set about it at once; and I sat suddenly up in my chair, as if I'd just come out of a sleep. And, looking at the statue, I saw it as it had seemed at first — all mis-shapen and out of drawing.

The very next moment, as I was rising, I sat down again as suddenly as if somebody had pulled me back.

Now a chap doesn't like to be changed about like that; so, without looking at Benlian, I muttered, a bit testily, 'Don't, Benlian!'

Then I heard him get up and knock his chair away. He was standing behind me.

'Pudgie,' he said, in a moved sort of voice, 'I'm no good to you. Get out of this. Get out —'

'No, no, Benlian!' I pleaded.

'Get out, do you hear, and don't come again! Go and live somewhere else — go away from London — don't let me know where you go —'

'Oh, what have I done?' I asked unhappily; and he was muttering again.

'Perhaps it would be better for me too,' he muttered; and then he added, 'Come, bundle out! —'

So in home I went, and finished my ivory for the firm; but I can't tell you how friendless and unhappy I felt.

Now I used to know in those days a little girl — a nice, warm-hearted little thing, just friendly, you know, who used to come to me sometimes in another place I lived at and mend for me and so on. It was an awful long time since I'd seen her; but she found me out one night — came to that yard, walked straight in, went straight to my linen-bag, and began to look over my things to see what wanted mending, just as she used to. I don't mind confessing that I was a bit sweet on her at one time; and it made me feel awfully mean, the way she came in, without asking any questions, and took up my mending.

So she sat doing my things, and I sat at my work, glad for a bit of company; and she chatted as she worked, just jolly and gentle, and not at all reproaching me.

But as suddenly as a shot, right in the middle of it all, I found myself wondering about Benlian again. And I wasn't only wondering; somehow, I was horribly uneasy about him. It came to me that he might be ill or something. And all the fun of her having come to see me was gone. I found myself doing all sorts of stupid things to my work, and glancing at my watch, that was lying on the table before me.

At last I couldn't stand it any longer. I got up.

'Daisy,' I said, 'I've got to go out now.'

She seemed surprised.

'Oh, why didn't you tell me I'd been keeping you!' she said, getting up at once.

I muttered that I was awfully sorry ...

I packed her off. I closed the door in the hoarding behind her. Then I walked straight across the yard to Benlian's.

He was lying on a couch, not doing anything.

'I know I ought to have come sooner, Benlian,' I said, 'but I had somebody with me.'

'Yes,' he said, looking hard at me; and I got a bit red.

'She's awfully nice,' I stammered; 'but you never bother with girls, and you don't drink or smoke —'

'No,' he said.

'Well,' I continued, 'you ought to have a little relaxation; you're knocking yourself up.' And, indeed, he looked awfully ill.

But he shook his head.

'A man's only a definite amount of force in him, Pudgie,' he said, 'and, if he spends it in one way he goes short in another. Mine goes — there.' He glanced at the statue. 'I rarely sleep now,' he added.

'Then you ought to see a doctor,' I said, a bit alarmed (I'd felt sure he was ill.)

'No, no, Pudgie. My force is all going there — all but the minimum that can't be helped, you know ... You've heard artists talk about "putting their soul into their work", Pudgie?'

'Don't rub it in about my rotten miniatures, Benlian,' I asked him.

'You've heard them say that; but they're charlatans, professional artists, all, Pudgie. They haven't got any souls bigger than a sixpence to put into it ... You know, Pudgie, that Force and Matter are the same thing — that it's decided nowadays that you can't define matter otherwise than as "a point of Force"?'

'Yes,' I found myself saying eagerly, as if I'd heard it dozens of times before.

'So that if they could put their souls into it, it would be just as easy for them to put their *bodies* into it? ...'

I had drawn very close to him, and again — it was not fancy — I felt as if somebody, not me, was using my mouth. A flash of comprehension seemed to come into my brain.

'*Not that, Benlian?*' I cried breathlessly.

He nodded three or four times, and whispered. I really don't know why we both whispered.

'Really, *that*, Benlian?' I whispered again.

'Shall I show you? ... I tried my hardest not to, you know ...' he still whispered.

'Yes, show me!' I replied in a suppressed voice.

'Don't breathe a sound then! I keep them up there ...'

He put his finger to his lips as if we had been two conspirators; then he tiptoed across the studio and went up to his bedroom in the gallery. Presently he tiptoed down again, with some rolled-up papers in his hand. They were photographs, and we stooped together over a little table. His hand shook with excitement.

'You remember this?' he whispered, showing me a rough print.

It was one of the prints from the fogged plates that I'd taken that first night.

'Come closer to me if you feel frightened, Pudgie,' he said. 'You said they were old plates, Pudgie. No, no; the plates were all right; it's *I* who am wrong!'

'Of course,' I said. It seemed so natural.

'This one,' he said, taking up one that was numbered '1', 'is a plain photograph, in the flesh, before it started; *you* know — Now look at this, and this —'

He spread them before me, all in order.

'2' was a little fogged, as if a novice had taken it; on '3' a sort of cloudy veil partly obliterated the face; '4' was still further smudged and lost; and '5' was a figure with gloved hands held up, as a man holds his hands up when he is covered by a gun. The face of this one was completely blotted out.

And it didn't seem in the least horrible to me, for I kept on murmuring, 'Of course, of course.'

Then Benlian rubbed his hands and smiled at me.

'I'm making good progress, am I not?' he said.

'Splendid!' I breathed.

'Better than you know, too,' he chuckled, 'for you're not properly under yet. But you will be, Pudgie, you will be —'

'Yes, yes! ... Will it be long, Benlian?'

'No,' he replied, 'not if I can keep from eating and sleeping and thinking of other things than the statue — and if you don't disturb me by having girls about the place, Pudgie.'

'I'm awfully sorry,' I said contritely.

'All right, all right; ssh! ... This, you know, Pudgie, is my own studio; I bought it; I bought it purposely to make my statue, my god. I'm passing nicely into it; and when I'm quite passed — *quite* passed, Pudgie — you can have the key and come in when you like.'

'Oh, thanks, awfully,' I murmured gratefully.

He nudged me.

'What would they think of it, Pudgie — those of the Exhibitions and Academies, who say "their hearts are in their work"? What would the cacklers think of it, Pudgie?'

'Aren't they fools!' I chuckled.

'And I shall have *one* worshipper, shan't I, Pudgie?'

'Rather!' I replied. 'Isn't it splendid! ... Oh, need I go back just yet?'

'Yes, you must go now; but I'll send for you again very soon ... You know I tried to do without you, Pudgie; I tried for thirteen days, and it nearly killed me! — that's past. I shan't try again — Now off you trot, my Pudgie —'

I winked at him knowingly, and came skipping and dancing across the yard.

III

It's just silly — that's what it is — to say that something of a man doesn't go into his work. Why, even those wretched little ivories of mine, the thick-headed fellows who paid for them knew my touch in them, and once spotted it instantly when I'd tried to slip in another chap's who was hard up. Benlian used to say that a man went about spreading himself over everything he came in contact with — diffusing some sort of influence (as far as I could make it out); and the mistake was, he said, that we went through the world just wasting it instead of directing it. And if Benlian didn't understand all about those things, I should jolly well like to know who does! A chap with a great abounding will and brain like him, it's only natural he should be able to pass himself on, to a statue or anything else, when he really tried — did without food and talk and sleep in order to save himself up for it!

'A man can't both *do* and *be*,' I remember he said to me once. 'He's so much force, no more, and he can either make himself with it or something else. If he tries to do both, he does both imperfectly. I'm going to do *one* perfect thing.' — Oh, he was a queer chap! Fancy, a fellow making a thing like that statue, out of himself, and then wanting somebody to adore him!

And I hadn't the faintest conception of how much I did adore him till yet again, as he had done before, he seemed to — you know — to take himself away from me again, leaving me all alone, and so wretched! ... And I was angry at the same time, for he'd promised me he wouldn't do it again ... (This was one night, I don't remember when.)

I ran to my landing and shouted down into the yard.

'Benlian! Benlian!'

There was a light in his studio, and I heard a muffled shout come back.

'Keep away — keep away — keep away!'

He was struggling — I knew he was struggling as I stood there on my landing — struggling to let me go. And I could only run and throw myself on my bed and sob, while he tried to set me free, who didn't want to be set free ... he was having a terrific struggle, all alone there ...

(He told me afterwards that he *had* to eat something now and then and to sleep a little, and that weakened him — strengthened him — strengthened his body and weakened the passing, you know.)

But the next day it was all right again. I was Benlian's again. And I wondered, when I remembered his struggle, whether a dying man had ever fought for life as hard as Benlian was fighting to get away from it and pass himself.

The next time after that that he fetched me — called me — whatever you like to name it — I burst into his studio like a bullet. He was sunk in a big chair, gaunt as a mummy now, and all the life in him seemed to burn in the bottom of his deep eye-sockets. At the sight of him I fiddled with my knuckles and giggled.

'You *are* going it, Benlian!' I said.

'Am I not?' he replied, in a voice that was scarcely a breath.

'You *meant* me to bring the camera and magnesium, didn't you?' (I had snatched them up when I felt his call, and had brought them.)

'Yes. Go ahead.'

So I placed the camera before him, made all ready, and took the magnesium ribbon in a pair of pincers.

'Are you ready?' I said; and lighted the ribbon.

The studio seemed to leap with the blinding glare. The ribbon spat and spluttered. I snapped the shutter, and the fumes drifted away and hung in clouds in the roof.

'You'll have to walk me about soon, Pudgie, and bang me with bladders, as they do the opium-patients,' he said sleepily.

'Let me take one of the statue now,' I said eagerly.

But he put up his hand.

'No, no. *That's* too much like testing our god. Faith's the food they feed gods on, Pudgie. We'll let the SPR people photograph it when it's all over,' he said. 'Now get it developed.'

I developed the plate. The obliteration now seemed complete.

But Benlian seemed dissatisfied.

'There's something wrong somewhere,' he said. 'It isn't so perfect as that yet — I can feel within me it isn't. It's merely that your camera isn't strong enough to find me, Pudgie.'

'I'll get another in the morning,' I cried.

'No,' he answered. 'I know something better than that. Have a cab here by ten o'clock in the morning, and we'll go somewhere.'

By half past ten the next morning we had driven to a large hospital, and had gone down a lot of steps and along corridors to a basement room. There was a stretcher couch in the middle of the room, and all manner of queer appliances, frames of ground glass, tubes of glass blown into extraordinary shapes, a dynamo, and a lot of other things all about. A couple of doctors were there too, and Benlian was talking to them.

'Well, try my hand first,' Benlian said by and bye.

He advanced to the couch, and put his hand under one of the frames of ground glass. One of the doctors did something in a corner. A harsh crackling filled the room, and an unearthly, fluorescent light shot and flooded across the frame where Benlian's hand was. The two doctors looked, and then started back. One of them gave a cry. He was sickly white.

'Put me on the couch,' said Benlian.

I and the doctor who was not ill lifted him on the canvas stretcher. The green-gleaming frame of fluctuating light was passed over the whole of his body. Then the doctor ran to a telephone and called a colleague.

We spent the morning there, with dozens of doctors coming

and going. Then we left. All the way home in the cab Benlian chuckled to himself.

'That scared 'em, Pudgie!' he chuckled. 'A man they can't X-ray — that scared 'em! We must put that down in the diary —'

'Wasn't it ripping!' I chuckled back.

He kept a sort of diary or record. He gave it to me afterwards, but they've borrowed it. It was as big as a ledger, and immensely valuable, I'm sure; they oughtn't to borrow valuable things like that and not return them. The laughing that Benlian and I have had over that diary! It fooled them all — the clever X-ray men, the artists of the Academies, everybody! Written on the fly-leaf was '*To My Pudgie.*' I shall publish it when I get it back again.

Benlian had now got frightfully weak; it's awfully hard work, passing yourself. And he had to take a little milk now and then or he'd have died before he had quite finished. I didn't bother with miniatures any longer, and when angry letters came from my employers we just put them into the fire, Benlian and I, and we laughed — that is to say, I laughed, but Benlian only smiled, being too weak to laugh really. He'd lots of money, so that was all right; and I slept in his studio, to be there for the passing.

And that wouldn't be very long now, I thought; and I was always looking at the statue. Things like that (in case you don't know) have to be done gradually, and I supposed he was busy filling up the inside of it and hadn't got to the outside yet — for the statue was much the same to look at. But, reckoning off his sips of milk and snatches of sleep, he was making splendid progress, and the figure must be getting very full now. I was awfully excited, it was getting so near ...

And then somebody came bothering and nearly spoiling it all. It's odd, but I really forget exactly what it was. I only know there was a funeral, and people were sobbing and looking at me, and somebody said I was callous, but somebody else said, 'No, look at him,' and that it was just the other way about. And I think I remember, now, that it wasn't in London, for I was in a train; but after the funeral I dodged them, and found myself back at Euston again. They followed me, but I shook them off. I locked my own studio up, and lay as quiet as a mouse in Benlian's place when they came hammering at the door ...

And now I must come to what you'll called the finish — though it's awfully stupid to call things like that 'finishes'.

I'd slipped into my own studio one night — I forget what for; and I'd gone quietly, for I knew they were following me, those people, and would catch me if they could. It was a thick, misty night, and the light came streaming up through Benlian's roof window, with the shadows of the window-divisions losing themselves like dark rays in the fog. A lot of hooting was going on down the river, steamers and barges ... oh, I know what I'd come into my studio for! It was for those negatives. Benlian wanted them for the diary, so that it could be seen there wasn't any fake about the prints — For he'd said he would make a final spurt that evening and get the job finished. It had taken a long time, but I'll bet *you* couldn't have passed *your*self any quicker.

When I got back he was sitting in the chair he'd hardly left for weeks, and the diary was on the table by his side. I'd taken all the scaffolding down from the statue, and he was ready to begin. He had to waste one last bit of strength to explain to me, but I drew as close as I could, so that he wouldn't lose much.

'Now, Pudgie,' I just heard him say, 'you've behaved splendidly, and you'll be quite still up to the finish, won't you?'

I nodded.

'And you mustn't expect the statue to come down and walk about, or anything like that,' he continued. '*Those* aren't the really wonderful things. And no doubt people will tell you it hasn't changed; but you'll know better! It's much more wonderful that I should be there than that they should be able to prove it, isn't it? ... And, of course, I don't know exactly how it will happen, for I've never done this before ... You have the letter for the SPR? They can photograph it if they want ... By the way: you don't think the same of my statue as you did at first, do you?'

'Oh, it's wonderful!' I breathed.

'And even if, like the God of the others, it doesn't vouchsafe a special sign and wonder, it's Benlian, for all that?'

'Oh, do be quick, Benlian! I can't bear another minute!'

Then, for the last time, he turned his great eaten-out eyes on me.

'*I seal you mine, Pudgie!*' he said.

Then his eyes fastened themselves on the statue.

I waited for a quarter of an hour, scarcely breathing. Benlian's breath came in little flutters, many seconds apart. He had a little clock on the table. Twenty minutes passed, and half an hour. I was a little disappointed, really, that the statue wasn't going to move; but Benlian knew best, and it was filling quietly up with him instead. Then I thought of those zigzag bunches of lightning they draw on the electric-belt advertisements, and I was rather glad after all that the statue *wasn't* going to move. It would have been a little cheap, that ... vulgar, in a sense ... He was breathing a little more sharply now, as if in pain, but his eyes never moved. A dog was howling somewhere, and I hoped that the hooting of the tugs wouldn't disturb Benlian ...

Nearly an hour had passed when, all of a sudden, I pushed my chair farther away and cowered back, gnawing my fingers, very frightened. Benlian had suddenly moved. He'd set himself forward in his chair, and he seemed to be strangling. His mouth was wide open, and he began to make long harsh '*Aaaaah-aaaah's!*' I shouldn't have thought passing yourself was such agony ...

And then I gave a scream — for he seemed to be thrusting himself back in his chair again, as if he'd changed his mind and didn't want to pass himself at all — But just you ask anybody: When you get yourself just over half-way passed, the other's *dragged* out of you, and you can't help yourself. His '*Aaaaah's!*' became so loud and horrid that I shut my eyes and stopped my ears ... Minutes that lasted; and then there came a high dinning that I couldn't shut out, and all at once the floor shook with a heavy thump. When all was still again I opened my eyes.

His chair had overturned, and he lay in a heap beside it.

I called 'Benlian!' but he didn't answer ...

He'd passed beautifully; quite dead. I looked up at the statue. It was just as Benlian had said — it didn't open its eyes, nor speak, nor anything like that. Don't you believe chaps who tell you that statues that have been passed into do that; they don't.

But instead, in a blaze and flash and shock, I knew now for the first time what a glorious thing that statue was! Have you ever seen anything for the first time like that? If you have, you never see very much afterwards, you know. The rest's all piffle after that. It was like coming out of fog and darkness into a split in the open heavens, my statue was so transfigured; and I'll bet if you'd been there you'd have clapped your hands, as I did, and chucked the tablecloth over the Benlian on the floor till they should come to cart that empty shell away, and patted the statue's foot, and cried, '*Is it all right, Benlian?*'

I did this; and then I rushed excitedly out into the street, to call somebody to see how glorious it was ...

They've brought me here for a holiday, and I'm to go back to the studio in two or three days. But they've said that before, and I think it's caddish of fellows not to keep their word — and not to return a valuable diary too! But there isn't a peephole in my room, as there is in some of them (the Emperor of Brazil told me that); and Benlian knows I haven't forsaken him, for they take me a message every day to the studio, and Benlian always answers that it's '*all right*, and I'm to stay where I am for a bit'. So as long as he knows I don't mind so much — But it is a bit rotten hanging on here, especially when the doctors themselves admit how reasonable it all is ... Still, if Benlian says it's '*All right*' ...

8 The Marble Hands (1915)

BERNARD CAPES

We left our bicycles by the little lych-gate and entered the old church yard. Heriot had told me frankly that he did not want to come; but at the last moment, sentiment or curiosity prevailing with him, he had changed his mind. I knew indefinitely that there was something disagreeable to him in the place's associations, though he had always referred with affection to the relative with whom he had stayed here as a boy. Perhaps she lay under one of these greening stones.

We walked round the church, with its squat, shingled spire. It was utterly peaceful, here on the brow of the little town where the flowering fields began. The bones of the hill were the bones of the dead, and its flesh was grass. Suddenly Heriot stopped me. We were standing then to the northwest of the chancel, and a gloom of motionless trees over-shadowed us.

'I wish you'd just look in there a moment,' he said, 'and come back and tell me what you see.'

He was pointing towards a little bay made by the low boundary wall, the green floor of which was hidden from our view by the thick branches and a couple of interposing tombs, huge, coffer-shaped, and shut within rails. His voice sounded odd; there was a 'plunging' look in his eyes, to use a gambler's phrase. I stared at him a moment, followed the direction of his hand; then, without a word, stooped under the heavy, brushing boughs, passed round the great tombs, and came upon a solitary grave.

It lay there quite alone in the hidden bay — a strange thing, fantastic and gruesome. There was no headstone, but a bevelled marble curb, without name or epitaph, enclosed a gravelled space from which projected two hands. They were of white marble, very faintly touched with green, and conveyed in that still, lonely spot a most curious sense of reality, as if actually thrust up, deathly and alluring, from the grave beneath. The impression grew upon me as I looked, until I could have thought they moved stealthily, consciously, turning in the soil as if to greet me. It was absurd, but — I turned and went rather hastily back to Heriot.

'All right. I see they are there still,' he said; and that was all. Without another word we left the place and, remounting, continued our way.

Miles from the spot, lying on a sunny downside, with the sheep about us in hundreds cropping the hot grass, he told me the story:

'She and her husband were living in the town at the time of my first visit there, when I was a child of seven. They were known to Aunt Caddie, who disliked the woman. I did not dislike her at all, because, when we met, she made a favourite of me. She was a little pretty thing, frivolous and shallow; but truly, I know now, with an abominable side to her. She was inordinately vain of her hands; and indeed they were the loveliest things, softer and shapelier than a child's. She used to have them photographed, in fifty different positions; and once they were exquisitely done in marble by a sculptor, a friend of hers. Yes, those were the ones you saw. But they were cruel little hands, for all their beauty. There was something wicked and unclean about the way in which she regarded them.

'She died while I was there, and she was commemorated by her own explicit desire after the fashion you saw. The marble hands were to be her sole epitaph, more eloquent than letters. They should preserve her name and the tradition of her most exquisite feature to remoter ages than any crumbling inscription could reach. And so it was done.

'That fancy was not popular with the parishioners, but it gave me no childish qualms. The hands were really beautifully modelled on the originals, and the originals had often caressed me. I was never afraid to go and look at them, sprouting like white celery from the ground.

'I left, and two years later was visiting Aunt Caddie a second time. In the course of conversation I learned that the husband of the woman had married again — a lady belonging to the place — and that the hands, only quite recently, had been removed. The new wife had objected to them — for some reason perhaps not difficult to understand — and they had been uprooted by the husband's order.

'I think I was a little sorry — the hands had always seemed somehow personal to me — and, on the first occasion that offered, I slipped away by myself to see how the grave looked without them. It was a close, lowering day, I remember, and the churchyard was very still. Directly, stooping under the branches, I saw the spot, I understood that Aunt Caddie had spoken prematurely. The hands had not been removed so far, but were extended in their old place and attitude, looking as if held out to welcome me. I was glad; and I ran and knelt, and put my own hands down to touch them. They were soft and cold like dead meat, and they closed caressingly about mine, as if inviting me to pull — to pull.

'I don't know what happened afterwards. Perhaps I had been sickening all the time for the fever which overtook me. There was a period of horror, and blankness — of crawling, worm-threaded immurements and heaving bones — and then at last the blessed daylight.'

Heriot stopped, and sat plucking at the crisp pasture.

'I never learned,' he said suddenly, 'what other experiences synchronized with mine. But the place somehow got an uncanny reputation, and the marble hands were put back. Imagination, to be sure, can play strange tricks with one.'

9 Hypnos (1923)

H P LOVECRAFT

> Apropos of sleep, that sinister adventure of all our nights,
> we may say that men go to bed daily with an audacity that
> would be incomprehensible if we did not know that it is
> the result of ignorance of the danger.
> — Baudelaire

May the merciful Gods, if indeed there be such, guard those hours when no power of the will, or drug that the cunning of man devises, can keep me from the chasm of sleep. Death is merciful, for there is no return therefrom, but with him who has come back out of the nethermost chambers of night, haggard and knowing, peace rests nevermore. Fool that I was to plunge with such unsanctioned phrensy into mysteries no man was meant to penetrate; fool or god that he was — my only friend, who led me and went before me, and who in the end passed into terrors which may yet be mine.

We met, I recall, in a railway station, where he was the centre of a crowd of the vulgarly curious. He was unconscious, having fallen in a kind of convulsion which imparted to his slight black-clad body a strange rigidity. I think he was then approaching forty years of age, for there were deep lines in the face, wan and hollow-cheeked, but oval and actually beautiful; and touches of grey in the thick, waving hair and small full beard which had once been of the deepest raven black. His brow was white as the marble of Pentelicus, and of a height and breadth almost godlike. I said to myself, with all the ardour of a sculptor, that this man was a faun's statue out of antique Hellas, dug from a temple's ruins and brought somehow to life in our stifling age only to feel the chill and pressure of devastating years. And when he opened his immense, sunken, and wildly luminous black eyes I knew he would be thenceforth my only friend — the only friend of one who had never possessed a friend before — for I saw that such eyes must have looked fully upon the grandeur and the terror of realms beyond normal consciousness and reality; realms which I had cherished in fancy, but vainly sought. So as I drove the crowd away I told him he must come home with me and be my teacher and leader in unfathomed mysteries, and he assented without speaking a word. Afterward I found that his voice was music — the music of deep viols and of crystalline spheres. We talked often in the night, and in the day, when I chiselled busts of him, and carved miniature heads in ivory to immortalize his different expressions.

Of our studies it is impossible to speak, since they held so slight a connexion with anything of the world as living men conceive it. They were of that vaster and more appalling universe of dim entity and consciousness which lies deeper than matter, time, and space, and whose existence we suspect only in certain forms of sleep — those rare dreams beyond dreams which come never to common men, and but once or twice in the lifetime of imaginative men. The cosmos of our waking knowledge, born from such an universe as a bubble is born from the pipe of a jester, touches it only as such a bubble may touch its sardonic source when sucked back by the jester's whim. Men of learning suspect it little, and ignore it mostly. Wise men have interpreted dreams, and the gods have laughed. One man with Oriental eyes has said that all time and space are relative, and men have laughed. But even that man with Oriental eyes has done no more than suspect. I had wished and tried to do more than suspect, and my friend had tried and partly succeeded. Then we both tried together, and with exotic drugs courted terrible and forbidden dreams in the tower studio chamber of the old manor-house in hoary Kent.

Among the agonies of these after days is that chief of torments — inarticulateness. What I learned and saw in those hours of impious exploration can never be told — for want of symbols or suggestions in any language. I say this because from first to last our discoveries partook only of the nature of sensations; sensations correlated with no impression which the nervous system of normal humanity is capable of receiving.

They were sensations, yet within them lay unbelievable elements of time and space — things which at bottom possess no distinct and definite existence. Human utterance can best convey the general character of our experiences by calling them plungings or soarings; for in every period of revelation some part of our minds broke boldly away from all that is real and present, rushing aerially along shocking, unlighted, and fear-haunted abysses, and occasionally tearing through certain well-marked and typical obstacles describable only as viscous, uncouth clouds or vapours. In these black and bodiless flights we were sometimes alone and sometimes together. When we were together, my friend was always far ahead; I could comprehend his presence despite the absence of form by a species of pictorial memory whereby his face appeared to me, golden from a strange light and frightful with its weird beauty, its anomalously youthful cheeks, its burning eyes, its Olympian brow, and its shadowing hair and growth of beard.

Of the progress of time we kept no record, for time had become to us the merest illusion. I know only that there must have been something very singular involved, since we came at length to marvel why we did not grow old. Our discourse was unholy, and always hideously ambitious — no god or daemon could have aspired to discoveries and conquests like those which we planned in whispers. I shiver as I speak of them, and dare not be explicit; though I will say that my friend once wrote on paper a wish which he dared not utter with his tongue, and which made me burn the paper and look affrightedly out of the window at the spangled night sky. I will hint — only hint — that he had designs which involved the rulership of the visible universe and more; designs whereby the earth and the stars would move at his command, and the destinies of all living things be his. I affirm — I swear — that I had no share in these extreme aspirations. Anything my friend may have said or written to the contrary must be erroneous, for I am no man of strength to risk the unmentionable warfare in unmentionable spheres by which alone one might achieve success.

There was a night when winds from unknown spaces whirled us irresistibly into limitless vacua beyond all thought and entity. Perceptions of the most maddeningly untransmissible sort thronged upon us; perceptions of infinity which at the time convulsed us with joy, yet which are now partly lost to my memory and partly incapable of presentation to others. Viscous obstacles were clawed through in rapid succession, and at length I felt that we had been borne to realms of greater remoteness than any we had previously known. My friend was vastly in advance as we plunged into this awesome ocean of virgin aether, and I could see the sinister exultation on his floating, luminous, too youthful memory-face. Suddenly that face became dim and quickly disappeared, and in a brief space I found myself projected against an obstacle which I could not penetrate. It was like the others, yet incalculably denser; a sticky, clammy mass, if such terms can be applied to analogous qualities in a non-material sphere.

I had, I felt, been halted by a barrier which my friend and leader had successfully passed. Struggling anew, I came to the end of the drug-dream and opened my physical eyes to the tower studio in whose opposite corner reclined the pallid and still unconscious form of my fellow-dreamer, weirdly haggard and wildly beautiful as the moon shed gold-green light on his marble features. Then, after a short interval, the form in the corner stirred; and may pitying heaven keep from my sight and sound another thing like that which took place before me. I cannot tell you how he shrieked, or what vistas of unvisitable hells gleamed for a second in black eyes crazed with fright. I can only say that I fainted, and did not stir till he himself recovered and shook me in his phrensy for someone to keep away the horror and desolation.

That was the end of our voluntary searchings in the caverns of dream. Awed, shaken, and portentous, my friend who had been beyond the barrier warned me that we must never venture within those realms again. What he had seen, he dared not tell me; but he said from his wisdom that we must sleep as little as possible, even if drugs were necessary to keep us awake. That he was right, I soon learned from the unutterable fear which engulfed me whenever consciousness lapsed. After each short and inevitable sleep I seemed older, whilst my friend aged with a rapidity almost shocking. It is hideous to see wrinkles form and hair whiten almost before one's eyes. Our mode of life was now totally altered. Heretofore a recluse so far as I know — his true name and origin never having passed his lips — my friend now became frantic in his fear of solitude. At night he would not be alone, nor would the company of a few persons calm him. His sole relief was obtained in revelry of the most general and boisterous sort; so that few assemblies of the young and the gay were unknown to us. Our appearance and age seemed to excite in most cases a ridicule which I keenly resented, but which my friend considered a lesser evil than solitude. Especially was he afraid to be out of doors alone when the stars were shining, and if forced to this condition he would often glance furtively at the sky as if hunted by some monstrous thing therein. He did not always glance at the same place in the sky — it seemed to be a different place at different times. On spring evenings it would be low in the northeast. In the summer it would be nearly overhead. In the autumn it would be in the northwest. In winter it would be in the east, but mostly in the small hours of morning. Midwinter evenings seemed least dreadful to him. Only after two years did I connect this fear with anything in particular; but then I began to see that he must be looking at a special spot on the celestial vault whose position at different times corresponded to the direction of his glance — a spot roughly marked by the constellation Corona Borealis.

We now had a studio in London, never separating, but never discussing the days when we had sought to plumb the mysteries of the unreal world. We were aged and weak from our drugs, dissipations, and nervous overstrain, and the thinning hair and beard of my friend had become snow-white. Our freedom from long sleep was surprising, for seldom did we succumb more than an hour or two at a time to the shadow which had now grown so frightful a menace. Then came one January of fog and rain, when money ran low and drugs were hard to buy. My statues and ivory heads were all sold, and I had no means to purchase new materials, or energy to fashion them even had I possessed them. We suffered terribly, and on a certain night my friend sank into a deep-breathing sleep from which I could not awaken him. I can recall the scene now — the desolate, pitch-black garret studio under the eaves with the rain beating down; the ticking of the lone clock; the fancied ticking of our watches as they rested on the dressing-table; the creaking of some swaying shutter in a remote part of the house; certain distant city noises muffled by fog and space; and worst of all the deep, steady, sinister breathing of my friend on the couch — a rhythmical breathing which seemed to measure moments of supernal fear and agony for his spirit as it wandered in spheres forbidden, unimagined, and hideously remote.

The tension of my vigil became oppressive, and a wild train of trivial impressions and associations thronged through my almost unhinged mind. I heard a clock strike somewhere — not ours, for that was not a striking clock — and my morbid fancy found in this a new starting-point for idle wanderings. Clocks — time — space — infinity — and then my fancy reverted to the local as I reflected that even now, beyond the roof and the fog and the rain and the atmosphere, Corona Borealis was rising in the northeast. Corona Borealis, which my friend had appeared to dread, and whose scintillant semicircle of stars must even now be glowing unseen through the measureless abysses of aether. All at once my feverishly sensitive ears seemed to detect a new and wholly distinct component in the soft medley of drug-magnified sounds — a low and damnably insistent whine from very far away; droning, clamouring, mocking, calling, from the northeast.

But it was not that distant whine which robbed me of my faculties and set upon my soul such a seal of fright as may never in life be removed; not that which drew the shrieks and excited the convulsions which caused lodgers and police to break down the door. It was not what I heard, but what I saw; for in that dark, locked, shuttered, and curtained room there appeared from the black northeast corner a shaft of horrible red-gold light — a shaft which bore with it no glow to disperse the darkness, but which streamed only upon the recumbent head of the troubled sleeper, bringing out in hideous duplication the luminous and strangely youthful memory-face as I had known it in dreams of abysmal space and unshackled time, when my friend had pushed beyond the barrier to those secret, innermost and forbidden caverns of nightmare.

And as I looked, I beheld the head rise, the black, liquid, and deep-sunken eyes open in terror, and the thin, shadowed lips part as if for a scream too frightful to be uttered. There dwelt in that ghastly and flexible face, as it shone bodiless, luminous, and rejuvenated in the blackness, more of stark, teeming, brain-shattering fear than all the rest of heaven and earth has ever revealed to me. No word was spoken amidst the distant sound that grew nearer and nearer, but as I followed the memory-face's mad stare along that cursed shaft of light to its source, the source whence also the whining came, I too saw for an instant what it saw, and fell with ringing ears in that fit of shrieking and epilepsy which brought the lodgers and the police. Never could I tell, try as I might, what it actually was that I saw; nor could the still face tell, for although it must have seen more than I did, it will never speak again. But always I shall guard against the mocking and insatiate Hypnos, lord of sleep, against the night sky, and against the mad ambitions of knowledge and philosophy.

Just what happened is unknown, for not only was my own mind unseated by the strange and hideous thing, but others were tainted with a forgetfulness which can mean nothing if not madness. They have said, I know not for what reason, that I never had a friend, but that art, philosophy, and insanity had filled all my tragic life. The lodgers and police on that night soothed me, and the doctor administered something to quiet me, nor did anyone see what a nightmare event had taken place. My stricken friend moved them to no pity, but what they found on the couch in the studio made them give me a praise which sickened me, and now a fame which I spurn in despair as I sit for hours, bald, grey-bearded, shrivelled, palsied, drug-crazed, and broken, adoring and praying to the object they found.

For they deny that I sold the last of my statuary, and point with ecstasy at the thing which the whining shaft of light left cold, petrified, and unvocal. It is all that remains of my friend; the friend who led me on to madness and wreckage; a godlike head of such marble as only old Hellas could yield, young with the youth that is outside time, and with beauteous bearded face, curved smiling lips, Olympian brow, and dense locks waving and poppy-crowned. They say that that haunting memory-face is modelled from my own, as it was at twenty-five, but upon the marble base is carven a single name in the letters of Attica — HYPNOS.

10 The Ceremony (1924)

ARTHUR MACHEN

From her childhood, from those early and misty days which began to seem unreal, she recollected the grey stone in the wood.

It was something between the pillar and the pyramid in shape, and its grey solemnity amidst the leaves and the grass shone and shone from those early years, always with some hint of wonder. She remembered how, when she was quite a little girl, she had strayed one day, on a hot afternoon, from her nurse's side, and only a little way in the wood the grey stone rose from the grass, and she cried out and ran back in panic terror.

'What a silly little girl,' the nurse had said. 'It's only the ... stone.' She had quite forgotten the name that the servant had given, and she was always ashamed to ask as she grew older.

But always that hot day, that burning afternoon of her childhood when she had first looked consciously on the grey image in the wood, remained not a memory but a sensation. The wide wood swelling like the sea, the tossing of the bright boughs in the sunshine, the sweet smell of the grass and flowers, the beating of the summer wind upon her cheek, the gloom of the underglade rich, indistinct, gorgeous, significant as old tapestry; she could feel it and see it all, and the scent of it was in her nostrils. And in the midst of the picture, where the strange plants grew gross in shadow, was the old grey shape of the stone.

But there were in her mind broken remnants of another and far earlier impression. It was all uncertain, the shadow of a shadow, so vague that it might well have been a dream that had mingled with the confused waking thoughts of a little child. She did not know that she remembered, she rather remembered the memory. But again it was a summer day, and a woman, perhaps the same nurse, held her in her arms, and went through the wood. The woman carried bright flowers in one hand; the dream had in it a glow of bright red, and the perfume of cottage roses. Then she saw herself put down for a moment on the grass, and the red colour stained the grim stone, and there was nothing else — except that one night she woke up and heard the nurse sobbing.

She often used to think of the strangeness of very early life; one came, it seemed, from a dark cloud, there was a glow of light, but for a moment, and afterwards the night. It was as if one gazed at a velvet curtain, heavy, mysterious, impenetrable blackness, and then, for the twinkling of an eye, one spied through a pin-hole a storied town that flamed, with fire about its walls and pinnacles. And then again the folding darkness, so that sight became illusion, almost in the seeing. So to her was that earliest, doubtful vision of the grey stone, of the red colour spilled upon it, with the incongruous episode of the nursemaid, who wept at night.

But the later memory was clear; she could feel, even now, the inconsequent terror that sent her away shrieking, running to the nurse's skirts. Afterwards, through the days of girlhood, the stone had taken it -s place amongst the vast array of unintelligible things which haunt every child's imagination. It was part of life, to be accepted and not questioned; her elders spoke of many things which she could not understand, she opened books and was dimly amazed, and in the Bible there were many phrases which seemed strange. Indeed, she was often puzzled by her parents' conduct, by their looks at one another, by their half-words, and amongst all these problems which she hardly recognized as problems, was the grey ancient figure rising from dark grass.

Some semi-conscious impulse made her haunt the wood where shadow enshrined the stone. One thing was noticeable; that all through the summer months the passers-by dropped flowers there. Withered blossoms were always on the ground, amongst the grass, and on the stone fresh blooms constantly appeared. From the daffodil to the Michaelmas daisy there was marked the calendar of the cottage gardens, and in the winter she had seen sprays of juniper and box, mistletoe and holly. Once she had been drawn through the bushes by a red glow, as if there had been a fire in the wood, and when she came to the place, all the stone shone and all the ground about it was bright with roses.

In her eighteenth year she went one day into the wood, carrying with her a book that she was reading. She hid herself in a nook of hazel, and her soul was full of poetry, when there was a rustling, the rapping of parted boughs returning to their place. Her concealment was but a little way from the stone, and she peered through the net of boughs, and saw a girl timidly approaching. She knew her quite well; it was Annie Dolben, the daughter of a labourer, lately a promising pupil at Sunday school. Annie was a nice-mannered girl, never failing in her curtsy, wonderful for her knowledge of the Jewish Kings. Her face had taken an expression that whispered, that hinted strange things; there was a light and a glow behind the veil of flesh. And in her hand she bore lilies.

The lady hidden in hazels watched Annie come close to the grey image; for a moment her whole body palpitated with expectation, almost the sense of what was to happen dawned upon her. She watched Annie crown the stone with flowers, she watched the amazing ceremony that followed.

And yet, in spite of all her blushing shame, she herself bore blossoms to the wood a few months later. She laid white hothouse lilies upon the stone, and orchids of dying purple, and crimson exotic flowers. Having kissed the grey image with devout passion, she performed there all the antique immemorial rite.

11 Bagnell Terrace (1925)

E F BENSON

I had been for ten years an inhabitant of Bagnell Terrace, and, like all those who have been so fortunate as to secure a footing there, was convinced that for amenity, convenience, and tranquillity it is unrivalled in the length and breadth of London. The houses are small; we could, none of us, give an evening party or a dance, but we who live in Bagnell Terrace do not desire to do anything of the kind. We do not go in for sounds of revelry at night, nor, indeed, is there much revelry during the day, for we have gone to Bagnell Terrace in order to be anchored in a quiet little backwater. There is no traffic through it, for the terrace is a cul-de-sac, closed at the far end by a high brick wall, along which, on summer nights, cats trip lightly on visits to their friends. Even the cats of Bagnell Terrace have caught something of its discretion and tranquillity, for they do not hail each other with long-drawn yells of mortal agony like their cousins in less well-conducted places, but sit and have quiet little parties like the owners of the houses in which they condescend to be lodged and boarded.

But, though I was more content to be in Bagnell Terrace than anywhere else, I had not got, and was beginning to be afraid I never should get, the particular house which I coveted above all others. This was at the top end of the terrace adjoining the wall that closed it, and in one respect it was unlike the other houses, which so much resemble each other. The others have little square gardens in front of them, where we have our bulbs abloom in the spring, when they present a very gay appearance, but the gardens are too small, and London too sunless to allow of any very effective horticulture. The house, however, to which I had so long turned envious eyes, had no garden in front of it; instead, the space had been used for the erection of a big, square room (for a small garden will make a very well-sized room) connected with the house by a covered passage. Rooms in Bagnell Terrace, though sunny and cheerful, are not large, and just one big room, so it occurred to me, would give the final touch of perfection to those delightful little residences.

Now, the inhabitants of this desirable abode were something of a mystery to our neighbourly little circle, though we knew that a man lived there (for he was occasionally seen leaving or entering his house), he was personally unknown to us. A curious point was that, though we had all (though rarely) encountered him on the pavements, there was a considerable discrepancy in the impression he had made on us. He certainly walked briskly, as if the vigour of life was still his, but while I believed that he was a young man, Hugh Abbot, who lived in the house next his, was convinced that, in spite of his briskness, he was not only old, but very old. Hugh and I, life-long bachelor friends, often discussed him in the ramble of conversation when he had dropped in for an after-dinner pipe, or I had gone across for a game of chess. His name was not known to us, so, by reason of my desire for his house, we called him Naboth. We both agreed that there was something odd about him, something baffling and elusive.

I had been away for a couple of months one winter in Egypt; the night after my return Hugh dined with me, and after dinner I produced those trophies which the strongest-minded are unable to refrain from purchasing, when they are offered by an engaging burnoused ruffian in the Valley of the Tombs of the Kings. There were some beads (not quite so blue as they had appeared there), a scarab or two, and for the last I kept the piece of which I was really proud, namely, a small lapis-lazuli statuette, a few inches high, of a cat. It sat square and stiff on its haunches, with upright forelegs, and, in spite of the small scale, so good were the proportions and so accurate the observation of the artist, that it gave the impression of being much bigger. As it stood on Hugh's palm, it was certainly small, but if, without the sight of it, I pictured it to myself, it represented itself as far larger than it really was.

'And the odd thing is,' I said, 'that though it is far and away the best thing I picked up, I cannot for the life of me remember where I bought it. Somehow I feel that I've always had it.'

He had been looking very intently at it. Then he jumped up from his chair and put it down on the chimneypiece.

'I don't think I quite like it,' he said, 'and I can't tell you why. Oh, a jolly bit of workmanship; I don't mean that. And you can't remember where you got it, did you say? That's odd ... Well, what about a game of chess?'

We played a couple of games, without much concentration or fervour, and more than once I saw him glance with a puzzled look at my little image on the chimneypiece. But he said nothing more about it, and when our games were over, he gave me the discursive news of the terrace. A house had fallen vacant and been instantly snapped up.

'Not Naboth's?' I asked.

'No, not Naboth's. Naboth is in possession still. Very much in possession; going strong.'

'Anything new?' I asked.

'Oh, just bits of things. I've seen him a good many times lately, and yet I can't get any clear idea of him. I met him three days ago, as I was coming out of my gate, and had a good look at him, and for a moment I agreed with you and thought he was a young man. Then he turned and stared me in the face for a second, and I thought I had never seen anyone so old. Frightfully alive, but more than old, antique, primeval.'

'And then?' I asked.

'He passed on, and I found myself, as has so often happened before, quite unable to remember what his face was like. Was he old or young? I didn't know. What was his mouth like, or his nose? But it was the question of his age which was the most baffling.'

Hugh stretched his feet out towards the blaze, and sank back in his chair, with one more frowning look at my lapis-lazuli cat.

'Though after all, what is age?' he said. 'We measure age by time, we say "so many years", and forget that we're in eternity here and now, just as we say we're in a room or in Bagnell Terrace, though we're much more truly in infinity.'

'What has that got to do with Naboth?' I asked.

Hugh beat his pipe out against the bars of the grate before he answered.

'Well, it will probably sound quite cracked to you,' he said, 'unless Egypt, the land of ancient mystery, has softened your rind of materialism, but it struck me then that Naboth belonged to eternity much more obviously than we do. We belong to it, of course, we can't help that, but he's less involved in this error or illusion of time than we are. Dear me, it sounds amazing nonsense when I put it into words.'

I laughed.

'I'm afraid my rind of materialism isn't soft enough yet,' I said. 'What you say implies that you think Naboth is a sort of apparition, a ghost, a spirit of the dead that manifests itself as a human being, though it isn't one!'

He drew his legs up to him again.

'Yes; it must be nonsense,' he said. 'Besides he has been so much in evidence lately, and we can't all be seeing a ghost. It doesn't happen. And there have been noises coming from his house, loud and cheerful noises, which I've never heard before. Somebody plays an instrument like a flute in that big, square room you envy so much, and somebody beats an accompaniment as if with drums. Odd sort of music; it goes on often now at night … Well, it's time to go to bed.'

Again he glanced up at the chimneypiece.

'Why, it's quite a little cat,' he said.

This rather interested me, for I had said nothing to him about the impression left on my mind that it was bigger than its actual dimensions.

'Just the same size as ever,' I said.

'Naturally. But I had been thinking of it as life-size for some reason,' said he.

I went with him to the door, and strolled out with him into the darkness of an overcast night. As we neared his house, I saw that big patches of light shone into the road from the windows of the square room next door. Suddenly Hugh laid his hand on my arm.

'There!' he said. 'The flutes and drums are at it tonight.'

The night was very still, but, listen as I would, I could hear nothing, but the rumble of traffic in the street beyond the terrace.

'I can't hear it,' I said.

Even as I spoke, I heard it, and the wailing noise whisked me back to Egypt again. The boom of the traffic became for me the beat of the drum, and upon it floated just that squeal and wail of the little reed pipes which accompany the Arab dances, tuneless and rhythm-less, and as old as the temples of the Nile.

'It's like the Arab music that you hear in Egypt,' I said.

As we stood listening it ceased to his ears as well as mine, as suddenly as it had begun, and simultaneously the lights in the windows of the square room were extinguished.

We waited a moment in the roadway opposite Hugh's house, but from next door came no sound at all, nor glimmer of illumination from any of its windows ...

I turned; it was rather chilly to one lately arrived from the South.

'Good night,' I said, 'we'll meet to-morrow sometime.'

I went straight to bed, slept at once, and woke with the impress of a very vivid dream on my mind. There was music in it, familiar Arab music, and there was an immense cat somewhere. Even as I tried to recall it, it faded, and I had but time to recognise it as a hash-up of the happenings of the evening before I went to sleep again.

The normal habits of life quickly reasserted themselves. I had work to do, and there were friends to see; all the minute events of each day stitched themselves into the tapestry of life. But somehow a new thread began to be woven into it, though at the time I did not recognise it as such. It seemed trivial and extraneous that I should so often hear a few staves of that odd music from Naboth's house, or that as often as it fixed my attention it was silent again, as if I had imagined, rather than actually heard it. It was trivial, too, that I should so often see

Naboth entering or leaving his house. And then one day I had a sight of him, which was unlike any previous experience of mine.

I was standing one morning in the window of my front room. I had idly picked up my lapis-lazuli cat, and was holding it in the splash of sunlight that poured in, admiring the soft texture of its surface which, though it was of hard stone, somehow suggested fur. Then, quite casually, I looked up, and there a few yards in front of me, leaning on the railings of my garden, and intently observing not me, but what I held, was Naboth. His eyes, fixed on it, blinked in the April sunshine with some purring sensuous content, and Hugh was right on the question of his age; he was neither old nor young, but timeless.

The moment of perception passed; it flashed on and off my mind like the revolving beam of some distant lighthouse. It was just a ray of illumination, and was instantly shut off again, so that it appeared to my conscious mind like some hallucination. He suddenly seemed aware of me, and turning, walked briskly off down the pavement.

I remember being rather startled, but the effect soon faded, and the incident became to me one of those trivial little things that make a momentary impression and vanish. It was odd, too, but in no way remarkable, that more than once I saw one of those discreet cats of which I have spoken sitting on the little balcony outside my front room, and gravely regarding the interior. I am devoted to cats, and several times I got up in order to open the window and invite it to enter, but each time on my movement it jumped down and slunk away. And April passed into May.

I came back after dining out one night in this month, and found a telephone message from Hugh that I should ring him up on my return. A rather excited voice answered me.

'I thought you would like to know at once,' he said. 'An hour ago a board was put up on Naboth's house to say that the freehold was for sale. Martin and Smith are the agents. Good night; I'm in bed already.'

'You're a true friend,' I said.

Early next morning, of course, I presented myself at the house-agent's. The price asked was very moderate, the title perfectly satisfactory. He could give me the keys at once, for the house was empty, and he promised that I could have a couple of days to make up my mind, during which time I was to have the prior right of purchase if I was disposed to pay the full price asked. If, however, I only made an offer, he could not guarantee that the trustees would accept it … Hot-foot, with the keys in my pocket, I sped back up the terrace again.

I found the house completely empty, not of inhabitants only, but of all else. There was not a blind, not a strip of drugget, not a curtain-rod in it from garret to cellar. So much the better, thought I, for there would be no tenant's fixtures to take on. Nor was there any débris of removal, of straw and waste paper; the house looked as if it was prepared for an occupant instead of just rid of one. All was in apple-pie order, the windows clean, the floors swept, the paint and woodwork bright; it was a clean and polished shell ready for its occupier. My first inspection, of course, was of the big built-out room, which was its chief attraction, and my heart leaped at the sight of its plain spaciousness. On one side was an open fireplace, on the other a coil of pipes for central heating, and at the end, between the windows, a niche let into the wall, as if a statue had once stood there; it might have been designed expressly for my bronze Perseus. The rest of the house presented no particular features; it was on the same plan as my own, and my builder, who inspected it that afternoon, pronounced it to be in excellent condition.

'It looks as if it had been newly done up, and never lived in,' he said, 'and at the price you mention a decided bargain.'

The same thing struck Hugh when, on his return from his office, I dragged him over to see it.

'Why, it all looks new,' he said, 'and yet we know that Naboth has been here for years, and was certainly here a week ago. And then there's another thing. When did he remove his furniture? There have been no vans at the house that I have seen.'

I was much too pleased at getting my heart's desire to consider anything except that I had got it.

'Oh, I can't bother about little things like that,' I said. 'Look at my beautiful big room. Piano there, bookcases all along the wall, sofa in front of the fire, Perseus in the niche. Why, it was made for me.'

Within the specified two days the house was mine, and within a month papering and distempering, electric fittings, and blinds and curtain rods were finished, and my move began. Two days were sufficient for the transport of my goods, and at the close of the second my old house was dismantled, except for my bedroom, the contents of which would be moved next day. My servants were installed in the new abode, and that night, after a hurried dinner with Hugh, I went back for a couple more hours' work of hauling and tugging and arranging books in the large room, which it was my purpose to finish first. It was a chilly night for May, and I had had a log-fire lit on the hearth, which from time to time I replenished, in intervals of dusting and arranging. Eventually, when the two hours had lengthened themselves into three, I determined to give over for the present, and, much tired, sat down for a recuperative pause on the edge of my sofa and contemplated with satisfaction the result of my labours. At that moment I was conscious that there was a stale, but aromatic, smell in the room that reminded me of the curious odour that hangs about an Egyptian temple. But I put it down to the dust from my books and the smouldering logs.

The move was completed next day, and after another week I was installed as firmly as if I had been there for years. May slipped by, and June, and my new house never ceased to give me a vivid pleasure: it was always a treat to return to it. Then came a certain afternoon when a strange thing happened.

The day had been wet, but towards evening it cleared up: the pavements soon dried, but the road remained moist and miry. I was close to my house on my way home, when I saw form itself on the paving-stones a few yards in front of me the mark of a wet shoe, as if someone invisible to the eye had just stepped off the road. Another and yet another briskly imprinted themselves going up towards my house. For the moment I stood stock still, and then, with a thumping heart I followed. The marks of these strange footsteps preceded me right up to my door: there was one on the very threshold faintly visible.

I let myself in, closing the door, I confess, very quickly behind me. As I stood there I heard a resounding crash from my room, which, so to speak, startled my fright from me, and I ran down the little passage, and burst in. There, at the far end of the room was my bronze Perseus fallen from its niche and lying on the floor. And I knew, by what sixth sense I cannot tell, that I was not alone in the room and that the presence there was no human presence.

Now fear is a very odd thing: unless it is overmastering and overwhelming, it always produces its own reaction. Whatever courage we have rises to meet it, and with courage comes anger that we have given entrance to this unnerving intruder. That, at any rate, was my case now, and I made an effective emotional resistance. My servant came running in to see what the noise was, and we set Perseus on his feet again and examined into the cause of his fall. It was clear enough: a big piece of plaster had broken away from the niche, and that must be repaired and strengthened before we reinstated him. Simultaneously my fear and the sense of an unaccountable presence in the room slipped from me. The footsteps outside were still unexplained and I told myself that if I was to shudder at everything I did not understand, there would be an end to tranquil existence for ever.

I was dining with Hugh that night: he had been away for the last week, only returning today, and he had come in before these slightly agitating events happened to announce his arrival and suggest dinner. I noticed that as he stood chatting for a few minutes, he had once or twice sniffed the air but he had made no comment, nor had I asked him if he perceived the strange faint odour that every now and then manifested itself to me. I knew it was a great relief to some secretly quaking piece of my mind that he was back, for I was convinced that there was some psychic disturbance going on, either subjectively in my mind, or a real invasion from without. In either case his presence was comforting, not because he is of that stalwart breed which believes in nothing beyond the material facts of life, and pooh-poohs these mysterious forces which surround and so strangely interpenetrate existence, but because, while thoroughly believing in them, he has the firm confidence that the deadly and evil powers which occasionally break through into the seeming security of existence are not really to be feared, since they are held in check by forces stronger yet, ready to assist all who realise their protective care. Whether I meant to tell him what had occurred today, I had not fully determined.

It was not till after dinner that such subjects came up at all, but I had seen there was something on his mind of which he had not spoken yet.

'And your new house,' he said at length, 'does it still remain as all your fancy painted?'

'I wonder why you ask that,' I said.

He gave me a quick glance.

'Mayn't I take any interest in your well-being?' he said.

I knew that something was coming, if I chose to let it.

'I don't think you've ever liked my house from the first,' I said. 'I believe you think there's something queer about it. I allow that the manner in which I found it empty was odd.'

'It was rather,' he said. 'But so long as it remains empty, except for what you've put in it, it is all right.'

I wanted now to press him further.

'What was it you smelt this afternoon in the big room?' I said. 'I saw you nosing and sniffing. I have smelt something, too. Let's see if we smelt the same thing.'

'An odd smell,' he said. 'Something dusty and stale, but aromatic.'

'And what else have you noticed?' I asked.

He paused a moment.

'I think I'll tell you,' he said. 'This evening from my window I saw you coming up the pavement, and simultaneously I saw, or thought I saw, Naboth cross the road and walk on in front of you. I wondered if you saw him, too, for you paused as he stepped on to the pavement in front of you, and then you followed him.'

I felt my hands grow suddenly cold, as if the warm current of my blood had been chilled.

'No, I didn't see him,' I said, 'but I saw his step.'

'What do you mean?'

'Just what I say. I saw footprints in front of me, which continued on to my threshold.'

'And then?'

'I went in, and a terrific crash startled me. My bronze Perseus had fallen from his niche. And there was something in the room.'

There was a scratching noise at the window. Without answering, Hugh jumped up and drew aside the curtain. On the sill was seated a large grey cat, blinking in the light. He advanced to the window, and on his approach the cat jumped down into the garden. The light shone out into the road, and we both saw, standing on the pavement just outside, the figure of a man. He turned and looked at me, and then moved away towards my house, next door.

'It's he,' said Hugh.

He opened the window and leaned out to see what had become of him. There was no sign of him anywhere, but I saw that light shone from behind the blinds of my room.

'Come on,' I said. 'Let's see what is happening. Why is my room lit?'

I opened the door of my house with my latch-key, and followed by Hugh went down the short passage to the room. It was perfectly dark, and when I turned the switch, we saw that it was empty. I rang the bell, but no answer came, for it was already late, and doubtless my servants had gone to bed.

'But I saw a strong light from the windows two minutes ago,' I said, 'and there has been no one here since.'

Hugh was standing by me in the middle of the room. Suddenly he threw out his arm as if striking at something. That thoroughly alarmed me.

'What's the matter?' I asked. 'What are you hitting at?'

He shook his head.

'I don't know,' he said. 'I thought I saw — But I'm not sure. But we're in for something if we stop here. Something is coming, though I don't know what.'

The light seemed to me to be burning dim; shadows began to collect in the corner of the room, and though outside the night had been clear, the air here was growing thick with a foggy vapour, which smelt dusty and stale and aromatic. Faintly, but getting louder as we waited there in silence, I heard the throb of drums and the wail of flutes. As yet I had no feeling that there were other presences in the place beyond ours, but in the growing dimness I knew that something was coming nearer. Just in front of me was the empty niche from which my bronze had fallen, and looking at it, I saw that something was astir. The shadow within it began to shape itself into a form, and out of it there gleamed two points of greenish light. A moment more and I saw that they were eyes of antique and infinite malignity.

I heard Hugh's voice in a sort of hoarse whisper.

'Look there!' he said. 'It's coming! Oh, my God, it's coming!'

Sudden as the lightning that leaps from the heart of the night it came. But it came not with blaze and flash of light, but, as it were, with a stroke of blinding darkness, that fell not on the eye, or on any material sense, but on the spirit, so that I cowered under it in some abandonment of terror. It came from those eyes which gleamed in the niche, and which now I saw to be set in the face of the figure that stood there. The form of it, naked, but for a loin-cloth, was that of a man, the head seemed now human, now to be that of some monstrous cat. And as I looked, I knew that if I continued looking there I should be submerged and drowned in that flood of evil that poured from it. As in some catalepsy of nightmare I struggled to tear my eyes from it, but still they were riveted there, gazing on incarnate hate.

Again I heard Hugh's whisper.

'Defy it,' he said. 'Don't yield an inch.'

A swarm of disordered and hellish images were buzzing in my brain, and now I knew as surely as if actual words had been spoken to us, that the presence there told me to come to it.

'I've got to go to it,' I said. 'It's making me go.'

I felt his hand tighten on my arm.

'Not a step,' he said. 'I'm stronger than it is. It will know that soon. Just pray — pray.'

Suddenly his arm shot out in front of me, pointing at the presence.

'By the power of God,' he shouted. 'By the power of God.'

There was dead silence. The light of those eyes faded, and then came dawn on the darkness of the room. It was quiet and orderly, the niche was empty, and there on the sofa by me was Hugh, his face white and streaming with sweat.

'It's over,' he said, and without pause fell fast asleep.

Now we have often talked over together what happened that evening. Of what seemed to happen, I have already given the account, which anyone may believe or not, precisely as they please. He, as I, was conscious of a presence wholly evil, and he tells me that all the time that those eyes gleamed from the niche, he was trying to realise what he believed, namely, that only one power in the world is Omnipotent, and that the moment he gained that realisation the presence collapsed ... What exactly that presence was it is impossible to say. It looks as if it was the essence or spirit of one of those mysterious Egyptian cults, of which the force survived, and was seen and felt in this quiet terrace. That it was embodied in Naboth seems (among all these incredibilities) possible, and Naboth certainly has never been seen again. Whether or not it was connected with the worship and cult of cats might occur to the mythological mind, and it is perhaps worthy of record that I found next morning my little lapis-lazuli image, which stood on the chimneypiece, broken into fragments. It was too badly damaged to mend, and I am not sure that, in any case, I should have attempted to have it restored.

Finally, there is no more tranquil and pleasant room in London than the one built out in front of my house in Bagnell Terrace.

12 At Simmel Acres Farm (1929)

ELEANOR SCOTT

I must explain first that I didn't know Markham very well. We lived on the same stair at Comyn (I don't think I'll give the real name of our college), but he was one of those large, vigorous people who live for Rugger and rowing, and I am no good at games on account of my short sight. I want to lay some stress on my sight, because it may account for other things. I don't believe it does, but it may. I hope it may.

It happened late in the Hilary term of our second year that Markham got rather badly damaged in a Rugger match. It was some injury to the back, not very serious, but it meant that he had to lie up for some weeks; and as we were of the same year and on the same stair, it also happened that I used to go in and see him a good deal; so when he asked me to come down to the Cotswolds with him for part of the vac I rather jumped at it. I haven't many friends of my own — I am dull and priggish — and I expect he didn't want any of his own hefty pals about while he was so badly out of it. So, odd as we were as a pair, we fitted in rather well.

He chose the place — said his family used to come from those parts, and he had a liking for the country. It was a farmhouse, standing alone in wide, prosperous fields. We went there by car, on account of Markham's back, and I shall never, even now, look back on that evening with anything but pleasure. It was the twentieth of March, I remember, and there was a kind of green bloom on the bare fields and a purple bloom on the bare woods that lay on the hill behind the farm. The house itself was like a dozen others in that country — long and low, built of the yellow Cotswold stone, with a beautifully pitched roof and mullioned windows. The stone barns grouped about it showed the same beauty of perfect proportion. The whole thing was as simple and direct as the country it stood in.

I said something of this to Markham, but he hardly answered.

He seemed fidgety and uneasy; I thought he was probably in pain, or overtired with the journey. Anyhow, he only growled, rather shortly, that it was all rot, one farm was like another, and he hoped they'd give us decent meals. But he threw a queer, almost suspicious glance round as he was being helped in. I dismissed it as of no importance.

In the morning he was more cheerful. It was a lovely day, soft as April, with a tender blue sky that showed up the bursting leaf-buds. It was not a day to be in, ill or well; so I consulted Mrs Stokes as to the possibility of getting Markham out. She had a sofa long and broad enough for him, and was perfectly willing that I should take it out; but when I asked her about a suitable spot to establish him in she rather hesitated.

'Haven't you a small garden or patch of grass somewhere near the house?' I asked.

She looked quite troubled and confused.

'Well, of course,' she said at last, 'there's the plot in there,' and she jerked her head at a high stone wall with a wooden door in it at one end of the yard; 'but I don't think your friend would like it, sir,' she added hurriedly. 'Nobody's been there for years, and it's likely all choked wi' nettles and rubbish.'

I was surprised to hear this. The farm was so well-ordered and the fields so clean that it seemed odd that a piece of ground so near the dwelling-house should be neglected.

'May I look at it?' I asked: and again I couldn't help seeing that she went for the key of the door with considerable reluctance.

While she was gone I studied the outside of this yard. It ran on to one end of the farmhouse, as if it had once been the flower-garden of some bygone farmer's wife; but instead of coming right up to the house wall, a high wall of its own cut it off from the house. This seemed absurd and ridiculously inconvenient, since of course it meant that the rooms on that side of the house could have no windows, whereas they might have looked out pleasantly on to a garden. The high wall ran round three sides of the little plot and at the fourth end, opposite the house, I could see the pointed end of a stone barn.

I'm sorry if I'm tedious, but I must explain this still more. This fourth wall was apparently the end of a ruined barn which had at one time, before the garden was made, run straight on to the house. You could tell this because a bit of the roof remained, projecting over the plot of grass like a penthouse roof. I had never seen traces of a large stone barn built straight on to a farmhouse before, and I was interested. I supposed that rats had made it inconvenient to have a barn on to the house, and that it had been destroyed and a garden made on its floor space; though why later farmers had abandoned the garden I could not imagine — still less why they had erected that wall between the grass plot and the house.

Mrs Stokes returned with the key. She still looked 'put about', as country people say, and I apologised for putting her to the trouble of opening the place.

'Oh, it isn't any trouble, sir,' she said, as she fitted the key into the big lock. 'Only — well, I'll tell you the truth, sir,' she burst out suddenly, standing upright and facing me. 'They do say as this place isn't — chancy. It's not the farm, it's just this one place. That's why they've walled it off. I don't know nothing myself,' she added hastily. 'I come from Dorset myself, and I've never heard nor seen a thing. But my husband's people, they've farmed this land for centuries, so they say, and there's not one of 'em as'll go anigh this plot.'

'Is there a story about it?' I asked. I am very keen on folklore and legends, and thought there might be something here.

'N — no,' she answered, rather reluctantly. And then, 'But if I was you, sir, I'd keep out o' Simmel Acres Plot.'

'Well, let's look at it, anyway,' I said; and with no more words we opened the door — the lock shrieked dismally, I remember — and went in.

It was by no means as bad as Mrs Stokes had painted it. The grass was long and rank, but the nettles had confined themselves to the shelter of the high stone walls. But the thing that drew my attention was the old gabled end of the barn. It was perhaps sixteen feet high, rounded off in a curiously rough and archaic form of arch. The roof, as I have said, projected in a kind of rugged penthouse, about two feet deep, and about half-way up the wall there was a niche with a stone bust of a man.

It was a very odd piece of work, worn by time and exposure, but quite complete enough for me. The top part of the head was the most disfigured; I could see some kind of fillet or crown, and some clumsy, conventional indications of hair. The blank eye-sockets were rather large, oddly rounded at the corners, and had in consequence an expression of ruthlessness. The nose was too worn to be in any way remarkable; but the mouth had the most subtle expression — at once cynical, suffering, cruel, undaunted and callous. The chin was square, but weak; the neck powerful, in a conventional manner. It was altogether a remarkable thing — almost savage in its clumsiness and crudity, and yet conveying a singular impression of truth to an original.

At first I thought it was a piece of decadent Roman sculpture; then I dismissed that as absurd. How could a Roman bust be in a barn in the Cotswolds? It might have been an eighteenth-century copy, but I didn't think so; it was too crude, too strong, too — I must use the word again — too archaic. Besides, when the eighteenth century copied Roman busts they were put in little pseudo-classical temples, not in niches in barns.

This was not quite all. Below the bust was a small semi-circular basin, floored with smooth pebbles, through which welled up water so clear as to be almost invisible — exactly like the Holy Wishing Wells one finds occasionally, decorated with pins and rags and other tributes to the presiding deity. But here there were no offerings.

The loveliness of the morning was even more apparent in the little enclosure. The soft sky gained colour from the grey walls, the grass smelt fresh and wet, the water mirrored the tiny white clouds. It was exactly the place for an invalid, I thought, restful, open and quiet. I told Mrs Stokes my decision, and she protested no more. Together we brought the sofa out into the plot; and Markham and I settled down there for the morning.

We had set the sofa against the farmhouse wall, at the end of the little plot away from the old barn-end with its bubbling spring. When he was established I went into the house for some books and notes — I had a lot of work to do that vac — and it was some minutes before I came out again. When I did, I noticed that Markham was not lying, as he should have been, flat on his back; he had rolled over on to his side and was staring with a frowning, puzzled look at the bust above the well.

'Hullo,' I said, 'oughtn't you to be on your back?'

He paid no attention. Indeed, I don't think he heard me. He was muttering something, like a man trying to remember a half-forgotten phrase.

'Damn it all, how did it go?' he broke out suddenly. '*Et te simulacrum ... Et te ...* Damn it! What was it?'

'What was what?' I asked, putting my books down on the table.

He looked round at me, and his face cleared a little.

'I — something came into my head — a sentence or something ... I can't remember. I read it once — or heard it — when I was a kid ... Some old book that belonged to some bloomin' ancestor. Dashed if I can remember ... *Et te simulacrum ...* Curse it! How did it go?'

'What about it?' I asked.

Again he made no answer — just lay, frowning a little and muttering. At last he said, 'What is it written under that head over there?'

'Under the bust? Nothing.'

'There is,' he insisted. 'What is it?'

Just to satisfy him I went and looked. He was quite right — there were words there.

'There is something,' I said, 'but I can't read it. I can only see bits of words here and there — nothing consecutive. *Simul*, I think that is —'

'*Simulacrum, et te — requiro ...*' muttered Markham.

I was very much surprised — for several reasons. First I was surprised that he should be interested at all; then that he should be quoting, however scrappily, a Latin sentence; and last that he could see that there was an inscription, let alone read the words. Kneeling on the ground before it, I could only just make out the defaced letters; and he was twenty yards away, lying flat.

'Can you read it right over there?' I called in astonishment.

'No — is it written there?' he cried back, wriggling round eagerly. 'Read it out, Norton — I can't remember how it goes.'

'I can't make out more than a word or two,' I said. 'And I don't know all the words — must be late Latin, I think. *Simul* — or perhaps you're right, *simulacrum* — something about water — and I think that's *lunae* — and — no, I can't read it.'

Markham seemed dissatisfied.

'There's more of it than that,' he insisted.

'Yes, there is,' I agreed, 'but it's so worn. But, I say, how did you know what it was? How did you know it was there?'

He looked puzzled.

'Damned if I know,' he began. He spoke slowly, like a man groping for words, or for ideas. 'I just knew ... We come from these parts, you know ... used to have a big place in the eighteenth century, or something. Rather rips, I believe we were — Hellfire Club and all that tosh ...'

He suddenly broke off. He made a quick gesture, like that of a man who remembers. His face cleared and his eyes shone. His lips moved a little as if he had caught the words he had been seeking.

'Got it?' I asked. I was rather thrilled; it was, I thought, a very interesting example of an inherited memory — something long forgotten and now recalled by equally forgotten associations.

He made no reply, so I asked again — 'Remembered it?'

He looked up at me, grinning, and wouldn't answer. It was a queer look, half ashamed, half malicious, wholly triumphant. Every now and then throughout the morning I caught him moving his lips as if he were repeating something he was anxious not to forget — like an amateur actor learning his part — and there was an odd, excited air about him like that of a small boy with a mischievous secret. He looked as if he were up to something recklessly silly, like an extra mad 'Cupper' rag. Of course I knew he couldn't be really, but I felt uneasy somehow. He'd always had the reputation for such daredevil games, and though he was tied to his couch he might be all the more restless, planning any monkey tricks. And he had a mocking light in his eye that irritated me badly. I know I'm not his type, but open mockery was a bit more than I could stick. I decided I'd leave him to himself in the afternoon and clear out for a good walk on my own.

He seemed quite pleased when I mentioned this. All he said was, just as I looked in to the little enclosure to say I was starting, 'Right. I say, you might just give me a drink before you go, will you? Some of that spring by the wall there.'

I said I'd go in and get him a drink; the spring looked good enough, but you never know, especially near a farmyard. But that wouldn't do him at all. He wanted the water from that well and nothing else. And when I said I wouldn't get it for him, he actually moved as if to get up and get it for himself.

Well, he wasn't a kid. He knew the risks of drinking the stuff as well as I did; so, still protesting, I scooped up about a spoonful of the water for him.

'I want to drink the old lad's health,' he said, half apologetically, when I handed it to him; and he held the glass up as if he really were drinking a health, and muttered some more nonsense about '*libatio aquae*'. It was too low for me to hear, and anyhow I was fed up with his nonsense. He still had the daring, wild expression I'd noticed in the morning, and he grinned at me in an absolutely impish way. I cleared out, annoyed and just a trifle uneasy.

I enjoyed my walk. Markham had ruffled me, and it was a real relief to be by myself for a bit. We hadn't anything in common, really. I'm a plodder by nature, and I had no sympathy with his wild outbursts of spirits and the mad enterprises that he alternated with training of a rigorous kind. Even since his illness, when we had seen a good deal of each other, I had never understood him much. I'd been surprised, for instance, to hear him quote Latin simply because I had taken it for granted that he was the ordinary beefy, brainless type; but I realised now that I had not the smallest reason, really, to think so. I knew nothing, quite literally nothing, of his mind. I began thinking of his queer behaviour that morning — his puzzled face, his relief at remembering some half-forgotten tag of dog-Latin seen in an old book, the dancing mockery of his eyes, that absurd business of the 'libation'. I began to wonder how long our companionship would last, and I thought that probably it would not be very long. There, at least, I was right.

I got in about six, perhaps a little earlier. I know dusk had not yet fallen; but the warmth was gone from the air, and the shadows were chill. I went out to the little grass plot at once to see if Markham had been moved in yet. I thought it might be risky for him after his illness to be lying out so late when April was not yet in.

He was still there, lying flat and rigid under the grey rug on the couch; and the dim colour of the rug and the stillness of his pose gave me quite a shock. He didn't look alive at all; he looked like a figure carved in grey stone on a tomb. It was the merest momentary impression, but for the instant it seemed to me as if even his face were — fixed. And there was something else about it ...

Then he opened his eyes and looked at me with the dazed sort of look a man has when he wakes suddenly — puzzled, rather appealing — you know what I mean, rather childlike somehow. And I suddenly had the oddest sort of guilty feeling, as if I'd been thinking something treacherous — planning some evil to him — I can't explain, it was all so vague, mixed up with that swiftly-lost impression of his set, still face and figure, like a debased statue on an evil tomb.

We had a door between our rooms in the farm. At first I used to leave it ajar, in case Markham should wake and want some small attention; but that night I closed it. I can't explain why, for I'd quite lost the irritation I'd felt earlier in the day; instead I had a queer sort of feeling, equally irrational, of pity, almost of grief; and yet I shut the door with a feeling of half-shamed relief such as one feels when one leaves a mourner one can't help.

I woke quite suddenly. Perhaps it was the big, bright moon, nearly full for Easter, that awakened me; but I had the impression that it was a voice. I sat up and listened. I thought I could hear it again — a voice (or was it two voices?) speaking quick and quiet in the next room.

'Want anything, Markham?' I called; and my voice sounded odd — anxious, and a little unsteady.

There was immediate and deathly silence — the kind of silence that follows on a furtive sound. I strained my ears to listen. I remember now how the flood of strong moonlight washed my room, and the look of the queer, sharp shadows that edged it. I could hear my own heart beating in the dead silence.

Nothing — not a whisper, not a rustle. Only that strained, aching, unnatural void, so different from real quiet, that you hear when you listen intently.

I waited a little, more uneasy than I liked to admit. I had, half unconsciously, in my mind the vision of Markham as I had seen him that afternoon, grey and rigid, with a set, altered, familiar, dreadful face ...

I twisted my legs round over the edge of my bed. The room had that half-familiar, half-magic look you get in full moonlight — solid and yet ethereal, real and still dreamlike ... I felt as if minutes passed in that dead, unnatural silence. It took more effort than I should have imagined possible to break through it.

'Markham!' I said again; and, though I pitched my voice low, it sounded horribly loud. It cracked upwards unexpectedly; and I knew then — and not till then — that I was — terrified.

No sound. Only the echo of that breaking, frightened, stranger's voice that had come from my own dry throat.

I got up and opened the door between our rooms.

The window, uncurtained, let the moonlight stream in. The shadows were massive, hard-edged, like odd shapes cut in a solid substance. I could see the bed, a patchwork of black and white, cut by the shadows of things in the room. One shadow was humped, rounded — I thought it moved, and spun round to see what threw it. There was nothing. When I turned back it had gone. Perhaps it had never been there ...

The pillow was, as it were, cut off from the whiteness of the bed by the straight, solid shadow of the curtain hanging beside the window. I could just see dimly in the blackness the blacker blot made by Markham's head. He lay as motionless as stone ...

I stood there in the chequered black and white. I don't think I *thought* at all. I just stood there, resisting with all my strength a wave of sheer panic that swept over me. It was as if in that silent room I stood on the verge of something too evil, too fearful, to understand. I could see nothing, hear nothing, but I felt evil, malignant, appalling, in the very air. And then quite silently the curtain at the window waved in some mysterious breath of night air — lifted for a second, and fell as silently. But in that single instant I had seen ...

Markham's head lay as if carved in stone on the pillow; the eyes were blankly lidded, the features altered — something twisted in the roughened hair, like a fillet — he smiled a little, an enigmatic, cruel and anguished smile ... Markham, yet not Markham ...

I forget what happened. A black wave seemed to engulf me. I heard the rush of it in my ears — I couldn't breathe for it ... Then I was standing in my own room, backing up to the open window, deadly cold, seeing that dreadful face. And then panic seized me — not for myself, but for Markham. What had happened? He was helpless ... I must go back — must help him — I couldn't let It ...

If there had been some sound it wouldn't have been so bad. A groan, a cry for help, even a whisper would have been more — more human. I should have known then that Markham really was there ...

I lit a candle. It took me, I knew, a very long time, I fumbled so. But at last I had a warm, friendly light instead of the mocking fantasy of moonlight. I went back.

The room looked just as usual. Markham lay, his brows a little drawn down, his mouth a little open, as if he were puzzled or expostulating — but it was Markham. There was no doubt of that. I felt a warm gush of sheer relief as I saw his familiar face. Oddly enough, I didn't, even then, feel at all ashamed of my terror. There *had* been something wrong, something appalling, ghastly, in that room. It was gone now, but it had been there ...

I went back to bed, but I did not sleep again. I listened, achingly, for a sound that never came.

I felt oddly embarrassed at the idea of meeting Markham in the morning. It was as if I had unwittingly surprised him in some secret, shameful and intimate. And I noticed that he, too, when we met, seemed unwilling to meet my eye. We were both conscious of something — some bond of knowledge that was at the same time a bar. And I think we both wondered what the other knew.

After a pretence of a meal I tried, feebly enough, to get something out of him.

'I don't think you'd better go out to-day,' I said, looking at him straight.

He changed colour at once.

'What d'you mean?' he asked, almost defiantly.

'I mean,' I said — carefully, because I wasn't myself sure of my own meaning — 'that I think Mrs Stokes is right. That enclosure isn't — healthy.'

He laughed, rather a mirthless, sneering sound.

'Too late to think of that now,' he said; and as our eyes met I saw a difference — his face looked strange, yet familiar, with its cynical, suffering mouth and expressionless eyes.

'Markham!' I cried, dropping all pretence. 'Markham — what is it? What have you done? Can't we ...?'

My voice died away.

He had said nothing. His whole face was set, rigid in that blank, cynical, anguished look. It was as if stricken to stone before my eyes. We sat, the spring sun on us, facing each other in horror and despair.

I said no more. I knew he was right — it was too late to avoid the enclosure, with its well and terrible bust. I stayed with Markham all that day, pretending to read as he lay motionless and silent in the air and sunshine of that haunted plot called Simmel Acre. I was tense the whole time, listening with strained ears, stealing furtive glances now at Markham's set face, now at the marred bust above the clear water of the spring. But nothing happened, except that once I thought I saw on the grass near the couch a crouching shadow ... It was not there when I looked sharply up. I had imagined it, perhaps.

But as evening drew on I felt we could not leave it like that. We must do something.

'Markham,' I said, as firmly as I could, 'I think I'd better sleep in your room to-night.'

He said nothing. He only turned his head a little and looked at me.

'You were restless last night,' I said feebly. 'You might need me.'

'*Restless?*' he half whispered, mockery in his tone.

I remembered that rigid form and terrible set face.

'You might need me,' I repeated.

'No. It's decent of you, Norton — but — no. I — I'd rather you didn't — I mean — I'm better alone.'

I don't know what made me say it.

'Where did you get the words from?' I asked.

He stared at me as if he would read my thoughts.

'*I don't know,*' he whispered; and his whole face was suddenly transfigured with sheer appalling panic. 'Norton — Norton,' he babbled, clutching at me, 'if I knew! If only I knew! I might find others — to undo it — Norton, can't you think? Where can I find out? What was the book?'

I was immensely relieved. It was far less dreadful put into words.

'I'll find out,' I said boldly. 'There'll be books — people must know ... I'll ask old Henderson, he's always working at these things, rites and old magic and things. He'll know, Markham, sure to. I'll go over to Oxford first thing to-morrow ...'

'No! No! To-night, Norton, it must be to-night. The moon's full to-night. You must, you simply must. You don't know — I — I can't ...'

He was nearly beside himself.

'I will,' I promised. 'I'll go now. I'll be in Oxford before eight. I'll find Henderson. It'll be all right, Markham, he's sure to know. It'll be all right ...'

I shall never forget that mad journey to Oxford. I cycled, as there was no quicker way to go; and it took me two hours, panting up hills, sweating as if I were on an errand of life and death. It was, I knew, even more serious than that ... And I had no clue — nothing but that Markham's family had once been connected with the village — that some ancestor had worshipped with the Hellfire Club ... that there had been a book ... Would it, could it be the faintest use? Could old Henderson — could anyone, pedant or priest, help us?

It seemed hours and hours before I got into the long roads of conventional houses that lie like a web about Oxford. The clocks were striking nine as I reached Carfax.

Henderson was away. Of course he was, in the vac. I stood stunned as the porter carefully explained it to me — I think he thought I was drunk. I could not take it in. Our last chance! ... The porter saw that it was something serious.

'Something urgent was it, sir?' he asked at last.

'Yes,' I whispered. My lips were almost too dry to speak.

'Well, sir — seein' as it's urgent ... Mr 'Enderson 'as a little 'ouse out near Kingston Bagpuize.'E don't like visitors there, not 'ouse out near Kingston Bagpuize.'E don't like visitors there, not in vacation, but seein' as it's urgent ... It ain't on the 'phone, but if you'd care to run out ...'

I was down the steps before he finished. He shouted the name of the house after me as I raced off. The moon, moving majestically and remorselessly up the sky, filled me with desperation. I should never, never be in time ...

I don't know what I said to Henderson. I thought I should never make him understand. I don't know why he listened — why he didn't write me down as mad, or drunk. But, thank God, he didn't; he made me sit down and drink something — I don't know what, I couldn't taste it, and my hands were shaking so that I couldn't drink without spilling the stuff — while he listened and nodded and consulted old books. He moved with the slowness of a very old man, taking down one book after another, consulting manuscripts, reading passages, while the minutes ticked away and the night crept on ... I can see him now, so old and bent, with his careful gestures clear in the steady lamplight, and the smell of old books in the air ...

The clocks were striking eleven as we rushed, in a hired car, out of the dim Oxford streets and struck up the glimmering white road to Simmel Acres Farm. I don't think we said a word. I know I sat with every muscle taut, straining with impatience, wild hope alternating with despair as I watched the moon rise higher and higher in the clear sky. We should never do it!

The moon was almost at the zenith when at last we reached the farm. I could not stand when I got out — old Henderson had to put his hand under my arm to keep me from falling.

I was making for the door, but he stopped me.

'No,' he said, 'the enclosure — the well. We must go there.'

He was muttering to himself, like a man saying prayers, but I knew that he was not praying to any Christian God.

The outer door was shut, but the key was in the lock, and we opened it easily.

The little yard looked quite empty. The royal moonlight flooded the young grass and the trees with leaves just unfolding. Only at the end the penthouse of stone threw a dark, menacing shadow. Beneath it came the tiny tinkle of water in the stone-edged spring. And, half in the shadow, half in the moonlight, I saw Markham lying — Markham, with a white, set face turned up to the moon. And his face was that of the sneering bust above him.

13 The Maker of Gargoyles (1932)

CLARK ASHTON SMITH

1

Among the many gargoyles that frowned or leered from the roof of the new-built cathedral of Vyones, two were pre-eminent above the rest by virtue of their fine workmanship and their supreme grotesquery. These two had been wrought by the stone-carver Blaise Reynard, a native of Vyones, who had lately returned from a long sojourn in the cities of Provence, and had secured employment on the cathedral when the three years' task of its construction and ornamentation was well-nigh completed. In view of the wonderful artistry shown by Reynard, it was regretted by Ambrosius, the archbishop, that it had not been possible to commit the execution of all the gargoyles to this delicate and accomplished workman; but other people, with less liberal tastes than Ambrosius, were heard to express a different opinion.

This opinion, perhaps, was tinged by the personal dislike that had been generally felt toward Reynard in Vyones even from his boyhood; and which had been revived with some virulence on his return. Whether rightly or unjustly, his very physiognomy had always marked him out for public disfavor: he was inordinately dark, with hair and beard of a preternatural bluish-black, and slanting, ill-matched eyes that gave him a sinister and cunning air. His taciturn and saturnine ways were such as a superstitious people would identify with necromantic knowledge or complicity; and there were those who covertly accused him of being in league with Satan; though the accusations were little more than vague, anonymous rumors, even to the end, through lack of veritable evidence.

However, the people who suspected Reynard of diabolic affiliations were wont for awhile to instance the two gargoyles as sufficient proof. No man, they contended, who was not inspired by the Arch-Enemy, could have carven anything so sheerly evil and malignant, could have embodied so consummately in mere stone the living lineaments of the most demoniacal of all the deadly Sins.

The two gargoyles were perched on opposite corners of a high tower of the cathedral. One was a snarling, murderous, cat-headed monster, with retracted lips revealing formidable fangs, and eyes that glared intolerable hatred from beneath ferine brows. This creature had the claws and wings of a griffin, and seemed as if it were poised in readiness to swoop down on the city of Vyones, like a harpy on its prey. Its companion was a horned satyr, with the vans of some great bat such as might roam the nether caverns, with sharp, clenching talons, and a look of Satanically brooding lust, as if it were gloating above the helpless object of its unclean desire. Both figures were complete, even to the hindquarters, and were not mere conventional adjuncts of the roof. One would have expected them to start at any moment from the stone in which they were mortised.

Ambrosius, a lover of art, had been openly delighted with these creations, because of their high technical merit and their verisimilitude as works of sculpture. But others, including many humbler dignitaries of the Church, were more or less scandalized, and said that the workman had informed these figures with the visible likeness of his own vices, to the glory of Belial rather than of God, and had thus perpetrated a sort of blasphemy. Of course, they admitted, a certain amount of grotesquery was requisite in gargoyles; but in this case the allowable bounds had been egregiously overpassed.

However, with the completion of the cathedral, and in spite of all this adverse criticism, the high-poised gargoyles of Blaise Reynard, like all other details of the building, were soon taken for granted through mere everyday familiarity; and eventually they were almost forgotten. The scandal of opposition died down, and the stone-carver himself, though the townsfolk continued to eye him askance, was able to secure other work through the favor of discriminating patrons. He remained in Vyones; and paid his addresses, albeit without visible success, to a taverner's daughter, one Nicolette Villom, of whom, it was said, he had long been enamored in his own surly and reticent fashion.

But Reynard himself had not forgotten the gargoyles. Often, in passing the superb pile of the cathedral, he would gaze up at them with a secret satisfaction whose cause he could hardly have assigned or delimited. They seemed to retain for him a rare and mystical meaning, to signalize an obscure but pleasurable triumph.

He would have said, if asked for the reason of his satisfaction, that he was proud of a skilful piece of handiwork. He would not have said, and perhaps would not even have known, that in one of the gargoyles he had imprisoned all his festering rancor, all his answering spleen and hatred toward the people of Vyones, who had always hated him; and had set the image of this rancor to peer venomously down for ever from a lofty place. And perhaps he would not even have dreamt that in the second gargoyle he had somehow expressed his own dour and satyr-like passion for the girl Nicolette — a passion that had brought him back to the detested city of his youth after years of wandering; a passion singularly tenacious of one object, and differing in this regard from the ordinary lusts of a nature so brutal as Reynard's.

Always to the stone-cutter, even more than to those who had criticized and abhorred his productions, the gargoyles were alive, they possessed a vitality and a sentiency of their own. And most of all did they seem to live when the summer drew to an end and the autumn rains had gathered upon Vyones. Then, when the full cathedral gutters poured above the streets, one might have thought that the actual spittle of a foul malevolence, the very slaver of an impure lust, had somehow been mingled with the water that ran in rills from the mouths of the gargoyles.

2

At that time, in the year of our Lord, 1138, Vyones was the principal town of the province of Averoigne. On two sides the great, shadow-haunted forest, a place of equivocal legends, of *loups-garous* and phantoms, approached to the very walls and flung its umbrage upon them at early forenoon and evening. On the other sides there lay cultivated fields, and gentle streams that meandered among willows or poplars, and roads that ran through an open plain to the high châteaux of noble lords and to regions beyond Averoigne.

The town itself was prosperous, and had never shared in the ill-fame of the bordering forest. It had long been sanctified by the presence of two nunneries and a monastery; and now, with the completion of the long-planned cathedral, it was thought that Vyones would have henceforward the additional protection of a more august holiness; that demon and *stryge* and incubus would keep their distance from its heaven-favored purlieus with a more meticulous caution than before.

Of course, as in all mediæval towns, there had been occasional instances of alleged sorcery or demoniacal possession; and, once or twice, the perilous temptations of succubi had made their inroads on the pious virtue of Vyones. But this was nothing more than might be expected, in a world where the Devil and his works were always more or less rampant. No one could possibly have anticipated the reign of infernal horrors that was to make hideous the latter month of autumn, following the cathedral's erection.

To make the matter even more inexplicable, and more blasphemously dreadful than it would otherwise have been, the first of these horrors occurred in the neighborhood of the cathedral itself and almost beneath its sheltering shadow.

Two men, a respectable clothier named Guillaume Maspier and an equally reputable cooper, one Gerome Mazzal, were returning to their lodgings in the late hours of a November eve, after imbibing both the red and white wines of the countryside in more than one tavern. According to Maspier, who alone survived to tell the tale, they were passing along a street that skirted the cathedral square, and could see the bulk of the great building against the stars, when a flying monster, black as the soot of Abaddon, had descended upon them from the heavens and assailed Gerome Mazzal, beating him down with its heavily flapping wings and seizing him with its inch-long teeth and talons.

Maspier was unable to describe the creature with minuteness, for he had seen it but dimly and partially in the unlit street; and moreover, the fate of his companion, who had fallen to the cobblestones with the black devil snarling and tearing at his throat, had not induced Maspier to linger in that vicinity. He had betaken himself from the scene with all the celerity of which he was capable, and had stopped only at the house of a priest, many streets away, where he had related his adventure between shudderings and hiccuppings.

Armed with holy water and aspergillus, and accompanied by many of the townspeople carrying torches, staves and halberds, the priest was led by Maspier to the place of the horror; and there they had found the body of Mazzal, with fearfully mangled face, and throat and bosom lined with bloody lacerations. The demoniac assailant had flown, and it was not seen or encountered again that night; but those who had beheld its work returned aghast to their homes, feeling that a creature of nethermost hell had come to visit the city, and perchance to abide therein.

Consternation was rife on the morrow, when the story became generally known; and rites of exorcism against the invading demon were performed by the clergy in all public places and before thresholds. But the sprinkling of holy water and the mumbling of stated forms were futile; for the evil spirit was still abroad, and its malignity was proved once more, on the night following the ghastly death of Gerome Mazzal.

This time, it claimed two victims, burghers of high probity and some consequence, on whom it descended in a narrow alley, slaying one of them instantaneously, and dragging down the other from behind as he sought to flee. The shrill cries of the helpless men, and the guttural growling of the demon, were heard by people in the houses along the alley; and some, who were hardy enough to peer from their windows, had seen the departure of the infamous assailant, blotting out the autumn stars with the sable and misshapen foulness of its wings, and hovering in execrable menace above the house-tops.

After this, few people would venture abroad at night, unless in case of dire and exigent need; and those who did venture went in armed companies and were all furnished with flambeaux, thinking thus to frighten away the demon, which they adjudged a creature of darkness that would abhor the light and shrink therefrom, through the nature of its kind. But the boldness of this fiend was beyond measure; for it proceeded to attack more than one company of worthy citizens, disregarding the flaring torches that were thrust in its face, or putting them out with the stenchful wind of its wide vans.

Evidently it was a spirit of homicidal hate; for all the people on whom it seized were grievously mangled or torn to numberless shreds by its teeth and talons. Those who saw it, and survived, were wont to describe it variously and with much ambiguity; but all agreed in attributing to it the head of a ferocious animal and the wings of a monstrous bird. Some, the most learned in demonology, were fain to identify it with Modo, the spirit of murder; and others took it for one of the great lieutenants of Satan, perhaps Amaimon or Alastor, gone mad with exasperation at the impregnable supremacy of Christ in the holy city of Vyones.

The terror that soon prevailed, beneath the widening scope of these Satanical incursions and depredations, was beyond all belief — a clotted, seething, devil-ridden gloom of superstitious obsession, not to be hinted in modern language. Even by daylight, the Gothic wings of nightmare seemed to brood in undeparting oppression above the city; and fear was everywhere, like the foul contagion of some epidemic plague. The inhabitants went their way in prayer and trembling; and the archbishop himself, as well as the subordinate clergy, confessed an inability to cope with the ever-growing horror. An emissary was sent to Rome, to procure water that had been specially sanctified by the Pope. This alone, it was thought, would be efficacious enough to drive away the dreadful visitant.

In the meanwhile, the horror waxed, and mounted to its culmination. One eve, toward the middle of November, the abbot of the local monastery of Cordeliers, who had gone forth to administer extreme unction to a dying friend, was seized by the black devil just as he approached the threshold of his destination, and was slain in the same atrocious manner as the other victims.

To this doubly infamous deed, a scarce-believable blasphemy was soon added. On the very next night, while the torn body of the abbot lay on a rich catafalque in the cathedral, and masses were being said and tapers burnt, the demon invaded the high nave through the open door, extinguished all the candles with one flap of its sooty wings, and dragged down no less than three of the officiating priests to an unholy death in the darkness.

Everyone now felt that a truly formidable assault was being made by the powers of Evil on the Christian probity of Vyones. In the condition of abject terror, of extreme disorder and demoralization that followed upon this new atrocity, there was a deplorable outbreak of human crime, of murder and rapine and thievery, together with covert manifestations of Satanism, and celebrations of the Black Mass attended by many neophytes.

Then, in the midst of all this pandemoniacal fear and confusion, it was rumored that a second devil had been seen in Vyones; that the murderous fiend was accompanied by a spirit of equal deformity and darkness, whose intentions were those of lechery, and which molested none but women. This creature had frightened several dames and demoiselles and maid-servants into a veritable hysteria by peering through their bedroom windows; and had sidled lasciviously, with uncouth mows and grimaces, and grotesque flappings of its bat-shaped wings, toward others who had occasion to fare from house to house across the nocturnal streets.

However, strange to say, there were no authentic instances in which the chastity of any woman had suffered actual harm from this noisome incubus. Many were approached by it, and were terrified immoderately by the hideousness and lustfulness of its demeanor; but no one was ever touched. Even in that time of horror, both spiritual and corporeal, there were those who made a ribald jest of this singular abstention on the part of the demon, and said that it was seeking throughout Vyones for someone whom it had not yet found.

3

The lodgings of Blaise Reynard were separated only by the length of a dark and crooked alley from the tavern kept by Jean Villom, the father of Nicolette. In this tavern, Reynard had been wont to spend his evenings; though his suit was frowned upon by Jean Villom, and had received but scant encouragement from the girl herself. However, because of his well-filled purse and his almost illimitable capacity for wine, Reynard was tolerated. He came early each night, with the falling of darkness, and would sit in silence hour after hour, staring with hot and sullen eyes at Nicolette, and gulping joylessly the potent vintages of Averoigne. Apart from their desire to retain his custom, the people of the tavern were a little afraid of him, on account of his dubious and semi-sorcerous reputation, and also because of his surly temper. They did not wish to antagonize him more than was necessary.

Like everyone else in Vyones, Reynard had felt the suffocating burden of superstitious terror during those nights when the fiendish marauder was hovering above the town and might descend on the luckless wayfarer at any moment, in any locality. Nothing less urgent and imperative than the obsession of his half-bestial longing for Nicolette could have induced him to traverse after dark the length of the winding alley to the tavern door.

The autumn nights had been moonless. Now, on the evening that followed the desecration of the cathedral itself by the murderous devil, a new-born crescent was lowering its fragile, sanguine-colored horn beyond the house-tops as Reynard went forth from his lodgings at the accustomed hour. He lost sight of its comforting beam in the high-walled and narrow alley, and shivered with dread as he hastened onward through shadows that were dissipated only by the rare and timid ray from some lofty window. It seemed to him, at each turn and angle, that the gloom was curded by the unclean umbrage of Satanic wings, and might reveal in another instant the gleaming of abhorrent eyes ignited by the everlasting coals of the Pit. When he came forth at the alley's end, he saw with a start of fresh panic that the crescent moon was blotted out by a cloud that had the semblance of uncouthly arched and pointed vans.

He reached the tavern with a sense of supreme relief, for he had begun to feel a distinct intuition that someone or something was following him, unheard and invisible — a presence that seemed to load the dusk with prodigious menace. He entered, and closed the door behind him very quickly, as if he were shutting it in the face of a dread pursuer.

There were few people in the tavern that evening. The girl Nicolette was serving wine to a mercer's assistant, one Raoul Coupain, a personable youth and a newcomer in the neighborhood, and she was laughing with what Reynard considered unseemly gayety at the broad jests and amorous sallies of this Raoul. Jean Villom was discussing in a low voice the latest enormities of the demons with two cronies at a table in the farthest corner, and was drinking fully as much liquor as his customers.

Glowering with jealousy at the presence of Raoul Coupain, whom he suspected of being a favored rival, Reynard seated himself in silence and stared malignly at the flirtatious couple. No one seemed to have noticed his entrance; for Villom went on talking to his cronies without pause or interruption, and Nicolette and her companion were equally oblivious. To his jealous rage, Reynard soon added the resentment of one who feels that he is being deliberately ignored. He began to pound on the table with his heavy fists, to attract attention.

Villom, who had been sitting all the while his back turned, now called out to Nicolette without even troubling to face around on his stool, telling her to serve Reynard. Giving a backward smile at Coupain, she came slowly and with open reluctance to the stone-carver's table.

She was small and buxom, with reddish-gold hair that curled luxuriantly above the short, delicious oval of her face; and she was gowned in a tight-fitting dress of apple-green that revealed the firm, seductive outlines of her hips and bosom. Her air was disdainful and a little cold, for she did not like Reynard and had taken small pains at any time to conceal her aversion. But to Reynard she was lovelier and more desirable than ever, and he felt a savage impulse to seize her in his arms and carry her bodily away from the tavern before the eyes of Raoul Coupain and her father.

'Bring me a pitcher of La Frênaie,' he ordered gruffly, in a voice that betrayed his mingled resentment and desire.

Tossing her head lightly and scornfully, with more glances at Coupain, the girl obeyed. She placed the fiery, blood-dark wine before Reynard without speaking, and then went back to resume her bantering with the mercer's assistant.

Reynard began to drink, and the potent vintage merely served to inflame his smoldering enmity and passion. His eyes became venomous, his curling lips malignant as those of the gargoyles he had carved on the new cathedral. A baleful, primordial anger, like the rage of some morose and thwarted faun, burned within him with its slow red fire; but he strove to repress it, and sat silent and motionless, except for the frequent filling and emptying of his wine-cup.

Raoul Coupain had also consumed a liberal quantity of wine. As a result, he soon became bolder in his love-making, and strove to kiss the hand of Nicolette, who had now seated herself on the bench beside him. The hand was playfully withheld; and then, after its owner had cuffed Raoul very lightly and briskly, was granted to the claimant in a fashion that struck Reynard as being no less than wanton.

Snarling inarticulately, with a mad impulse to rush forward and slay the successful rival with his bare hands, he started to his feet and stepped toward the playful pair. His movement was noted by one of the men in the far corner, who spoke warningly to Villom. The tavern-keeper arose, lurching a little from his potations, and came warily across the room with his eyes on Reynard, ready to interfere in case of violence.

Reynard paused with momentary irresolution, and then went

on, half insane with a mounting hatred for them all. He longed to kill Villom and Coupain, to kill the hateful cronies who sat staring from the corner; and then, above their throttled corpses, to ravage with fierce kisses and vehement caresses the shrinking lips and body of Nicolette.

Seeing the approach of the stone-carver, and knowing his evil temper and dark jealousy, Coupain also rose to his feet and plucked stealthily beneath his cloak at the hilt of a little dagger which he carried. In the meanwhile, Jean Villom had interposed his burly bulk between the rivals. For the sake of the tavern's good repute, he wished to prevent the possible brawl.

'Back to your table, stone-cutter,' he roared belligerently at Reynard.

Being unarmed, and seeing himself outnumbered, Reynard paused again, though his anger still simmered within him like the contents of a sorcerer's cauldron. With ruddy points of murderous flame in his hollow, slitted eyes, he glared at the three people before him, and saw beyond them, with instinctive rather than conscious awareness, the leaded panes of the tavern window, in whose glass the room was dimly reflected with its glowing tapers, its glimmering tableware, the heads of Coupain and Villom and the girl Nicolette, and his own shadowy face among them.

Strangely, and, it would seem, inconsequently, he remembered at that moment the dark, ambiguous cloud he had seen across the moon, and the insistent feeling of obscure pursuit while he had traversed the alley.

Then, as he still gazed irresolutely at the group before him, and its vague reflection in the glass beyond, there came a thunderous crash, and the panes of the window with their pictured scene were shattered inward in a score of fragments. Ere the litter of falling glass had reached the tavern floor, a swart and monstrous form flew into the room, with a beating of heavy vans that caused the tapers to flare troublously, and the shadows to dance like a sabbat of misshapen devils. The thing hovered for a moment, and seemed to tower in a great darkness higher than the ceiling above the heads of Reynard and the others as they turned toward it. They saw the malignant burning of its eyes, like coals in the depth of Tartarean pits, and the curling of its hateful lips on the bared teeth that were longer and sharper than serpent-fangs.

Behind it now, another shadowy flying monster came in through the broken window with a loud flapping of its ribbed and pointed wings. There was something lascivious in the very motion of its flight, even as homicidal hatred and malignity were manifest in the flight of the other. Its satyr-like face was twisted in a horrible, never-changing leer, and its lustful eyes were fixed on Nicolette as it hung in air beside the first intruder.

Reynard, as well as the other men, was petrified by a feeling of astonishment and consternation so extreme as almost to preclude terror. Voiceless and motionless, they beheld the demoniac intrusion; and the consternation of Reynard, in particular, was mingled with an element of unspeakable surprise, together with a dreadful recognizance. But the girl Nicolette, with a mad scream of horror, turned and started to flee across the room.

As if her cry had been the one provocation needed, the two demons swooped upon their victims. One, with a ferocious slash of its outstretched claws, tore open the throat of Jean Villom, who fell with a gurgling, blood-choked groan; and then, in the same fashion, it assailed Raoul Coupain. The other, in the meanwhile, had pursued and overtaken the fleeing girl, and had seized her in its bestial forearms, with the ribbed wings enfolding her like a hellish drapery.

The room was filled by a moaning whirlwind, by a chaos of wild cries and tossing, struggling shadows. Reynard heard the guttural snarling of the murderous monster, muffled by the body of Coupain, whom it was tearing with its teeth; and he heard the lubricous laughter of the incubus, above the shrieks of the hysterically frightened girl. Then the grotesquely flaring tapers went out in a gust of swirling air, and Reynard received a violent blow in the darkness — the blow of some rushing object, perhaps of a passing wing, that was hard and heavy as stone. He fell, and became insensible.

4

Dully and confusedly, with much effort, Reynard struggled back to consciousness. For a brief interim, he could not remember where he was nor what had happened. He was troubled by the painful throbbing of his head, by the humming of agitated voices about him, by the glaring of many lights and the thronging of many faces when he opened his eyes; and, above all, by the sense of nameless but grievous calamity and uttermost horror that weighed him down from the first dawning of sentiency.

Memory returned to him, laggard and reluctant; and with it, a full awareness of his surroundings and situation. He was lying on the tavern floor, and his own warm, sticky blood was rilling across his face from the wound on his aching head. The long room was half filled with people of the neighborhood, bearing torches and knives and halberds, who had entered and were peering at the corpses of Villom and Coupain, which lay amid pools of wine-diluted blood and the wreckage of the shattered furniture and tableware.

Nicolette, with her green gown in shreds, and her body crushed by the embraces of the demon, was moaning feebly while women crowded about her with ineffectual cries and questions which she could not even hear or understand. The two cronies of Villom, horribly clawed and mangled, were dead beside their overturned table.

Stupefied with horror, and still dizzy from the blow that had laid him unconscious, Reynard staggered to his feet, and found himself surrounded at once by inquiring faces and voices. Some of the people were a little suspicious of him, since he was the sole survivor in the tavern, and bore an ill repute; but his replies to their questions soon convinced them that the new crime was wholly the work of the same demons that had plagued Vyones in so monstrous a fashion for weeks past.

Reynard, however, was unable to tell them all that he had seen, or to confess the ultimate sources of his fear and stupefaction. The secret of that which he knew was locked in the seething pit of his tortured and devil-ridden soul.

Somehow, he left the ravaged inn, he pushed his way through the gathering crowd with its terror-muted murmurs, and found himself alone on the midnight streets. Heedless of his own possible peril, and scarcely knowing where he went, he wandered through Vyones for many hours; and somewhile in his wanderings, he came to his own workshop. With no assignable reason for the act, he entered, and re-emerged with a heavy hammer, which he carried with him during his subsequent peregrinations. Then, driven by his awful and unremissive torture, he went on till the pale dawn had touched the spires and the house-tops with a ghostly glimmering.

By a half-conscious compulsion, his steps had led him to the square before the cathedral. Ignoring the amazed verger, who had just opened the doors, he entered and sought a stairway that wound tortuously upward to the tower on which his own gargoyles were ensconced.

In the chill and livid light of sunless morning, he emerged on the roof; and leaning perilously from the verge, he examined the carven figures. He felt no surprise, only the hideous confirmation of a fear too ghastly to be named, when he saw that the teeth and claws of the malign, cat-headed griffin were stained with darkening blood; and that shreds of apple-green cloth were hanging from the talons of the lustful, bat-winged satyr.

It seemed to Reynard, in the dim ashen light, that a look of unspeakable triumph, of intolerable irony, was imprinted on the face of this latter creature. He stared at it with fearful and agonizing fascination, while impotent rage, abhorrence, and repentance deeper than that of the damned arose within him in a smothering flood. He was hardly aware that he had raised the iron hammer and had struck wildly at the satyr's horned profile, till he heard the sullen, angry clang of impact, and found that he was tottering on the edge of the roof to retain his balance.

The furious blow had merely chipped the features of the gargoyle, and had not wiped away the malignant lust and exultation. Again Reynard raised the heavy hammer.

It fell on empty air; for, even as he struck, the stone-carver felt himself lifted and drawn backward by something that sank into his flesh like many separate knives. He staggered helplessly, his feet slipped, and then he was lying on the granite verge, with his head and shoulders over the dark, deserted street.

Half swooning, and sick with pain, he saw above him the other gargoyle, the claws of whose right foreleg were firmly embedded in his shoulder. They tore deeper, as if with a dreadful clenching. The monster seemed to tower like some fabulous beast above its prey; and he felt himself slipping dizzily across the cathedral gutter, with the gargoyle twisting and turning as if to resume its normal position over the gulf. Its slow, inexorable movement seemed to be part of his vertigo. The very tower was tilting and revolving beneath him in some unnatural nightmare fashion.

Dimly, in a daze of fear and agony, Reynard saw the remorseless tiger-face bending toward him with its horrid teeth laid bare in an eternal rictus of diabolic hate. Somehow, he had retained the hammer. With an instinctive impulse to defend himself, he struck at the gargoyle, whose cruel features seemed to approach him like something seen in the ultimate madness and distortion of delirium.

Even as he struck, the vertiginous turning movement continued, and he felt the talons dragging him outward on empty air. In his cramped, recumbent position, the blow fell short of the hateful face and came down with a dull clangor on the foreleg whose curving talons were fixed in his shoulder like meat-hooks. The clangor ended in a sharp cracking sound; and the leaning gargoyle vanished from Reynard's vision as he fell. He saw nothing more, except the dark mass of the cathedral tower, that seemed to soar away from him and to rush upward unbelievably in the livid, starless heavens to which the belated sun had not yet risen.

It was the archbishop Ambrosius, on his way to early mass, who found the shattered body of Reynard lying face downward in the square. Ambrosius crossed himself in startled horror at the sight; and then, when he saw the object that was still clinging to Reynard's shoulder, he repeated the gesture with a more than pious promptness.

He bent down to examine the thing. With the infallible memory of a true art-lover, he recognized it at once. Then, through the same clearness of recollection, he saw that the stone foreleg, whose claws were so deeply buried in Reynard's flesh, had somehow undergone a most unnatural alteration. The paw, as he remembered it, should have been slightly bent and relaxed; but now it was stiffly outthrust and elongated, as if, like the paw of a living limb, it had reached for something, or had dragged a heavy burden with its ferine talons.

14 The Man of Stone (1932)

HAZEL HEALD, WITH H P LOVECRAFT

Chapter I

Ben Hayden was always a stubborn chap, and once he had heard about those strange statues in the upper Adirondacks, nothing could keep him from going to see them. I had been his closest acquaintance for years, and our Damon and Pythias friendship made us inseparable at all times. So when Ben firmly decided to go — well, I had to trot along too, like a faithful collie.

'Jack,' he said, 'you know Henry Jackson, who was up in a shack beyond Lake Placid for that beastly spot in his lung? Well, he came back the other day nearly cured, but had a lot to say about some devilish queer conditions up there. He ran into the business all of a sudden and can't be sure yet that it's anything more than a case of bizarre sculpture; but just the same his uneasy impression sticks.

'It seems he was out hunting one day, and came across a cave with what looked like a dog in front of it. Just as he was expecting the dog to bark he looked again, and saw that the thing wasn't alive at all. It was a stone dog — but such a perfect image, down to the smallest whisker, that he couldn't decide whether it was a supernaturally clever statue or a petrified animal. He was almost afraid to touch it, but when he did he realized it was surely made of stone.

'After a while he nerved himself up to go in the cave — and there he got a still bigger jolt. Only a little way in there was another stone figure — or what looked like it — but this time it was a man's. It lay on the floor, on its side, wore clothes, and had a peculiar smile on its face. This time Henry didn't stop to do any touching, but beat it straight for the village, Mountain Top, you know. Of course he asked questions — but they did not get him very far. He found he was on a ticklish subject, for the natives only shook their heads, crossed their fingers, and muttered something about a "Mad Dan" — whoever he was.

'It was too much for Jackson, so he came home weeks ahead of his planned time. He told me all about it because he knows how fond I am of strange things — and oddly enough, I was able to fish up a recollection that dovetailed pretty neatly with his yarn. Do you remember Arthur Wheeler, the sculptor who was such a realist that people began calling him nothing but a solid photographer? I think you knew him slightly. Well, as a matter of fact, he ended up in that part of the Adirondacks himself. Spent a lot of time there, and then dropped out of sight. Never heard from again. Now if stone statues that look like men and dogs are turning up around there, it looks to me as if they might be his work — no matter what the rustics say, or refuse to say, about them. Of course a fellow with Jackson's nerves might easily get flighty and disturbed over things like that: but I'd have done a lot of examining before running away.

'In fact, Jack, I'm going up there now to look things over — and you're coming along with me. It would mean a lot to find Wheeler — or any of his work. Anyhow, the mountain air will brace us both up.'

So less than a week later, after a long train ride and a jolting bus trip through breathlessly exquisite scenery, we arrived at Mountain Top in the late, golden sunlight of a June evening. The village comprised only a few small houses, a hotel, and the general store at which our bus drew up; but we knew that the latter would probably prove a focus for such information. Surely enough, the usual group of idlers was gathered around the steps; and when we represented ourselves as health-seekers in search of lodgings they had many recommendations to offer.

Though we had not planned to do any investigating till the next day, Ben could not resist venturing some vague, cautious questions when he noticed the senile garrulousness of one of the ill-clad loafers. He felt, from Jackson's previous experience, that it would be useless to begin with references to the queer statues; but decided to mention Wheeler as one whom we had known, and in whose fate we consequently had a right to be interested.

The crowd seemed uneasy when Sam stopped his whittling and started talking, but they had slight occasion for alarm. Even this barefoot old mountain decadent tightened up when he heard Wheeler's name, and only with difficulty could Ben get anything coherent out of him.

'Wheeler?' he had finally wheezed, 'Oh, yeh — that feller as was all the time blastin' rocks and cuttin' 'em up into statues. So yew knowed him, hey? Wal, they ain't much we kin tell ye, and mebbe that's too much. He stayed out to Mad Dan's cabin in the hills — but not so very long. Got so he wa'nt wanted no more … by Dan, that is. Kinder soft-spoken and got around Dan's wife till the old devil took notice. Pretty sweet on her, I guess. But he took the trail sudden, and nobody's seen hide nor hair of him since. Dan must a told him sumthin' pretty plain — bad feller to git agin ye, Dan is! Better keep away from thar, boys, for they ain't no good in that part of the hills. Dan's ben workin' up a worse and worse mood, and ain't seen about no more. Nor his wife, neither. Guess he's penned her up so's nobody else kin make eyes at her!'

As Sam resumed his whittling after a few more observations, Ben and I exchanged glances. Here, surely, was a new lead which deserved intensive following up. Deciding to lodge at the hotel, we settled ourselves as quickly as possible; planning for a plunge into the wild hilly country on the next day.

At sunrise we made our start, each bearing a knapsack laden with provisions and such tools as we thought we might need. The day before us had an almost stimulating air of invitation — through which only a faint undercurrent of the sinister ran. Our rough mountain road quickly became steep and winding, so that before long our feet ached considerably

After about two miles we left the road — crossing a stone wall on our right near a great elm and striking off diagonally toward a steeper slope according to the chart and directions which Jackson had prepared for us. It was rough and briery traveling, but we knew that the cave could not be far off. In the end we came upon the aperture quite suddenly — a black, bush-grown crevice where the ground shot abruptly upward, and beside it, near a shallow rock pool, a small, still figure stood rigid — as if rivalling its own uncanny petrification.

It was a grey dog — or a dog's statue — and as our simultaneous gasp died away we scarcely knew what to think. Jackson had exaggerated nothing, and we could not believe that any sculptor's hand had succeeded in producing such perfection. Every hair of the animal's magnificent coat seemed distinct, and those on the back were bristled up as if some unknown thing had taken him unaware. Ben, at last half-kindly touching the delicate stony fur, gave vent to an exclamation.

'Good God, Jack, but this can't be any statue! Look at it — all the little details, and the way the hair lies! None of Wheeler's technique here! This is a real dog — though Heaven only knows how he ever got in this state. Just like stone — feel for yourself. Do you suppose there's any strange gas that sometimes comes out of the cave and does this to animal life? We ought to have looked more into the local legends. And if this is a real dog — or was a real dog — then that man inside must be the real thing too.'

It was with a good deal of genuine solemnity — almost dread — that we finally crawled on hands and knees through the cave mouth, Ben leading. The narrowness looked hardly three feet, after which the grotto expanded in every direction to form a damp, twilight chamber floored with rubble and detritus. For a time we could make out very little, but as we rose to our feet and strained our eyes we began slowly to descry a recumbent figure amidst the greater darkness ahead. Ben fumbled with his flashlight, but hesitated for a moment before turning it on the prostrate figure. We had little doubt that the stony thing was what had once been a man, and something in the thought unnerved us both.

When Ben at last sent forth the electric beam we saw that the object lay on its side, back toward us. It was clearly of the same material as the dog outside, but was dressed in the mouldering and unpetrified remains of rough sport clothing. Braced as we were for a shock, we approached quite calmly to examine the thing; Ben going around to the other side to glimpse the averted face. Neither could possibly have been prepared for what Ben saw when he flashed the light on those stony features. His cry was wholly excusable, and I could not help echoing it as I leaped to his side and shared the sight. Yet it was nothing hideous or intrinsically terrifying. It was merely a matter of recognition for beyond the least shadow of a doubt this chilly rock figure with its half-frightened, half-bitter expression had at one time been our old acquaintance, Arthur Wheeler.

Some instinct sent us staggering and crawling out of the cave, and down the tangled slope to a point whence we could not see the ominous stone dog. We hardly knew what to think, for our brains were churning with conjections and apprehensions. Ben, who had known Wheeler well, was especially upset; and seemed to be piecing together some threads I had overlooked.

Again and again as we paused on the green slope he repeated 'Poor Arthur, poor Arthur!' but not till he muttered the name 'Mad Dan' did I recall the trouble into which, according to old Sam Poole, Wheeler had run just before his disappearance. Mad Dan, Ben implied, would doubtless be glad to see what had happened. For a moment it flashed over both of us that the jealous host might have been responsible for the sculptor's presence in this evil cave, but the thought went as quickly as it came.

The thing that puzzled us most was to account for the phenomenon itself. What gaseous emanation or mineral vapor could have wrought this change in so relatively short a time was utterly beyond us. Normal petrification, we know, is a slow chemical replacement process requiring vast ages for completion; yet here were two stone images which had been living things — or at least Wheeler had — only a few weeks before. Conjecture was useless. Clearly, nothing remained but to notify the authorities and let them guess what they might; and yet at the back of Ben's head that notion about Mad Dan still persisted. Anyhow, we clawed our way back to the road, but Ben did not turn toward the village, but looked along upward toward where old Sam had said Dan's cabin lay. It was the second house from the village, the ancient loafer had wheezed, and lay on the left far back from the road in a thick copse of scrub oaks. Before I knew it Ben was dragging me up the sandy highway past a dingy farmstead and into a region of increasing wildness.

It did not occur to me to protest, but I felt a certain sense of mounting menace as the familiar marks, of agriculture and civilization grew fewer and fewer. At last the beginning of a narrow, neglected path opened up on our left, while the peaked roof of a squalid, unpainted building showed itself beyond a sickly growth of half-dead trees. This, I knew, must be Mad Dan's cabin; and I wondered that Wheeler had ever chosen so unprepossessing a place for his headquarters. I dreaded to walk up that weedy, uninviting path, but could not lag behind when Ben strode determinedly along and began a vigorous rapping at the rickety, musty-smelling door.

There was no response to the knock, and something in its echoes sent a series of shivers through one. Ben, however, was quite unperturbed; and at once began to circle the house in quest of unlocked windows. The third that he tried — in the rear of the dismal cabin — proved capable of opening, and after a boost and a vigorous spring he was safely inside and helping me after him.

The room in which we landed was full of limestone and granite blocks, chiselling tools and clay models, and we realized at once that it was Wheeler's erstwhile studio. So far we had not met with any sign of life, but over everything hovered a damnably ominous dusty odor. On our left was an open door evidently leading to a kitchen on the chimney side of the house, and through this Ben started, intent on finding anything he could concerning his friend's last habitat. He was considerably ahead of me when he crossed the threshold, so that I could not see at first what brought him up short and wrung a low cry of horror from his lips.

In another moment, though, I did see — and repeated his cry as instinctively as I had done in the cave. For here in this cabin

163

far from any subterranean depths which could breed strange gases and work strange imitations — were two stony figures which I knew at once were no products of Arthur Wheeler's chisel. In a rude armchair before the fireplace, bound in position by the lash of a long rawhide whip, was the form of a man — unkempt, elderly, and with a look of fathomless horror on its evil, petrified face.

On the floor beside it lay a woman's figure; graceful, and with a face betokening considerable youth and beauty. Its expression seemed to be one of sardonic satisfaction, and near its outflung right hand was a large tin pail, somewhat stained on the inside, as with a darkish sediment.

Chapter II
The Diary of 'Mad Dan'

We made no move to approach these inexplicably petrified bodies, nor did we exchange any but the simplest conjectures. That this stony couple had been Mad Dan and his wife we could not well doubt, but how to account for their present condition was another matter. As we looked horrifiedly around we saw the suddenness with which the final development must have come — for everything about is seemed, despite a heavy coating of dust, to have been left in the midst of commonplace household activities.

The only exception to this rule of casualness was on the kitchen table; in whose cleared center, as if to attract attention, lay a thin, battered, blank-book weighted down by a sizable tin funnel. Crossing to read the thing, Ben saw that it was a kind of diary or set of dated entries, written in a somewhat cramped and none too practiced hand. The very first words riveted my attention, and before ten seconds had elapsed he was breathlessly devouring the halting text — I avidly following as I peered over his shoulder. As we read on — moving as we did so into the less loathsome atmosphere of the adjoining room — many obscure things became terribly clear to us, and we trembled with a mixture of complex emotions.

This is what we read — and what the coroner read later on. The public has seen a highly twisted and sensationalized version in the cheap newspapers, but not even that has more than a fraction of the genuine terror which the simple original held for us as we puzzled it out alone in that musty cabin among the wild hills, with two monstrous stone abnormalities lurking in the deathlike silence of the next room. When we had finished Ben pocketed the book with a gesture half of repulsion, and his first words were 'Let's get out of here.'

Silently and nervously we stumbled to the front of the house, unlocked the door, and began the long tramp back to the village. There were many statements to make and questions to answer in the days that followed, and I do not think that either Ben or I can ever shake off the effects of the whole harrowing experience. Neither can some of the local authorities and city reporters who flocked around — even though they burned a certain book and many papers found in attic boxes, and destroyed considerable apparatus in the deepest part of that sinister hillside cave. But here is the text itself:

'Nov 5 — My name is Daniel Morris. Around here they call me "Mad Dan" because I believe in powers that nobody else believes in nowadays. When I go up on Thunder Hill to keep the Feast of the Foxes they think I am crazy — all except the back country folks that are afraid of me. They try to stop me from sacrificing the Black Goat at Hallow Eve, and always prevent my doing the Great Rite that would open the gate. They ought to know better, for they know I am a Van Kauran on my mother's side, and anybody this side of the Hudson can tell what the Van Kaurans have handed down. We come from Nicholas Van Kauran, the wizard, who was hanged in Wijtgaart in 1587, and everybody knows he had made the bargain with the Black Man.

'The soldiers never got his Book of Eibon when they burned his house, and his grandson, William Van Kauran, brought it over when he came to Rensselaerwyck and later crossed the river to Esopus. Ask anybody in Kingston or Hurley about what the William Van Kauran line could do to people that got in their way. Also, ask them if my uncle Hendrick didn't manage to keep hold of the Book of Eibon when they ran him out of town and he went up the river to this place with his family.

'I am writing this — and am going to keep on writing this — because I want people to know the truth after I am gone. Also, I am afraid I shall really go mad if I don't set things down in plain black and white. Everything is going against me, and if it keeps up I shall have to use the secrets in the Book and call in certain Powers. Three months ago that sculptor Arthur Wheeler came to Mountain Top, and they sent him up to me because I am the only man in the place who knows anything except farming, hunting, and fleecing summer boarders. The fellow seemed to be interested in what I had to say, and made a deal to stop here for $13.00 a week with meals. I gave him the back room beside the kitchen for his lumps of stone and his chiselling, and arranged with Nate Williams to tend to his rock blasting and haul his big pieces with a drag and yoke of oxen.

'That was three months ago. Now I know why that cursed son of hell took so quick to the place. It wasn't my talk at all, but the looks of my wife Rose, that is Osborn Chandler's oldest girl. She is sixteen years younger than I am, and is always casting sheep's eyes at the fellows in town. But we always managed to get along fine enough till this dirty rat showed up, even if she did balk at helping me with the Rites on Roodmas and Hallowmass. I can see now that Wheeler is working on her feelings and getting her so fond of him that she hardly looks at me, and I suppose he'll try to elope with her sooner or later.

'But he works slow like all sly, polished dogs, and I've got plenty of time to think up what to do about it. They don't either of them know I suspect anything, but before long they'll both realize it doesn't pay to break up a Van Kauran's home. I promise them plenty of novelty in what I'll do.

'Nov 25 — Thanksgiving Day! That's a pretty good joke! But at that I'll have something to be thankful for when I finish what I've started. No question but that Wheeler is trying to

steal my wife. For the time being, though, I'll let him keep on
being a star boarder. Got the Book of Eibon down from Uncle
Hendrik's old trunk in the attic last week, and am looking
up something good which won't require sacrifices that I can't
make around here. I want something that'll finish these two
sneaking traitors, and at the same time get me into no trouble.
If it has a twist of drama in it, so much the better. I've thought
of calling in the emanation of Yoth, but that needs a child's
blood and I must be careful about the neighbors. The Green
Decay looks promising, but that would be a bit unpleasant for
me as well as for them. I don't like certain sights and smells.

'Dec 10 — *Eureka!* I've got the very thing at last! Revenge
is sweet — and this is the perfect climax! Wheeler, the
sculptor — this is too good! Yes, indeed, that damned sneak
is going to produce a statue that will sell quicker than any
of the things he's been carving these past weeks! A realist,
eh? Well — the new statuary won't lack any realism! I found
the formula in a manuscript insert opposite page 679 of the
Book. From the handwriting I judge it was put there by my
great-grandfather Bareut Picterse Van Kauran — the one who
disappeared from New Paltz in 1839. *Iä! Shub-niggurath!* The
Goat With a Thousand Young!

'To be plain, I've found a way to turn those wretched rats into
stone statues. It's absurdly simple, and really depends more on
plain chemistry than on the Outer Powers. If I can get hold of
the right stuff I can brew a drink that'll pass for home-made
wine, and one swig ought to finish any ordinary being short
of an elephant. What it amounts to is a kind of petrification
infinitely speeded up. Shoots the whole system full of calcium
and barium salts and replaces living cells with mineral matter
so fast that nothing can stop it. It must have been one of
those things my great-grandfather got at the Great Sabbat on
Sugar-Loaf in the Catskills. Queer things used to go on
there. Seems to me I heard of a man in New Paltz — Squire
Hasbrouck — turned to stone or something like that in 1834.
He was an enemy of the Van Kaurans. First thing I must do
is order the five chemicals I need from Albany and Montreal.

Plenty of time later to experiment. When everything is over I'll round up all the statues and sell them as Wheeler's work to pay for his overdue board bill! He always was a realist and an egoist — wouldn't it be natural for him to make a self-portrait in stone, and to use my wife for another model — as indeed he's really been doing for the past fortnight? Trust the dull public not to ask *what quarry* the queer stone came from!

'Dec 25 — Christmas. Peace on earth, and so forth! Those two swine are goggling at each other as if I didn't exist. They must think I'm deaf, dumb, and blind! Well, the barium sulphate and calcium chloride came from Albany last Thursday, and the acids, catalytics, and instruments are due from Montreal any day now. The mills of the gods — and all that! I'll do the work in Allen's Cave near the lower wood lot, and at the same time will be openly making some wine in the cellar here. There ought to be some excuse for offering a new drink — though it won't take much planning to fool those moonstruck nincompoops. The trouble will be to make Rose take wine, for she pretends not to like it. Any experiments that I make on animals will be down at the cave, and nobody ever thinks of going there in winter. I'll do some woodcutting to account for my time away. A small load or two brought in will keep him off the track.

'Jan 20 — It's harder work than I thought. A lot depends on the exact proportions. The stuff came from Montreal, but I had to send again for some better scales and an acetylene lamp. They're getting curious down at the village. Wish the express office weren't in Steenwyck's store. Am trying various mixtures on the sparrows that drink and bathe in the pool in front of the cave — when it's melted. Sometimes it kills them, but sometimes they fly away. Clearly, I've missed some important reaction. I suppose Rose and that upstart are making the most of my absence — but I can afford to let them. There can be no doubt of my success in the end.

'Feb 11 — Have got it at last! Put a fresh lot in the little pool — which is well melted today — and the first bird that drank toppled over as if he were shot. I picked him up a second later, and he was a perfect piece of stone, down to the smallest claws and feather. Not a muscle changed since he was poised for drinking, so he must have died the instant any of the stuff got to his stomach. I didn't expect the petrification to come so soon. But a sparrow is a fair test of the way the thing would act with a large animal. I must get something bigger to try it on, for it must be the right strength when I give it to those swine. I guess Rose's dog Rex will do. I'll take him along the next time and say a timber wolf got him. She thinks a lot of him, and I shan't be sorry to give her something to sniffle over before the big reckoning. I must be careful where I keep this book. Rose sometimes pries around in the queerest places.

'Feb 15 — Getting warm! Tried it on Rex and it worked like a charm with only double the strength. I fixed the rock pool and got him to drink. He seemed to know something queer had hit him, for he bristled and growled, but he was a piece of stone before he could turn his head. The solution ought to have been stronger, and for a human being ought to be very much stronger. I think I'm getting the hang of it now, and am about ready for that cur Wheeler. The stuff seems to be tasteless, but to make sure I'll flavor it with the new wine I'm making up at the house. Wish I were surer about the tastelessness, so I could give it to Rose in water without trying to urge wine on her. I'll get the two separately — Wheeler out here and Rose at home. Have just fixed a strong solution and cleared away all strange objects in front of the cave. Rose whimpered like a puppy when I told her a wolf had got Rex, and Wheeler gurgled a lot of sympathy.

'March 1 — *Iä R'lyeh!* Praise the Lord Tsathoggua! I've got that son of hell at last! Told him I'd found a new ledge of friable limestone down this way, and he trotted after me like the yellow cur he is! I had the wine-flavored stuff in a bottle on my hip, and he was glad of a swig when we got here. Gulped it down without a wink — and dropped in his tracks before you could count three. But he knows I've had my vengeance, for I made a face at him that he couldn't miss. I saw the look of understanding come into his face as he keeled over. In two minutes he was solid stone.

'I dragged him into the cave and put Rex's figure outside again. That bristling dog shape will help to scare people off. It's getting time for the spring hunters, and besides, there a damned "lunger" named Jackson in a cabin over the hill who does a lot of snooping around in the snow. I wouldn't want my laboratory and storeroom to be found just yet! When I got home I told Rose that Wheeler had found a telegram at the village summoning him suddenly home. I don't know whether she believed me or not but it doesn't matter. For form's sake, I packed Wheeler's things and took them down the hill, telling her I was going to ship them after him. I put them in the dry well at the abandoned Rapelye place. Now for Rose!

'March 3 — Can't get Rose to drink any wine. I hope that stuff is tasteless enough to go unnoticed in water. I tried it in tea and coffee, but it forms a precipitate and can't be used that way. If I use it in water I'll have to cut down the dose and trust to a more gradual action. Mr and Mrs Hoog dropped in this noon, and I had hard work keeping the conversation away from Wheeler's departure. It mustn't get around that we say he was called back to New York when everybody at the village knows no telegram came, and that he didn't leave on the bus. Rose is acting damned queer about the whole thing. I'll have to pick a quarrel with her and keep her locked in the attic. The best way is to try to make her drink that doctored wine — and if she does give in, so much the better.

'March 7 — Have started in on Rose. She wouldn't drink the wine so I took a whip to her and drove her up in the attic. She'll never come down alive. I pass her a platter of salty bread and salt meat, and a pail of slightly doctored water, twice a day. The salt food ought to make her drink a lot, and it can't be long before the action sets in. I don't like the way she shouts about Wheeler when I'm at the door. The rest of the time she is absolutely silent.

'March 9 — It's damned peculiar how slow that stuff is in getting hold of Rose. I'll have to make it stronger — probably she'll never taste it with all the salt I've been feeding her. Well, if it doesn't get her there are plenty of other ways to fall back on. But I would like to carry this neat statue plan through! Went to the cave this morning and all is well there. I sometimes hear Rose's steps on the ceiling overhead, and I think they're getting more and more dragging. The stuff is certainly working, but it's too slow. Not strong enough. From now on I'll rapidly stiffen up the dose.

'March 11 — It is very queer. She is still alive and moving. Tuesday night I heard her piggling with a window, so went up and gave her a rawhiding. She acts more sullen than frightened, and her eyes look swollen. But she could never drop to the ground from that height and there's nowhere she could climb down. I have had dreams at night, for her slow, dragging pacing on the floor above gets on my nerves. Sometimes I think she works at the lock of the door.

'March 15 — Still alive, despite all the strengthening of the dose. There's something queer about it. She crawls now, and doesn't pace very often. But the sound of her crawling is horrible. She rattles the windows, too, and fumbles with the door. I shall have to finish her off with the rawhide if this keeps up. I'm getting very sleepy. Wonder if Rose has got on her guard somehow. But she must be drinking the stuff. This sleepiness is abnormal — I think the strain is telling on me. I'm sleepy ...'

(Here the cramped handwriting trails out in a vague scrawl, giving place to a note in a firmer, evidently feminine handwriting, indicative of great emotional tension.)

'March 16 — 4 AM — This is added by Rose C Morris, about to die. Please notify my father, Osborne E Chandler, Route 2, Mountain Top, NY. I have just read what the beast has written. I felt sure he had killed Arthur Wheeler, but did not know how till I read this terrible notebook. Now I know what I escaped. I noticed the water tasted queer, so took none after the first sip. I threw it all out of the window. That one sip has half paralyzed me, but I can still get about. The thirst was terrible, but I ate as little as possible of the salty food and was able to get a little water by setting some old pans and dishes that were up here under places where the roof leaked.

'There were two great rains. I thought he was trying to poison me, though I didn't know what the poison was like. What he has written about himself and me is a lie. We were never happy together and I think I married him only under one of those spells that he was able to lay on people. I guess he hypnotized both my father and me, for he was always hated and feared and suspected of dark dealings with the devil. My father once called him The Devil's Kin, and he was right.

'No one will ever know what I went through as his wife. It was not simply common cruelty — though God knows he was cruel enough, and beat me often with a leather whip. It was more — more than anyone in this age can ever understand. He was a monstrous creature, and practised all sorts of hellish ceremonies handed down by his mother's people. He tried to make me help in the rites — and I don't dare even hint what they were. I would not, so he beat me. It would be blasphemy to tell what he tried to make me do. I can say he was a murderer even then, for I know what he sacrificed one night on Thunder Hill. He was surely the Devil's Kin. I tried four times to run away, but he always caught and beat me. Also, he had a sort of hold over my mind, and even over my father's mind.

'About Arthur Wheeler I have nothing to be ashamed of. We did come to love each other, but only in an honorable way. He gave me the first kind treatment I had ever had since leaving my father's, and meant to help me get out of the clutches of that fiend. He had several talks with my father, and was going to help me get out west. After my divorce we would have been married.

'Ever since that brute locked me in the attic I have planned to get out and finish him. I always kept the poison overnight in case I could escape and find him asleep and give it to him somehow. At first he waked easily when I worked on the lock of the door and tested the conditions at the windows, but later he began to get more tired and sleep sounder. I could always tell by his snoring when he was asleep.

'Tonight he was so fast asleep that I forced the lock without waking him. It was hard work getting downstairs with my partial paralysis, but I did. I found him here with the lamp burning — asleep at the table, where he had been writing in this book. In the corner was the long rawhide whip he had so often beaten me with. I used it to tie him to the chair so he could not move a muscle. I lashed his neck so that I could pour anything down his throat without his resisting.

'He waked up just as I was finishing and I guess he saw right off that he was done for. He shouted frightful things and tried to chant mystical formulas, but I choked him off with a dish towel from the sink. Then I saw this book he had been writing in, and stopped to read it.

The shock was terrible, and I almost fainted four or five times. My mind was not ready for such things. After that I talked to that fiend for two or three hours steady. I told him everything I had wanted to tell him through all the years I had been his slave, and a lot of other things that had to do with what I had read in this awful book.

'He looked almost purple when I was through, and I think he was half delirious. Then I got a funnel from the cupboard and jammed it into his mouth after taking out the gag. He knew what I was going to do, but was helpless. I had brought down the pail of poisoned water, and without a qualm, I poured a good half of it into the funnel.

'It must have been a very strong dose, for almost at once I saw that brute begin to stiffen and turn a dull stony grey. In ten minutes I knew he was solid stone. I could not bear to touch him, but the tin funnel *clinked* horribly when I pulled it out of his mouth. I wish I could have given that Kin of the Devil a more painful, lingering death, but surely this was the most appropriate he could have had.

'There is not much more to say. I am half-paralyzed, and with Arthur murdered I have nothing to live for. I shall make things complete by drinking the rest of the poison after placing this book where it will be found. In a quarter of an hour I shall be a stone statue. My only wish is to be buried beside the statue that was Arthur — when it is found in that cave where the fiend left it. Poor trusting Rex ought to lie at our feet. I do not care what becomes of that stone devil tied in the chair ...'

15 The Menhir (1934)

N DENNETT

The village, which lay in a pocket of the great rolling moorland hills, was approached by a steep, narrow road — a road inclining so deeply that midway the stranger felt he were descending directly upon the spire of the old grey church, which rose like a warning finger from the depth below.

Once down, however, the village spread itself out in the pleasant desultory fashion peculiar to such places. There were the usual high-banked lanes, over which could be glimpsed meadowland of a lush and vivid green, the usual cluster of cool white cottages, with farmhouses at widening distances, the inn, which was also shop and post-office — the ancient and creeper-lined church itself, which seemed to be dreaming gently of things long past and forgotten.

All delightfully rural and peaceful: this, at least, is the impression of the casual visitor, which Mr Melsome received before he knew it to be erroneous. Its peacefulness, he decided, was not so much peace as that strange calm which precedes a storm. There was the same waiting stillness before the first thunder claps break …

Justly annoyed at himself for this fanciful notion, which was so foreign to him, Mr Melsome walked on at a quicker pace.

He had crossed the endless open moorland, where no sound came to his ear but the whispering sibilance of the wind in the dry grasses and the chaffering heather fronds, where no sight met his gaze but the far-off sky-line serrated by faint, mist-crowned tors, or a tall, single-armed finger-post in the near distance, that looked somehow sinister in those boundless solitudes, with the stranger's usual sensation of fascination and awe. It was with a sigh of relief that he had seen the loneliness yield to signs of habitation; but now that he was arrived in the village, he felt by no means happy in it.

To be sure, it was a wet, lowering evening, growing early dark, and a chilly wind blowing, but that did not altogether account for his sense of depression. The few people he had met appeared subdued, with a certain nervousness about them that he could neither understand nor account for. They walked as though beneath a burden, as a man might who was haunted by either dread or remorse ... Mr Melsome stopped suddenly dead.

Yes, that was what it was: it was a haunted village, a village that went in daily fear of something ...

Oppressed by the weight of his own imaginings Mr Melsome tried to shake off his vague alarm. Not a soul seemed to be stirring, the village deserted, hidden away behind fast-shut doors. He began to experience a curious expectancy and to dislike turning a corner, as if he feared to meet with some danger. Rain had fallen heavily some hours before, and earth and sky were drained of colour. He began to dislike the sound of his own footsteps on the muddy road, and trod gingerly, almost on tiptoe. A streak of amber in the west washed with a cold, cheerless light the windows of the cottages, and lay reflected in the wind-ruffled pools.

Presently he came in sight of the cemetery, a dim, melancholy place given up to silence, trees black and shining with wet, and sodden earth.

Then, just outside the iron gates, and in the shadow of a great yew-tree, Mr Melsome saw it for the first time — a curious, lichen-grown pillar-stone. There was something so impressive, so suggestive of hidden power about this grey, rough-hewn Menhir, barring, as it were, the entrance to the cemetery, that with a quickening of the pulses Mr Melsome had a sudden impulse to move forward and look more closely at it, noting with some surprise as he did so that bunches of flowers and other small offerings were laid at the foot.

The Menhir, which had evidently been carved into a rude female figure with closed or downcast eyes, was much defaced by time and weather; but, as if to belie this peaceful aspect, the expression was startingly evil. Her gargoyle face, with flat, sloping forehead, pointed ears, and sharp, narrow jaw, was so brutal as to be three-parts animal — the personification of vice incarnate. She stood there sombrely, malevolently, with curling, sneering lips — silent, unmoving, but strangely suggestive of latent power. By some curious accident in the carving she appeared to be leaning forward, as if to clutch anyone unwary enough to venture near enough to her. Mr Melsome was not usually an imaginative man, nor one particularly timid, but a sensation of acute discomfort grew and strengthened the longer he stood looking at the thing.

He averted his eyes; peered about him nervously: already the semi-luminous light of the sunset had dwindled, and a mist was gathering. In faint, tenuous vapours it writhed and crept among the trees and up the narrow lane, shutting off and closing Mr Melsome in from the outside world. As in a narrow circle he stood there facing the evil, vulpine face of the Menhir. At his back, across the road, an old tumbledown cottage stared at him with blind eyes; before him, beyond the low wall, the tombstones in the sad, neglected-looking churchyard glimmered palely. Raindrops fell with an everlasting patter off the bare branches upon the graves, whose stained and fading flowers looked even more melancholy.

Suddenly, with a strange unhuman cry, a figure rushed from the darkness surrounding the gate, and disappeared down the mist-filled lane bordered by its dripping trees.

This, combined with the dampness, the dreamy graveyard and the malevolent-looking Menhir, finished Mr Melsome. His heart beating uncomfortably fast, he turned and hurried away from the spot with a feeling of ridiculous panic.

He had intended to look in at the church, which, as its new curate, he supposed was a serious omission; but now his chief concern was a good rest and a cup of really hot tea.

He reflected that he had perhaps been a little foolish to accept the curacy without coming to see the place first; but the idea of a country church, after one situated in the slum of a busy city — besides having been advised by his doctor to make a complete change for the good of his health — had so appealed to him that he had eagerly seized the chance that a friend had put in his way.

Seated before the peat fire of The Three Chimneys, presently some of its rosy glow stole over his spirit as it rubified his body. After all, he'd done a pretty good jaunt, and he wasn't so young as he was, he thought: probably he'd feel differently about it all in the morning, and when he had once settled down and become accustomed to the change. He began to scoff at himself and wondered how he could have been intimidated by really nothing at all but his sense of the dull day, the gloom of the churchyard, and the natural weariness attendant on a long walk over the moors ... He commenced to feel quite jovial, and in need of conversation.

The landlord of The Three Chimneys was a fat, stocky man, with a face as round and red as an apple. But his comfortable contour did not agree with his expression, since it was glum and stolid; and when Mr Melsome, in the relief of finding his depression had vanished, inquired almost jocularly about the very peculiar-looking statue-menhir at the entrance of the churchyard, mine host became, if anything, more morose and disinclined to talk than before.

'I don't know what tes, sir; tes bin 'ere so long, like,' he answered at last, unwillingly, when he could no longer ignore Mr Melsome's questions.

'Then perhaps you can tell me why fruit and flowers are presented to it; surely that is a very heathenish thing to do?'

Either the mild rebuke in Mr Melsome's voice, or the slightly scandalized look in the pale-blue eyes behind the large spectacles, stung the man into speech, for he answered quite heatedly:

'Mebbe tes; but Law' bless 'ee, if you was so scared o' the wicked oa' toad as us be, you would too. They flowers and such don't do no harm, if en don't do no gude. The curse o' the village her be, for certain sure,' he added, almost under his breath.

Mr Melsome, considerably intrigued, hastened to put more

queries, but the man was not to be drawn. Indeed, he appeared to regret that he had said as much as he had, and soon after disappeared through a doorway into an inner room, while Mr Melsome sat sipping his tea slowly and rather thoughtfully.

On the landlord presently re-entering the room, he asked: 'Has the cottage opposite the main gate of the churchyard been empty for long? I shall be coming to live here shortly; I'm Mr Melsome, the new curate —'

'Aw, be you, sir?' said the man, taken by surprise. 'Well, I be mortal pleased to see 'ee, sir; but don't 'ee go for to live in thicky cottage, whatever 'ee do. Why, tes jus' opposite the graveyard, and *faces the Grey Gammer*!' His voice expressed the horror he felt.

'But it looks such a picturesque old place, though certainly rather neglected. Besides, what harm could the Grey Gammer, as you call it, do me?'

The man hesitated.

'I shouldn't like to say, sir; but round these yur parts nobody'll a-live in thicky cottage; and wouldn't for awl the money in the world. Last one as lived there, her went mad, and one afore that, he killed hisself, sir. So tes bin left empty ever since.'

Really, thought Mr Melsome, this ignorant superstition should be stamped out. It was a disgrace in a civilised country, and above all in the present year of grace 1934.

He accordingly spoke a little sharply: 'Nonsense, nonsense! Doesn't Mr Vince, the vicar, tell you so?'

'Aw, he says so,' said the landlord heavily, 'but he don't sound as if 'ee meant it. Tidden as if 'ee didn't know, the same as us do.'

'And does he countenance all this flower and fruit business, these offerings, as if it were an image of worship?' persisted Mr Melsome.

'Not worship; tidden worship at awl, sir; jus' to keep en in gude humour, so en won't plague us, see? Mr Vince, he tried to stop us when he first comed, but bless 'ee, 'twarn't no manner o' use. And now he jus' lets 'em stay: tes safer, like.'

'But what does the Grey Gammer do, that you must so placate

her?' asked Mr Melsome, feeling as if he had lost himself in a foreign country.

The man's face closed, became secretive.

'Tes best not to say, sir,' he said; but after some pressing, vouchsafed reluctantly that at every funeral the corpse must be carried round her three times before entering the churchyard, or those who carried it would die within the year.

It had happened that very week, too; for either forgetting, or scorning to follow the procedure, the pall-bearers had taken the coffin straight away in. 'But,' said the landlord, sinking his voice to a mere whisper, 'but the very next day they was all dead — yes, the four ov 'em' — two, it appeared, from a mysterious accident, when they were found apparently crushed to death; one from the effects of some fright, that left on his face a look of fear and loathing; and the other who, grazing his thumb on the Menhir as he brushed by, developed lockjaw and died in agony.

Nor was that all, went on the landlord, his tongue fairly unlocked now he had once began, like a stream in spate. There was an old rhyme in the district, which ran:

'From the Shade and the ravening Ghoul,
Save, O Lord, my living soul.'

For the Gammer of the churchyard was reputed to be jealous of the living and sought to draw them into her clutch, as she did the dead in the cemetery.

'Did 'ee see anywheres about a lad wi' an awful face? A year ago he was the brightest lad o' the village, then one night the Ghoul got en; and now he'm for ever hanging about the Grey Gammer as if he'm looking for sommat he can't find — and never will no more. I tell 'ee, tes more'n your life's worth to go past en at night.' And the burly landlord shuddered and crossed his fingers.

Feeling comfortable and warm in the cosy black-raftered parlour, Mr Melsome could afford to smile at the childishness of it all. These country people were astonishing sometimes; he supposed the remoteness from modernizing influences was responsible; and went to bed privately vowing to have a quiet word with the vicar on the subject.

The next morning, getting up to brilliant sunshine, birds singing, and the air full of the promise of spring, Mr Melsome was soon striding happily along in the direction of the vicarage. He stared boldly at the Gammer of the Churchyard, who gazed stonily and malevolently in front of her, and who had somehow lost some of her terror in the bright morning light; then, after wandering into the church, which was very small and old, the air vitiated by damp walls and stale incense, he proceeded to call on Mr Vince. After the preliminaries of welcome and so forth had been finished with, Mr Melsome presently broached the subject of his night's meditations.

Mr Vince, however, proved less amenable to reason than he had expected.

'My dear Melsome,' he said, with a shrug, 'superstition is bred in their very bones. A good number of years ago the Menhir was an idol, and used to have human sacrifices presented to it. They believe it still hungers for them; hence the flowers and fruit and so on, in the hope of assuaging its terrible appetite. It is hopeless to try to stop it. The only way to root it out would be to rid the village of the monolith, and that, my friend — I frankly admit it — would take a braver man that I. It is a strange, weird thing. Live here a time, and discover it for yourself,' he added, on perceiving the other's look of mingled disgust and scepticism; 'live here a while, and discover it for yourself — as I have.' And the vicar's face on a sudden wore, to the further disconcerting of Mr Melsome, a look of plain, unmistakable fear.

A week later found the new curate, with the obstinacy of a man fighting against his own instincts, installed in the old cottage facing the churchyard. He'd show 'em he was made of sterner stuff than to be scared of an old image! Pack of frightened Isaacs, so they were, to believe in such stuff and nonsense.

Tryphena, his sister, heartily supported him in this opinion. She was one of those elderly English virgins whose uprightness of mind corresponds with a back as straight as a ramrod. Not possessing an ounce of imagination or nerves of any sort, the good lady was not unduly troubled by dear Edwin's choice of abode, and paid less attention to the tales regarding the Grey Gammer than she would have upon hearing that Patch, the dog, had been involved in a dog-fight.

A further week went by, during which Mr Melsome became quite settled down in the village, with nothing untoward happening to cause him to regret his foolhardiness. Then the test came, when he had either to stand by his opinions or own himself as weak as the rest of them. He had proclaimed loudly and widely during this short period that he would stand for none of their heathenish practices; and condemned wholesale their ridiculous fear of the Menhir, so that when he had to take the funeral of a small child who had recently died, he emphatically forbade the thrice-repeated circumambulation of the corpse before entering the graveyard. When at the gate the bearers obstinately refused to enter without so doing, he had perforce been obliged to take the small coffin from them and carry it in himself before the Service could proceed. Even then the men could scarcely be induced to go on, and remained throughout uneasy and apprehensive; and had at length departed, throwing scared looks behind them.

Mr Melsome had forgotten all about the affair when, about nine o'clock that evening, he thought he would go for a short stroll with the dog. No sooner had he shut the front-door behind him, however, and stepped out into the lane, than, with a whine, his hair bristling, Patch bolted madly down the road, his tail between his legs. And at the same instant, as he took a step or two forward, Mr Melsome became aware of a hostile and sinister presence, an aura of evil that gradually enveloped him, radiating from the strange pillar-stone where it stood half lost in the shadow of the great tree. There seemed also a kind of mist or cloud writhing about it, that stretched out and reached towards him with searching tentacles ...

All at once real, naked fear seized him as he stood there in the silence and darkness, the yew-trees in the churchyard beyond seeming unusually impenetrable and secret, the monuments unusually white and ghostly. It was due only to his strength of will that he forced himself on towards the gate.

A waning moon, gliding from behind troubled clouds, suddenly spilled a flood of cold and frozen moonlight on the earth below.

He sprang back with a startled exclamation. The expression of the Menhir, always evil, was now malign and unspeakably foul under the influence of night. The eyes were wide open, the lips drawn back in a grinning snarl, the head thrust forward ... the face of a fiend, rapacious, terrifying.

Dark, motionless, she yet gave an impression of dormant activity; a brooding and sinister quiet that might at any moment leap forth to destroy and devour ... With the shades of night — so different from her peaceful aspect by day — she appeared to be wide awake, so that she looked alive ... Almighty powers, she WAS alive! For one horrible, palpitating second Mr Melsome thought she was going to spring upon him ... With a hoarse cry, in unconditional panic, he tore across the road and into the house, locking and bolting the door after him.

Considerably ashamed of this exhibition, he attempted to explain it away by deciding it was merely a sudden attack of nerves; and gave himself a severe lecture.

A grey, rough-hewn statue, lichen-coated and scarred by time and weather; and yet, by the power of suggestion and mental association, it had become a thing of superstitious fear, and terrorized a whole village. Puerile, ridiculous nonsense, and he and everyone else ought to be thoroughly ashamed of themselves.

Notwithstanding this sensible attitude, Mr Melsome could not rid himself of his nameless apprehension, for now, to his annoyance, he discovered in himself a decided reluctance to pass the Menhir at night, and took to leaving and entering the house by the back-door. He also used this roundabout way — shamefacedly and with much self-scorn — to go to and from the church, which method was quickly noticed by the villagers with general whispering and nudging.

'Ha-ha, Melsome! the Grey Gammer getting too much for you already?' twitted the vicar, with a certain amount of satisfaction, for it is never pleasant to have to own oneself as cowardly as one's flock.

Mr Melsome denied it indignantly; and to prove how very far from the truth the vicar's accusation was, the very next night he walked boldly out of the cottage by the front door, but clutching Patch, it must be admitted, by the collar with a grip unconsciously tight.

No sooner was he within ten yards of the thing, however, than again that wave of horror flowed out to him, and with a yelp, Patch burst frantically from the restraining hold, leaving the collar in his master's hand.

His heart thumping painfully, Mr Melsome's courage failed him; he fled as ignominiously as upon the first occasion. And now he knew it was no use continuing the unequal struggle. He was afraid, definitely afraid, of the Grey Gammer, and might as well own it. And owning it, he became possessed by a nervous dread that he could not overcome.

Even when he sat warm and comfortable before the fire, the curtains drawn against the windows and the night without, he felt her, saw her there in the darkness by the churchyard gate, obscene and hideous; felt it was useless to turn his back; even through the curtains he was certain she was aware of his regard ... was looking at him with evil, watching eyes ... He grew pale and strained.

'Why don't you say straight out that you've allowed the thing to get on your nerves, Edwin?' said Miss Tryphena acidly, when at last, unable to bear sitting in the front room any longer, he suggested occupying one to the rear of the house.

Pathetically he strove to protect his dignity. 'Nothing of the sort, Tryphena; nothing of the sort. You know quite well the light is bad here; you've complained of it yourself.'

'Humph! have it your own way, then,' she retorted, and the change was soon after made, for even she, which she would not have acknowledged for any money in the world, had come to loathe the sight of the evil-looking Menhir across the way.

Here, at least, Mr Melsome thought he was safe. And for a night or two he did find some relief. Then one evening there came a soft, insistent pressure that drove him to his feet ... drew him with irresistible force out of the shelter and security of the house into the hostile darkness without. Like a man mesmerized, like a sleep-walker, Mr Melsome stepped out into the lane, went slowly forward ...

Dark, motionless, compelling, the Gammer crouched, waiting in the shadow of the great yew ... Suddenly, urged forward by a power outside his control, Mr Melsome ran forward and flung himself at her feet ... Round his head swirled the malodorous mist; he knew thoughts and desires he had formerly thought of with disgust and loathing; he quailed and blenched beneath an intolerable weight of evil. Helpless, he stared up at the bestial face above him — cruel, lowering, vampire-like, with eyes set slit-wise, her teeth bared ... teeth sharp and pointed ... a creature hailing only from some Bourg of Night. The foul and evil personality, bound and impotent during the hours of daylight, was now an active, unclean force ... He felt his soul being drawn from his body, as if some fearful thing were sucking and pulling it forth ... A faintness stole over him; his heart began to beat slower and slower ...

Faintly, as from an infinite distance, he heard the sound of a dog's howling — Patch, who with nose pointed to the evening sky, was pouring out his instinctive defiance and terror of death. Gradually, and with infinite pain, his soul drew back, returned little by little; revitalized his body. Weak, trembling, Patch's howls sounding like trumps of doom in the still air, Mr Melsome dragged himself away and fell senseless on the doorstep of the cottage ...

Like a shadow of himself he went about his daily duties. His changed appearance was commented upon by the villagers with ominous shakes of the head, and the scared view that the Grey Gammer had marked him for her own ... A man haunted, his eyes sunk in the greyish pallor of his face, Mr Melsome seemed daily to be slipping out of life — a fact which was duly observed with half-fascinated, half-morbid curiosity and lively fear.

Again that soft, compelling force reached him where he sat before the fire one night, vainly trying to read and forget. And he knew, with fearful certitude, that did he obey this time, he were a dead man ...

And now there began a hideous struggle. Impotently, despairingly, Mr Melsome fought; for an overwhelming influence forced him to his feet, drove him out into the passage towards the door ... Outside, in saturnine triumph, the Gammer smiled and smiled ... Mr Melsome, sobbing, fell on his knees, grasping the handle, fighting desperately not to open the door, to go out to his destruction in the pitchy darkness ...

How long this tussle continued he did not know; but presently he felt the devouring clutch of the thing weaken, the insistent demand lessen; and, bathed in sweat, and shivering in every limb as from a fever, he rolled over on the floor, tears of relief running down his face. As strength returned he became filled with a great thankfulness and exultation; he rose to his full height, crying aloud: 'I've conquered, I've conquered! Oh, merciful Heaven, I'm saved — saved!' And went to bed, and slept the first real sleep he had had for weeks. Rising the next morning, the colour had returned to his cheeks, the light to his eyes. He felt, and was, a new man.

Confident, wreathed in smiles, he bustled about like a busy and energetic sparrow. Coming back from the church, where he had been preparing the Sunday's service, instead of taking the long way round, as he did usually to avoid the Gammer of the Churchyard, he came buoyantly down the long yew-tree-edged path, careless and carefree.

This mood did not desert him even when he stood in front of her, with a new spirit of criticism and a new wonder that it could have been actually himself who had knelt there in subjection, half-crazed with terror; for even upon this Sunday morning the Menhir looked, in the shade of the yew-tree, dark, sinister, monstrous, full of an evil power.

With a sudden spasm of hatred, of contempt, Mr Melsome struck her across the face.

'Do your damnedest, you fiend! You shan't get me a third time ... do you hear? I defy you utterly and completely!'

He raised his hand to give her a final blow when, out of a clear sky, there came a sudden and solitary growl of thunder.

With a face out of which all colour had been startled, Mr Melsome, with a scared look at the seemingly quiet grey figure, turned and ran, rather than walked, down the sun-splashed lane, seeing, in place of the brightness before him, only a black and noisome pit.

Followed a period of fear worse than any he had previously passed. His days were a series of creeping terror; he waited, sick and shivering, for he knew not what.

And then, down from the hills that towered far above the hamlet, on every side descended a storm that had never before been known; the air became a roar, the wind a devastating fury. It tore and blustered and rioted, rushed upon the houses and tore the roofs away, felled trees and wrought incalculable mischief. Then there came upon the valley as deep a calm; and presently people reported with awe that a mist, like a gigantic spider's web, was gathering round the Grey Gammer, which with every hour spread, until it became a thick, evil-smelling vapour that never lifted, so that lights had to be kept continually burning, and people groped their way about as best they could.

Soon, terrified whispers went abroad that the Grey Gammer was seeking vengeance ... A number of violent deaths occurred, the result of strange and inexplicable accidents. By a stranger coincidence, all those who died suddenly and horribly bore on their features a look of fear and loathing, while their bodies appeared to have been crushed by some heavy weight ...

Shudderingly, Mr Melsome knew he was the cause of it; knew that it was through him, and for him, this horror had descended upon the village ... He began to be haunted by a dreadful sound as of something that followed him, keeping pace with him like a dog; something that loomed up in the mist huge and dark, and then dropped back again as he leapt aside, but always with him ... something, he knew, would get him sooner or later ...

He could neither rest nor eat, and reduced Miss Tryphena
— who deplored the strange fatalities, and grumbled about the
everlasting mist that was so depressing — to as near distraction
as that level-headed spinster could go.

'For mercy's sake take a tonic, Edwin; you're getting as
nervous as a cat!' she exclaimed irritably, when, upon accidently
dropping a lump of coal, he sprang out of his chair, with his
eyes staring out of his head and his hands clutching his hair.

Still this maddening sound followed him, sometimes nearer,
sometimes further: a slow, lugubrious dragging, as if something
heavy were slurring over the ground ... Twice that day it had
been almost on his heels, but that he had saved himself in the
nick of time; once by rushing into a nearby cottage, and once
by climbing a tree. He had now got into such a state that he
was afraid to set his foot out of doors at all, and sat huddled
over the fire in the back room, starting at every sound and
disliking to be left.

Miss Tryphena, who was by now thoroughly alarmed for her
brother's reason — which characteristically she hid under a
hard, bright manner — finally hectored him into bestirring
himself enough to do a little shopping for her. The walk, she
declared, would do him infinitely more good than moping
over the fire.

Wearily Mr Melsome obeyed her, more than ashamed of
his cowardice; and trying to persuade himself that the whole
thing was due simply to imagination. His purchases made, he
returned, feeling, in spite of the choking mist, considerably
brighter and more hopeful, since not once had he heard that
terrible dragging sound behind him.

And then he made a shocking discovery: mistaking his way
in the obscurity, he had come through the churchyard, and *the
Grey Gammer was not there in her usual place.*

Stark, unreasoning terror seized him; his heart surged up
in his throat, beat suffocatingly. It was, then, no imagination;
no product of tired nerves. The Ghoul *was* after him; and
inevitably, sooner or later, she would catch him and crush him
to pulp ...

He staggered into the house, sat down limply. He was doomed, he knew it; had known it from the beginning.

Miss Tryphena bustled in soon after. Taking in his air of collapse, but appearing not to, she began to talk in a brisk, matter-of-fact voice: 'Oh, so you're back, Edwin. I suppose the mist shows no sign of lifting; extraordinary, isn't it, how it hangs about ...'

She clucked her teeth in annoyance upon taking out of the basket a bundle of flowers.

'Why did you get *white* ones, Edwin? I distinctly said daffodils,' she said.

Mr Melsome looked up from his brooding survey of the fire.

'I did get daffodils. Let me look,' he said, rousing himself sufficiently to get up from his chair.

He started back, his face blanching.

'A sign!' he muttered. 'A sign; it won't be long now ...'

'What are you talking about?' asked Miss Tryphena sharply, alarmed by his white face and wild expression.

'They are asphodels, Tryphena; asphodels, that grow in the meadows of the dead ...'

And with that, he reeled, and fell heavily upon the floor.

But now, as his hope was gone, his courage came back. True, it was the courage of despair; but now he took risks, where formerly he had fled, pale and quaking; took delight in seeing how long and how far he could outwit the devilish thing that sought him. Often through the mist he caught sight of the evil, vulpine face, with its glittering, slanting eyes and cruel jaw, and chuckled to himself with a glee that had more than a hint of hysteria in it.

The death of the burly landlord of The Three Chimneys pulled him up with a jerk. He, too, had been found terribly crushed, with that look of horror frozen on his features ... Mr Melsome could not but feel that here was another tragedy that should be laid at his door; for in her merciless, juggernaut-like pursuit of him, the fiend that was the Grey Gammer took everything in her path.

Thinking deeply, he was walking down a steep-banked cart-road, which sloped sharply uphill behind him, the mist completely hiding everything in a thick woolly blanket, when he came to a sudden halt, rooted to the spot by a sense of impending danger. That waiting was more awful than anything that had gone before. He heard Doom approaching him — a heavy, muffled, slurring sound that made his heart stand still. Then, dimly outlined in the murk, there loomed up before him a clutching, malignant Shape, with eyes that pierced ... He gave one look, shrieked, and fled into the writhing mist.

Unknown to himself, a strange, high scream came from his lips; he could neither see where he was going, nor run, for a queer sensation about his feet, as if something were clinging around them and impeding his progress.

Stumbling, panting, sobbing for breath, he rushed on; up that interminable hill, wild with fear and the awful expectation of being overtaken at any moment ... He could hear the lugubrious, muffle-footed sound close behind him; could visualize the hideous, devilish face, alight with a fearful greed; but dared not turn his head. He knew that if he stumbled his fate was sealed ... It was a flight that was the quintessence of nightmare.

Oh, the mist that swirled endlessly about him, blinded his eyes, seemed so heavy he could scarcely breathe! ... He thrust frantic hands out in an effort to push it from him, but soundlessly it evaded him, slipped in again, closed over his head like intangible water ...

He must run. He must go on, go on ... go on! ... Quicker, quicker yet, or *that thing* would clutch him and he would be done for ... Uncanny, to go running on like this in the silence and mist — silence, that was, except for that remorseless, dragging sound behind him.

And now the moon appeared above and glimmered through — a pale, tissue-paper moon ... the ghost of a moon, to add to the weirdness.

Exhausted — he was almost exhausted; his aching legs refused to hurry, his throat was dry and parched.

Ah-a-h! Ah-h! thank God, he was up the hill, and now he was running along the level road. Round and round curved the lane like a complicated letter 'S'; then a wall appeared, the vague outline of the church ... through the lich-gate, and into the graveyard ... He tried to whip his flagging strength into making a final sprint, for home was in sight — just there — beyond the — iron — gates — quite near — now. Safe, he would be safe — there. He could see — the chimneys — almost —

Behind him, close behind him, almost on him now, was the Shape in the Darkness, of which he could see only the piercing eyes ... The malinfluence that radiated from it seemed stronger, the tugging sensation overwhelming, so that every step he took forward was a terrible struggle ... sometimes he faltered and fell back a pace, then, released, plunged on again, as a mouse caught by a cat is let go, only to be captured and drawn back by the enemy it cannot escape ...

He took one quick look behind him, shrieked, and fled onward once more, past the grove-like walks, the silent graves ... Then, beside one half-dug, lay a mattock, thrown down by the sexton and forgotten.

He had just time to seize it and run for the gate, when, merciful Heaven, the Gammer was upon him! — a devouring, shadowy form, exuding venom and malevolence.

Crying out wildly, frenziedly, Mr Melsome raised his weapon in a last desperate effort ... faced the advancing Terror, seeing vaguely only a dreadful, rapacious face ...

There struck him like a wave between the shoulders an engulfing shadow — a blackness, whose suction power was of some overpowering current of air blowing up from an infernal terminus ...

The next morning, which dawned clear and sunny, a farm-hand going to work discovered, at the foot of the Grey Gammer, a mattock and a pair of spectacles, but of Mr Melsome himself there was no trace.

Nor was there any found; he appeared to have vanished off the face of the earth. There were many conjectures as to his possible fate; the newspapers holding the view that, while wandering over the moor in the thick mist, the unfortunate man must have either fallen over one of the many precipices or become caught in a bog. The villagers, themselves, however, have a different opinion, which is not spoken of except with bated breath.

The few strangers who come to the isolated village, when told the tale of the curate's brief stay among them, murmur politely, and pass on. They, too, stop and look with repugnance at the strange Menhir at the churchyard gate, which somehow now has the appearance of licking its lips, as some beast might over the carcase of its victim. A further thing they notice with some perplexity is the curious-looking lump on its head, which could almost be taken for headgear of some kind—and in shape is not unlike a clergyman's hat …

16 The Living Stone (1939)

E R PUNSHON

'Life sleeps in the stone, dreams in the plant, wakens in the animal.'
— Ancient Hindu saying

1

There was a general giggle.

The quaint little gentleman from London, beaming on them through his enormous horn-rimmed glasses, might be as learned as learned professors must always be, but fancy asking a question like that when the name of their little inn, The Missing Men, was the general jest all through this lonely Cornish district. Why, whenever any of the local inhabitants was missing from his own hearthside, here in the comfortable warm bar of The Missing Men was the place to seek and generally to find. One or two of those present laboriously explained the point of the pleasantry, and the little professor listened gravely.

'I see,' he said.

It was the chair of comparative religion at the Great Southern University that he held, and though few there knew what comparative religion was, and probably none had ever heard of his great work on Human Sacrifice in which was traced the history of that dark, evil rite from early days — the days of Abraham and Isaac — down to the faint traces of it still surviving, as when the small boy in city streets asks for a penny for the guy he means presently to offer up in fire, or, more sinister, in the offering of the youth of the nation on the sacrificial altar of that new god, the State, yet all knew what awe and reverence are a professor's due. For a professor is a person of strange knowledge, and therefore of strange powers, since knowledge is always power.

But now they felt more at their ease, now that he had shown he shared their common humanity by asking so simple a question and needing to have so simple a pleasantry explained to him. The professor took the giggling in good part. He wondered how long the name had been in use. No one knew. Most thought name and inn were co-existent.

'I asked,' explained the professor, 'because I noticed on the map there's a lane near here that seems to be called Missing Lane.'

The jesting suddenly ceased, as abruptly as though those fatal words: 'Time, gentlemen, time,' had boomed out suddenly from behind the bar.

'I was wondering,' the professor explained, 'whether the inn took its name from the lane, or the lane from the inn.'

No one seemed to know. No one seemed to care. The conversation showed a tendency to revert to football pools, an engrossing if limited topic. The professor did not seem interested in football pools. He had arrived by car that afternoon from London, a late survival of the touring season since now it was dark and chilly November when motorist and hiker alike seek their repose. He took an opportunity of a pause, while all were wrapped in silent contemplation of the curious fact that others habitually won enormous prizes in the pools, but none of them ever did, to remark:

'I couldn't make out from the map where that lane led.'

'Well, it doesn't rightly lead nowheres in particular,' explained the landlord.

'Well, now, that's odd,' murmured the professor. 'If it goes nowhere, why is it at all?'

No one seemed to know that either. It was just there. It had always been there. That was all. Went to the top of the hill, and, so to say, got lost there.

'Missing Lane, in fact,' mused the professor. 'Perhaps how it got its name. I suppose, if it goes nowhere, it's not often used?'

It began to appear that the lane was in fact very seldom used. Continued over the hill it would have provided a short and convenient way to the nearest market town. Only, somehow, no one seemed ever to have thought of that. Men working in the fields by which it ran used it sometimes, and, in the autumn, blackberrying parties, since the summit of the hill, where finally the lane lost itself, was famous for blackberries. But the blackberry pickers went always in parties, it seemed, and never stayed late.

'Not if they've sense, they don't,' said an old man who hitherto had hardly spoken. 'And if they do, maybe it's them that's missing or some of 'em.'

'Now grandpa,' interposed the landlord warningly.

'Thirty years ago,' said the old man, 'and never none to tell to this day what became of Polly Hill.'

'Wasn't there something in the paper the other day about a young woman who had disappeared from somewhere about here?' asked the professor.

'That would be Aggie, little Aggie Polton,' said someone else.

'Good-looking piece,' said the landlord. 'Lordy, when girls take themselves off, they have their own reasons. Flighty, that was Aggie.'

It appeared that Aggie had had something of a reputation. Most evenings, the tale went, she had a 'date' with one or other of the young men of the neighbourhood. On one occasion, a little time previously, there had been one of these 'dates' with the son of the local butcher. He had not been able to keep it. His mother had had suspicions, and naturally looked higher than poor little Aggie for her son, no matter how fascinating Aggie's blue eyes and curls might be. The general opinion was that Aggie had 'taken the huff', had been afraid of being laughed at, and had gone off to London, as she had often spoken of doing, in order to become one of those fascinating young ladies known as Nippies whose portraits in the papers had aroused her mingled admiration and envy.

Only it was true no trace of her in London had as yet been found.

'No great loss, a girl like her, setting all the lads at odds,' said someone else. 'But I reckon Mr Phelps up at Tor Farm would give a deal to know what's become of Beauty of Bolton Three.'

'What's that?' asked the professor.

He was told that Beauty of Bolton Three was a prize bull, worth some two or three hundred pounds, perfect in every way, and so tame and peaceable that it was allowed to graze out in the fields without any special precautions being taken. It was always brought in at night, but the other evening, when a farm lad went to fetch it as usual, though at a later hour than was customary, it wasn't there. No sign of it. Nothing to show what had happened to it.

'Curious,' said the professor. 'Curious, too, about Polly Hill thirty years ago. Curious again that in the Annual Register of sixty years back there's mention of a valuable stallion that vanished in this neighbourhood. Supposed to have been stolen by the groom, as he vanished himself next day.'

'That's sixty years gone,' said the landlord doubtfully. 'I wasn't born then,' and he had the air of suggesting that what happened before he was born really didn't matter very much.

'Lot of interesting reading in the Annual Register,' observed the professor, 'and odd how often there is a mention of this neighbourhood at intervals of thirty years. Was Mr Phelps's bull in the field near the Hunting Stone? That stands at the top of Missing Lane, doesn't it?'

'That's right,' said the landlord, somewhat surprised at this display of local knowledge; 'but there's no mystery about the bull being missing. Worth a mort of money. 'Ticed away and hidden somewhere till he can be smuggled off to foreign parts.'

'Not so easy to 'tice away,' interposed the old man who had spoken of the missing Polly Hill of long ago, 'and someone got hurt, too, for there was blood on the Hunting Stone. I seen it myself and didn't stop to look for long, neither.'

'Why is it called the Hunting Stone?' asked the professor.

The landlord said he supposed it had always been called that. The professor asked if the stains supposed to be blood

seen on the base of the Hunting Stone had been examined
or analysed. No one had thought of having that done. There
seemed no reason. It was mentioned that the only trace of the
recently vanished Aggie, the girl with the fondness for making
'dates' and the ambition some day to become a Nippy, had been
her handbag found near this same Hunting Stone. Probably
her 'date' with the youthful heir of the local butcher had been
made for the foot of Missing Lane. When he failed to keep
it, she might well have wandered up the lane rather than go
straight home, but what had happened to her after that was
entirely a matter for conjecture.

The door opened and an elderly woman looked in.

'Our Tim here?' she asked. 'He's not been home.'

No one had seen her Tim and she went away grumblingly.
The landlord winked at the professor.

'Out after rabbits,' he said, 'that's where her Tim is, and he'll
be copped some day. But there's a mort of them up by that
there Hunting Stone.'

The old man in the corner got up to go. In the doorway he
turned: 'Tim's a fool if he goes after rabbits there,' he said, 'for
if there's rabbits there, there's more than rabbits, too.'

He went out, and the landlord laughed, though a trifle
uneasily.

'To hear him talk,' he said, 'there might be something queer
about that there lump of granite what's been standing up on
the hill ever since the Flood, so to say.'

'I think I'll have a look at it myself,' observed the professor,
'but not tonight.'

'No, I wouldn't tonight,' agreed the landlord.

2

It was in fact high noon before the professor next day walked
slowly and warily up the Missing Lane that was hardly a lane
at all but rather a rough track with fields on one side — the
south — and the bare slope of the hill on the other, the north.
Where the cultivated land ceased and the ground grew rough

and bare with scattered blackberry bushes at intervals and many rabbit holes all around, stood the Hunting Stone, a huge upright oblong block of granite, standing on a sort of rough base. It was some eight or nine feet high and must have weighed many tons. On its face were carved signs that once may have been letters or symbols of some kind but that the wind and the rain of innumerable years had worn in part away. Reared by who could tell what strange distant tribe of men in what strange dawn of humanity, or by what pain or sacrifice in dragging that enormous weight from the distant quarry where it had been carved, all through the slow centuries it had stood on this bare hillside. Now at its base there sat a burly man in plus fours, smoking a pipe, and the professor nodded a greeting.

'Nice morning, chief inspector,' he said, 'but I wouldn't sit there if I were you.'

Chief Inspector Harris of Scotland Yard looked surprised, but got up all the same, for his was a disciplined mind and for all professors he had a proper respect.

'Why not?' he asked. 'It's firm enough. I thought I felt a tremor when I sat down, but it won't fall over just yet.'

The professor said: 'Know anything about a local lad called Tim something?'

'Reported missing,' said the chief inspector. 'You heard about that?'

'Yes,' said the professor.

'Maybe he had something to do with the Beauty of Bolton Three case,' observed the inspector musingly, 'but it's not so likely a smart, lively young girl like this Aggie Polton would mix up with cattle thieving.'

'No,' said the professor.

'Well, there you are,' said the chief inspector.

'Noticed anything about here?' asked the professor.

'Not a thing, except —' and he pointed to a strange, plainly marked trail on the ground as though something immensely heavy had passed that way. 'Looks like a steam roller has been by,' he remarked, 'only there can't have been, can there?'

'No,' said the professor. 'Noticed that?'

He pointed to a reddish-brown stain on the stone base just where the chief inspector had been sitting. The chief inspector shook his head. 'What is it?' he asked.

'I don't know,' said the professor, 'but I think it might be blood.'

He walked away a little distance and presently paused where the rabbit holes seemed most numerous in a low bank at a little distance. It was a fragment of a net he had picked up and he came back carrying it in his hand.

'Useful for snaring rabbits?' he suggested.

'Might be,' agreed the chief inspector. 'Why?'

'In the pub they seemed to think Tim was very likely out after rabbits,' the professor explained.

'Well then,' said the chief inspector. 'Don't think someone's kidnapped him, do you?'

'Not kidnapped, no,' said the professor.

The chief inspector strolled away and seated himself again on the base of the Hunting Stone. He got up hurriedly. He said: 'Gosh! I believe you're right.'

'What's that?' asked the professor, turning sharply.

'I thought I felt the thing move,' the chief inspector answered. 'When I sat down, I mean. A sort of movement, a tremor. As if it might topple over.' He put his hand against the stone and pushed. 'Seems firm enough,' he said.

The professor was looking at the sky. 'High noon,' he said. 'Just as well. No, I don't think there's any chance of its toppling over.'

'Well, then,' said the chief inspector. He looked very worried and a trifle pale. He said: 'I'll swear I felt — something.' After a pause, during which the professor was silent, he added: 'If I didn't know I hadn't, I should think I had been drinking.'

'I think we'll go, shall we?' said the professor.

The chief inspector agreed, somewhat hurriedly. He was looking back over his shoulder as they walked away. He said: 'It must be the mist; it gives the thing a sort of swaying sort of look, sort of to and fro, if you know what I mean.'

'There isn't any mist,' said the professor.

He was walking very quickly. At times he almost ran.

The chief inspector said: 'What's the hurry?'

'I don't know,' answered the professor. He added presently: 'I think where you were sitting is where the victims were offered when that was a stone of sacrifice.'

'Ugh,' said the chief inspector. 'Enough to make anyone a bit jittery if they knew that.'

'Or even if they didn't,' said the professor. When they had come to the bottom of the lane, he said: 'I want you to get me a bullock, white, without spot or blemish.'

'Eh?' said the chief inspector. 'What's that?'

The professor explained. The chief inspector said firmly: 'That's plumb crazy.'

'Yes, I know,' said the professor.

'If it hadn't been for what I felt up there ...' said the chief inspector.

'White from head to tail, without spot or blemish,' the professor repeated.

'Right-oh,' said the chief inspector. 'It's a screwy business,' he said. 'I feel I want to report myself off my head.'

'You mean you want to report me,' said the professor grimly. 'I know. Only what happened to little Aggie Polton? Where is she? What's become of Mr Phelps's prize bull? Where's Tim who went up there snaring rabbits, and now it seems he isn't anywhere? And why almost every thirty years does the Annual Register report some mysterious disappearance in this district?'

'Oh, have it your own way,' said the chief inspector angrily. 'I don't believe a word of it, and what's more, I don't know where to get a what-is-it white bullock without spot or blemish! We aren't cattle-dealers at the Yard.'

The professor gave him an address.

'Friend of mine,' he said. 'Big noise in the farming way. Ring him up. I asked him to see what he could do.'

The chief inspector went away to find a telephone. It was dusk when there arrived a lorry containing a fine young bullock, its hide snowy white, no spot or blemish on it from head to tail.

The professor looked it over carefully and seemed satisfied. Later on, as it drew towards midnight, by the light of the moon could have been seen the unusual sight of a learned professor and a chief inspector of Scotland Yard solemnly driving a snow-white ox up a steep and narrow lane.

It was a perfect night. The moonlight lay on the land like a faint and silvery sea, lending to all things a distant, wan enchantment. Not a breath of wind stirred. Not a living creature was abroad. It might have been a land from which all life had fled, and through it there passed slowly that small and strange procession — the snow-white bullock and the two men behind.

'Keep well back,' the professor whispered.

The chief inspector needed no such warning. He muttered presently: 'There's lots of rabbits here, but there's none about tonight.'

'They know,' the professor said.

Before them, plain in the white moonlight, the great stone showed, upright and waiting.

The chief inspector said: 'This moonlight plays queer tricks with a man's eyes.'

'So it does,' agreed the professor.

They walked on a little way. They were quite near now, or rather the bullock was quite near. The two men were some yards behind. The bullock paused and lowed uneasily and the sound seemed to travel far through the heavy silence of the moonlit night.

'I've got the jitters,' said the chief inspector. 'I've no drink taken all this day, but I could have sworn the stone was on the right-hand side of the lane.'

'So it was,' said the professor. He added: 'So it is.'

The chief inspector stood and stared.

'Well, it was on our left just now,' he said.

'So it was,' said the professor.

They stood still. The ox lowed again, a long low call. The professor took his companion by the arm. He said: 'We won't go any nearer.'

'No,' said the chief inspector. He said: 'What's that noise?'
'I think it's your teeth chattering,' said the professor. 'Or else
it's mine.'

The ox moved on. Again it lowed. It stood still and then once
more moved forward, very slowly, as if irresistibly impelled.
'Look,' screamed the professor.

They saw. In the pale moonlight they saw clearly. They
saw the great stone as it were heaving itself forward. Plainly
they saw how it lifted itself from its base and propelled itself
upon the approaching ox. Earth and sky were still, still and
motionless were the two men, the ox was as still as they, as
the vast immobile block of that huge stone lifted itself, left
its firm base, flung itself in great leaps upon the motionless
bullock. The chief inspector turned and ran. The professor
followed. They ran as they had never run before, as few indeed
have ever run but they, since few but they have ever had such
need for fearful speed. Once the chief inspector fell, and as
he fell, he screamed, for he had felt something plucking at
his ankle. It was only a bramble that had tripped him, but he
was still screaming as he got to his feet and ran on again, nor
indeed has he ever been quite the same man again.

Not till they were near the inn, not till lights showed close
ahead, not till friendly human voices could be heard, did they
cease that wild and dreadful flight.

When at last they were both safe in the professor's room at
the inn, the professor said: 'I knew. At least I think I knew.
But it's a different thing when you see it for yourself.'

'No one will believe us,' muttered the chief inspector. 'I don't
think I believe it any more myself. I thought it had me when
that thing caught my ankle.' He said fiercely: 'What's it mean?'

'No one will believe us,' agreed the professor. 'Why should
they? For how long, no one can even guess, but all through
the centuries that thing stood there and was offered every day
perhaps the blood of living victims, human victims, too, till at
last, for the blood is the life, it began to have a life of its own,
as evil as what caused that life, and when its worshippers no
longer brought it victims then it began to seek them for itself,

so to preserve with their blood the dim life the blood of others had begun to create within itself.'

'You mean the beastly thing grew alive?'

'I think it was wakening to life,' the professor answered.

The chief inspector went to the window and looked out into the palely lit night.

'I don't think I shall go to bed,' he said. 'I should dream — dream of that beastly thing making its way down here, crashing in the door or the walls — what could any man do against fifty tons of granite made animate?'

'It'll be safe tonight,' the professor answered. 'Safe and satiate. Satiate. Probably for another thirty years. Asleep again, the life within it. We won't risk another wakening though.' He motioned towards his luggage. 'There's enough high explosive there,' he said, 'to blow up half the hill. We'll wait till high noon.'

'No one will believe us,' the chief inspector repeated. 'I don't think I do quite myself. If I did, I think I should go mad.'

'We'll neither of us believe it,' agreed the professor. 'Safer not to.' After a time, he added: 'Not only in those days of the dawn of humanity have men made for themselves a god to destroy themselves.'

17 The Statue (1943)

JAMES CAUSEY

Jerome Winters pursed his lips.

'Young man,' he said coldly, 'a bargain is a bargain.'

'But can't you give me just a little more time!' The young man's eyes were dark and pleading against the pallor of his face. 'Another two months. Another month! I could surely find some way —'

His voice trailed off. Winters was shaking his head from side to side, staring at him with his frosty blue eyes.

'Three months you were given,' he said curtly. 'Seventy-five dollars. You've had time enough, my good man. Plenty of time. Seventy-five dollars, with interest. And — you don't have it, do you?' His voice was faintly mocking.

The young sculptor buried his face in his hands. 'No,' he said hoarsely. 'I haven't. But I could surely scrape up the money some way — if only —'

Winters looked queerly at him. He stood up. He was a short, slight man, small and withered as an old persimmon, his blue eyes wearing a perpetually frosty gaze.

In the little town of Hammondville, Winters was by far the wealthiest — as well as the most hated. His loans bordered upon usury — and those who could not pay were given no mercy. He had caused more than one suicide, and a very appreciable amount of misery and suffering. A wizened, dried-up little spider he was, who spun his web carefully, showing not the slightest pity to those unfortunate enough to fall into it.

Just now, contrary to his usual satisfaction when foreclosing a mortgage, he felt curiously frustrated. Perhaps — he had not made enough profit this time.

'Young man,' his voice was thin and sharp, 'three months ago you came to me with a desperate plea for money — on my terms. As security, I was given a small bit of sculpture, unfinished at that.' His voice hardened. 'It is not my usual policy to be so generous —'

'Generous!' The young sculptor's face twisted. His voice was bitter. 'You speak of generosity! The Dawn Child — my statue. Seventy-five dollars! Finished, I could very easily sell that statue for —'

'For some considerable sum, I suppose?' Winters' words dripped cold. 'Remember. The statue is incomplete. I may have a hard time disposing of it, for that very reason.'

He frowned petulantly.

The young man stared at Winters as if seeing him for the first time. Slowly Winters flushed, and his eyes fell under that penetrating gaze.

'So,' De Roults said softly. 'I might have known.'

He straightened, drew a deep breath, and looked at Winters again. 'It is absolutely useless to ask for more time, I see.'

'Absolutely,' Winters said, some of his poise returning to him.

'Then —' Two spots of color appeared in the young man's cheeks. 'Then, sir, may I see that statue? May I? Just once, since it is for the last time.'

There was no harm in letting him see it. Winters shrugged. 'Why not?'

He made his way toward the back of the study, where he opened the door to a closet. De Roults followed him slowly. In one corner of the closet stood a shapeless something on a pedestal, draped in a sheet.

'Your statue, young man.' Winters turned sideways, and lifted the sheet. In spite of himself, a small glint of appreciation came to his eyes as he looked at the statue.

It was the nude figure of a child. Exquisitely carved, it was, in pink marble, life size. The statue stood on tiptoe, a smile on its rosy face — a childish, contented smile, both arms stretching skyward, as to greet the sun.

But the hands — they were unfinished. The fingers were crudely blocked out — rough, like marble mittens. Evidently, some work was needed before the whole was completed.

But even as it was, the statue was beautiful. Winters, in spite of himself, had to admit that. Unconsciously, his fingers caressed the marble in a possessive gesture. He turned to look at the young man.

De Roults was standing there, leaning against the door jamb, gazing at the statue intently. There was an odd expression on his face — a strained, rapt expression.

'But it is unfinished,' he breathed. 'It is unfinished.'

'Eh?' said Winters sharply.

De Roults started. He turned slowly, and looked at Winters. He looked then, at the statue, caressing it with his eyes.

'I put my soul into that statue,' he murmured softly. 'I labored to produce a masterpiece, a work of art that would endure —' He broke off.

'Winters,' he said, his face strangely white, his voice suddenly hoarse. 'Could I — finish the Dawn Child. Her hands — they are incomplete. She — would not like that. It is hard to reach for the sun, when one's hands are — ugly. Would it be possible? Even though the statue is yours now. I could do the work in this room here. With chisel and hammer —' His eyes held the quality of a prayer, his voice trembled.

'Could I — finish it, sir?'

Winters looked at him. A faint streak of perversity — which, incidentally, was to cost him his life, rose in his brain.

'I see no reason why I should,' he snapped. 'You have looked at the statue. It was enough that I should let you do so. Quite enough. I expect to have the statue disposed of by the end of this week, unfinished as it is. Of course, the profit will be negligible, but —' He spread his hands, indicative of his disinterest in the matter.

'Good-day, sir.'

De Roults turned slowly ashen.

'Then — then you will not allow me to finish —' he said, almost childlike.

'Precisely.'

The young sculptor walked slowly toward the door, his head bowed. At the threshold, he turned, and looked first at Winters, then at the Dawn Child. There was an enigmatic expression on his face.

'Nevertheless,' he whispered, 'the Dawn Child shall be finished. Soon. I asked you for but a week more, Winters. *I give you a week, now.*'

He turned and walked stiffly out.

Winters raised his eyebrows.

It was, perhaps, thirty seconds later that he heard the crash. He hurried out of the house, his pale blue eyes curious behind the glasses. There was a rather large crowd clustered in the middle of the street, muttering excitedly. The truck stood by, its fender rather badly dented, with a splotch of red. The truck driver was standing by, addressing empty air for the most part, and telling how, 'He just walked right out in the street, front of my truck. Wasn't *my* fault. Can't help it if a man walks out'n the street in front of a truck, and doesn't even look where he's going. He walked out —'

Winters pursed his thin lips, then he turned back into his study, where he made certain entries in a large black ledger. On impulse, he checked up upon De Roults. The young sculptor had lived alone in a garret in the poorer section of town, and from what Winters could ascertain — seemed passionately devoted to his work. He was poor — very. Indeed, Winters wondered how he had ever managed to keep body and soul together.

It certainly was not *his* fault, if De Roults paid no attention to where he was walking, while crossing the street. The remainder of the day Winters spent in his usual pleasant fashion — that of figuring how to dispossess certain hapless clients.

It was late that night, around eleven-thirty, when Winters awoke suddenly, with the conviction that someone, or something was making strange sounds downstairs. He lay awake for some minutes, staring into the blackness, and suddenly he sat bolt upright in bed. The sound was repeated. It was an odd scraping, and scratching noise.

Muttering to himself, Winters got out of bed, put on his robe and slippers, and shuffled out into the hall. As near as he could determine, the sounds were coming from downstairs

— in the general direction of his study. He shuffled downstairs, and into his study, where he turned on the light.

The glare of the light exploded whitely, throwing everything in the room into harsh relief. Black ugly shadows. Dark corners illumined.

There was nothing in the room.

Winters grunted, and reached again for the light switch. He froze. The sound had recommenced; it was distinctly audible, and it seemed to come from the closet.

Winters went over and opened the closet door. Probably rats, he thought, peering through the darkness of the closet.

No rats.

Winters frowned and looked more carefully. There was no corner where a rat might hide. Winters looked at the statue, standing there in the corner, and his breath hissed softly between his teeth. He distinctly remembered having draped a sheet over it, before going to bed.

But now the sheet lay on the floor.

Well, then.

Rats could drag down sheets.

Large rats.

Frowning, Winters picked up the sheet and stood staring at the statue, before covering it. The general appearance of the statue had changed; it was not quite right somehow.

Winters shook his head angrily, and went back to his room. Rats, no doubt. He was not the sort of man to be bothered by such occurrences. Perhaps half an hour after going to bed, he was roused again.

The same sounds. Grating, rasping, scratching noises. Oddly muffled they were. Coming from downstairs. Winters swore softly and tried to sleep.

The next day Winters examined the statue critically. There was, he observed, a peculiar quality to the Dawn Child's smile — an oddly unpleasant quality — and the arms of the statue did not look quite right.

And the hands, Winters could see — were changed. As if someone had been working on them. With a sculptor's chisel!

He did not bother to puzzle the matter out. Methodical and precise as ever, he cleaned up the shards of marble, and went about his business for the day.

Possibly some prankster — or his imagination. Or it might be the rats. Gnawing. No matter. He would make sure.

A substantial remainder of the morning, he spent in setting rat traps in likely spots throughout the house. Later, he would see about selling the statue.

That afternoon, Winters called several dealers in antiques, and *objets d'art*. There was, it seemed, little or no demand, for unfinished statues. No, he could find no buyer anywhere. After the dozenth call, Winters hung up, disgusted, and sat meditatively staring into space for several seconds. His thoughts were not pleasant. It was probably the first time in his life he had failed to come out winner in a business transaction.

The remainder of the afternoon, he brooded over it. Mentally he kicked himself a dozen times for having failed to take advantage of the young sculptor's offer. He should have let De Roults finish —

Winters' brows furrowed. Had not De Roults said something about — *about finishing the statue!*

But — De Roults was dead.

Mentally Winters kicked himself again.

That night, before going to bed, Winters investigated the entire study thoroughly. Everything was in perfect order. The statue was covered, the closet was locked, the windows and the doors were all barred.

Winters grunted in satisfaction and then went to bed.

Three hours later he was roused suddenly. He could hear nothing now, save the faint echo of a somehow familiar sound, seeming to echo in his ears. Possibly one of the rat traps going off, he decided in some satisfaction, and so deciding, turned over again on his side.

Abruptly he raised himself on one elbow and glared through the darkness toward the hall. The sound had been repeated. He could hear it now — the same *chipping* sound. Winters cursed silently, and got up, taking care not to creak the bedsprings.

Very stealthily, he tiptoed downstairs. He opened the study door silently, and quite suddenly snapped on the light and stood on the threshold blinking.

There was no one in the room. Winters looked around. The closet door was still locked. Muttering querulously to himself, he opened it, and looked inside. For an instant he wondered if his eyes were beginning to play tricks on him.

Then he took a step backwards.

The statue's hands were beginning to take definite form. Moreover, the arms had moved. Moved a good three inches.

Winters rubbed his chin doubtfully, and wondered how he could have ever thought the face of the statue beautiful. The lips were not smiling at all, and the whole face seemed to have a definitely unpleasant cast.

'Humph,' said Winters.

He retrieved the sheet and placed it upon the statue. He looked around the study carefully, and into each corner of the closet, more than once narrowly escaping the sticking of his foot into a rat trap.

Before going back to bed, he eyed the tiny pile of marble chips around the pedestal of the statue, and though his lips moved queerly, he said nothing.

Jerome Winters got very little sleep that night. He heard the chipping, scraping sounds from downstairs quite audibly, no matter how hard he tried to bury his head underneath the covers.

Next day, business did not go well at all. Every little thing seemed to go wrong, his papers were not where they should be, and he forgot several important matters relating to interest payments and debts.

But he would not admit, even to himself, that he was worried. Toward noon, Winters received an unexpected telegram. He scowled at it, and pursed his lips.

This was decidedly unfortunate. He had planned to get rid of that statue today. To take it to some antique dealer, and — and give it away if he had to.

What was he thinking of! Give something away that had cost him seventy-five dollars. And for that matter — two sleepless nights. But after all — De Roults had said that the statue would be finished within a week. And the look on the face of the statue last night — possibly there was something to the young sculptor's threat, after all.

Winters dismissed the thought.

At any rate, he would be out of town for the next four days on business. A piece of property he had acquired from some poor debtor must be appraised. Well, he could get rid of the statue in the city. At some small profit, of course. It would be comparatively simple, since the statue was almost finished.

So it was that while away from Hammondville, Winters saw and interviewed the manager of a certain prominent antique shop, one Sir Arthur Manwell, in regard to coming out to Hammondville to see a very valuable statue he possessed.

Yes, the statue was easily worth five hundred dollars. Exquisitely carved, it was. By a young sculptor named De Roults. What? Oh no. The young man had met with a very tragic accident. Yes. Too bad.

And he would come out to Hammondville today, to appraise the statue? What? Not until tomorrow. But the week would be up then. What? Oh nothing. Nothing at all. Tomorrow then.

Winters arrived home that afternoon with a curious feeling of mingled relief and apprehension. The very first thing he did was to open the closet door. There was absolutely no doubt about it this time. The arms of the statue had moved downward to an almost horizontal position. The hands — they were nearly completed! But they had changed. The fingers were bent as if to grasp something — they looked like small pink claws.

The marble dust, Winters saw, was thick about the base of the statue. One foot was poised, with knee lifted high *as though the statue were about to step off the pedestal!*

Winters slowly raised his eyes and looked at the face. It was twisted in a rather frightful leer. Winters shut the closet door and leaned weakly against it. He locked it carefully and walked out of the study, mopping his damp face with a handkerchief. His mouth was strangely dry, and his face was pale.

Tomorrow would be the seventh day.

Late that night, he heard the now familiar chipping of stone. The noise this time, was fast and furious, almost — eager. Winters did not get out of bed. He knew it would be no use. After a little while, the sounds ceased. The statue, then, was finished.

Winters did not venture downstairs next morning until almost noon. When he did, he stayed as far away as possible from his study. In an agony of dread and apprehension he waited for the arrival of Sir Arthur, from the city.

Sir Arthur did not come.

By mid-afternoon, Winters was almost frantic.

Finally, he tiptoed into his study. There was a telephone on his desk.

Swiftly he dialed the operator, and staring fixedly at the closet door, waited for his call to be put through.

Sir Arthur Manwell, dealer in antiques and *objets d'art* answered. Yes, he was sorry, he was desolated, but he had not been able to keep the appointment. No, he would not be able to come down to make the appraisal until tomorrow. Sometime in the morning — What? What was the matter?

But it was impossible. An important matter had come up — he had to remain at the shop — and —

'I don't care!' Winters shrieked into the mouthpiece, suddenly panic-stricken. 'You've got to come down! Today, you hear? I've got the damned thing locked up in the closet, but the week's up, I tell you. The week's up!'

Sir Arthur informed him politely — and frigidly, that he would arrive tomorrow morning.

'But the statue!' shrilled Winters. '*The statue!*'

There was the audible click of the man hanging up.

'Operator, operator!' Winters dialed frantically.

Abruptly he froze.

Behind him. The sound of a splintering wood. A door smashing open ...

The *closet door* . . .?

Involuntarily, Winters dropped the receiver on its hook, and trembling, stared straight ahead.

A soft thud of something striking the carpet. Then the quick pattering of footsteps across the floor.

Winters worked his mouth convulsively, but before he could scream, he was seized by the throat.

Like Winters, Sir Arthur Manwell was a very punctilious man. So it was that he arrived in Hammondville early the next day to see Winters on the matter of the statue. It so happened that when he arrived, there was a rather large crowd of people clustered about Winters' house. Managing to get in, he saw the police and the coroner probing about Winters' study.

Winters had been found in his overturned chair, and the studio in his immediate vicinity was somewhat messy. His head had been almost torn from his body. Indeed, the coroner was quite puzzled.

'Strangled,' he murmured gravely. 'Um — handprints like those of a small ape. Or possibly those — of a child.'

Manwell was extremely shocked.

'Yes,' he explained. 'I came out here to see the poor chap about a statue he intended to sell. Any idea how it happened?'

The coroner had no idea.

As he turned to leave, Manwell caught sight of the closet door at the back of the room. The lock was ripped away, and the door hung loose on its hinges. Manwell frowned, puzzled.

'Winters mentioned the closet,' he murmured under his breath. On sudden impulse, Manwell looked around to see if he were being observed. Everyone's interest was focused upon what lay in the center of the room. Manwell went slowly to the closet door. He opened it. He drew a slow deep breath of awe.

'Superb,' he breathed.

The Dawn Child stood on tiptoe, both arms stretching high, its face smiling in contentment. Manwell looked at it for a long minute. Quite suddenly he stiffened. He glanced back to where Winters lay.

He looked again at the statue.

Then, his face very white, and his hands shaking, he shut the closet door softly. His lips were a jagged thin line, as he strode slowly outside. He recalled again the words of the coroner.

'Very tiny handprints …'

He remembered Winters' frantic shrieking over the phone.

And on the soft pink of the statue's hands, he had seen a deeper, more ominous stain of red.

Notes on the text

KATE MACDONALD

1 Master Sacristan Eberhart

bulls eye, quarries: bulls eye glass is the thicker central part of a pane of glass blown using centrifugal force, so the thickest part of the glass rests in the centre. Quarries are pieces of glass cut into geometric shapes to form a regular pattern within a leaded framework. The quarries would be much clearer than the bulls-eye glass.

leads: the tiled roof; lead was used extensively as a roofing material for its waterproof and sealing qualities.

common deal: pine, a fast-growing wood used for cheap furniture.

gurgoils: one of several variant spellings used before 1860 for gargoyles.

Te lucis ante terminum: the Latin hymn chanted at the end of the day's work.

shooting lips: the exaggerated stone lips through which rainwater was expected to flow.

St Simon Stylites:a fifth-century Christian monk who lived for 37 years on top of a pillar in Syria, near Aleppo.

Æolian: from the Greek gods of the winds.

the death watch: the death watch beetle, so named for its audible clicking which can be heard clearly in a quiet house.

luffer boards: louvre-boards, thin boards fixed at an angle in a door or window frame to form a partial screen open to air and light.

2 The Marble Hands

prie-dieu chair: originally a desk designed for kneeling at while reading a devotional work in private prayer; later evolved into a small kneeling stool with a raised arm-rest or shelf for a prayerbook or for the hands to rest on while praying.

3 The Mask

The King in Yellow: an invented play by Chambers that recurs as a motif of horror throughout his linked short story collection *The King in Yellow* (1895).

mahl-stick: a short stick or rod with a padded head used to support a painter's arm while they work on a detailed part of the painting.

morion: an iron soldier's helmet from the sixteenth century.

signed myself: made the sign of the Cross.

academic: a piece of art demonstrating or exhibiting technical achievement, but which might lack aesthetic perfection.

Beaux Arts: intended to suggest a Parisian art school, an École de Beaux Arts, rather than the Académie de Beaux Arts itself.

J'avais bien l'honneur, madame: French, I had the honour, Madam.

À la bonheur!: French, To happiness! O Happiness!

hôtel: French; not an inn, but a private house.

'over the mouth's good mark, that made the smile': a quotation from Robert Browning's long poem *Andrea del Sarto* (1855), about an artist and his art.

6 The Duchess at Prayer

escutcheon: heraldic shield, or a carved coat of arms

laminae: Latin, a thin sheet.

saurian: lizard-like.

Como: Lake Como, at the foothills of the Alps where summer weather is cooler than in southern Italy.

Proprio: Italian, just so, that's right.

scagliola volutes: ornamental scrollwork made from crushed pigment in plaster.

badalchin: ornamental canopy.

Bernini: the leading sculptor of the seventeenth century.

fraise: a delicate ruff rising from the neckline to frame the head.

suffered: endured, allowed to remain.

abates: possibly the Italian for abbots or confessors.

cadet: a younger son.

***pezzi grossi* of the Golden Book**: a leading family in the *Libro d'Oro*, the directory of the noble families of the Venetian Republic.

bravi: Italian, a superior henchman or follower.

the Ten: presumably the leaders of the Republic.

cabinet: an adjoining room to her bedroom.

7 Benlian

Prussian: Prussian Blue, an intense dark blue pigment.

ivory: miniatures have been painted on ivory plaques since the eighteenth century, since these are easier to prepare than vellum and support flesh tones more effectively.

zygomatics: his cheekbones.

hyper-space: this is one of the earliest known uses of this term in a non-mathematical setting.

Noah's ark figure: toy sets of Noah's Ark animal and figures often had the Biblical characters as columnar figures in long robes, easy to manufacture while suggesting Palestinian robes.

SPR: Society for Psychical Research, founded in 1881.

8 The Marble Hands

plunging: liable to play a risky move, to bet all.

9 Hypnos

Pentelicus: a mountain north-east of Athens, famous for the pure quality of its marble.

11 Bagnell Terrace

Naboth: Naboth owned a vineyard which was much coveted by King Ahab, and who was executed when he would not give it up (1 Kings 21 1–16).

12 At Simmel Acres Farm

stair: students at Oxford colleges who lived on the same staircase had rooms above and below each other, and consequently saw more of each other than other students in the same college.

Hilary term: the Oxford term between January and March.

vac: university vacation, the long break over Easter.

penthouse: a projecting porch formed by the roof alone, without walls or sides.

Et te simulacrum: Latin, 'and the image of you'.

Simulacrum, et te — require: Latin, 'image, and you – I require'.

Cupper rag: a Cupper is slang for a competition between Oxford and Cambridge university sports teams; a rag is a prank, a showy performance to tease and enrage the opposing team.

I could stick: I could endure.

libatio aquae: Latin, libation of water.

fillet: a ribbon or headband on classical statuary to keep the hair in place.

13 The Maker of Gargoyles

ferine: feral, wild.

vans: wings supported by struts or (in animals) bone or cartilage.

loups-garous: French, werewolves.

stryge: a winged creature of ill-omen; also a name for a witch.

aspergillus: an aspergillum, a holy-water sprinkler.

14 The Man of Stone

Damon and Pythias: two close friends from Classical Greek legend who trusted each other so much that Damon offered himself as a hostage to prove the integrity of Pythias's promise to return.

The mills of the gods: a proverb about inexorable Fate dating from Classical Greek times, now most well-known from a quotation from Longfellow: 'The mills of God grind slowly but they grind exceedingly small', from his 'Retribution' (1846).

15 The Menhir

tors: distinctive outcrops of rock in open moorland, often weathered or eroded into arresting shapes.

finger-post: a direction sign on a tall pole.

rubified: made red in colour.

Isaacs: this may be an anti-Semitic slur, suggesting that Jews were more likely to be afraid of superstition than Christians.

16 The Living Stone

Ancient Hindu saying: the quotation has also been attributed to Pythagoras, Ibn Arabi and Rumi.

Nippies: the name for waitresses at the chain of Lyons tea-shops.